The Witch and the City

Jake Burnett

SOUTH
WINDOW
PRESS

SOUTH WINDOW PRESS

1

An old woman limped through a place of infinite forgetting.

When the forest grew too dim to go on, Hecate slashed the acrid bark of a tanner's oak. A blot of red sap oozed grudgingly out. She tucked her flint witch-blade into her belt, dabbed the tip of her staff in the sap, and stuck one tiny moonflower to the daub. She patted the tree.

"Heal and grow."

She kissed the white petals. Her whispering breath brought a glow to the frail bloom. Thus lit, she hobbled into the near-pitch of the wood.

The crone followed a mossy trail. Easy to miss, the narrow strip of time-gnawed stone through the undergrowth must have been a wide road long ago, before the forest had eaten Osylum's Eighth Ward whole. Before Hecate could remember. Before anyone now living knew.

Despite the dark, the trees chattered with the mindless this-and-that of birds and small beasts—fearful, feral sounds. Burden-bent branches moaned a slow, mournful counterpoint. The whispers of thick leaves and creeping vines tied the glum sylvan concerto together.

Hecate chirped a fearless tune back at the forest.

Her nonsense clicks and chitters wove a cheerful umbrella against the wild menace. The last scraps of vellum harvested from the ruins of Osylum's largest library crammed her satchel. No grim wood could smother the joy sparked by a haul of new things to read.

A glint flashed from the brush.

The witch paused. She cocked her head to one side then the other and squinted into the thicket, waving her light-tipped staff. The glimmer danced.

"Reflection." She spoke aloud to herself, in the habit of one used to long hours alone. "Maybe."

She looked both ways down the trail. No obvious ambush. Of course, that was the way of ambushes, not to be obvious. One did not get old in the Prison City avoiding only the obvious.

"Hrm. Double hrm and a handful of huhn."

She crooked one spotted finger towards the twinkle.

"Little wisp, little wisp, if wisp ye be, show yourself and come to me."

No movement from the other light.

"Not a wisp, you. Oh, I should be home by now. Yet..."

Curiosity beat caution. It always had and likely always would, no matter how long she lived nor how much better she knew. Turning from the homeward trail, she picked a careful way through blackthorn tendrils, towards the unexpected reflection.

She did not have to go far.

The glint came from a thin shiv that had fallen point-end into the loam beneath a corpse's hand. The dead man hung from a broad tree trunk, pinned from behind. Prying branches cracked open his ribs. One of the more malevolent oaks.

"Here-now!" the crone clucked. "Filthy nails and filed teeth. A Ratkipper you, and out here?"

His exposed viscera had stopped throbbing. The worms had not had time to sprout. A puddle of blood grew in dribs and clots beneath his dangling feet. Hecate dipped a finger. Warm. Fresh. She wiped her finger clean on the corpse's forehead, swiping the design of the Lady's Eye. A dark joke. His eyes bulged beneath the sigil, straining upwards at the canopy.

"These are the pearls that were his eyes..." she sang, absent-mindedly.

She inspected the scene up and down, left and right, with myopic attention.

She prodded the leaf-strewn ground with her staff. The bright knife, a few sliver-gemmed rings, and a pouch of dubious leather filled with the fragments of nibbled fingers were all the Ratkipper's wealth beneath the sky. His clothes, mis-matched and ill-fit, bore several brown-rimmed slits in strategic locations—testimony to their violent acquisition.

All signs attested to a back-stabbing scavenger from the Seventh Ward who took what he wanted and had, at last, gotten what he gave. Had she found him tacked to a tenement wall in that Ward, she wouldn't have stopped to wonder.

But this was the Eighth.

"Just you and me and the Lady makes three," she said to the corpse. "What brought you here, mumblebone?"

She hunkered next to him on a burl that fit the curve of her haunches just right. She sucked her teeth in thought.

"Flight? Unlikely. What could be worse in the rookery than what you knew you'd find in here?"

To illustrate her point, a sharp-pointed branch surreptitiously rested itself on her shoulder. A loose root looped slowly around her bony ankle. Without even looking, she struck the gnarled trunk with her staff.

"Eat the loam, drink the rain, grow to touch the sky. Eat a witch, drink her blood, wither in pain and die."

Chastened, the branch and root withdrew. Once more for good measure, she thumped the trunk. She continued her one-sided interrogation of the Ratkipper's corpse.

"If not flight, hunger? Fear and feeding. The only two things your kind know. So what meal could you hope to make so tasty? Are they really out of unready morts in the Seventh Ward?"

She tapped her chin.

"Or was it Eschatos who sent you out and about, claiming the Lady's will? Yes. Call it that. That would-be Warden sent you here on some mission. Eschatos."

She spat. Her old enemy's name left a nasty taste on her tongue.

The corpse stared upwards, unresponding. His hand, already half-covered by the Eating Oak's bark, reached in the direction of his gaze. The crone thrust her stick higher. At the edge of the moonflower's glow, she spotted a lump of woven branches and leaves.

"That's not a feeder's boll. Or a sparrow's home."

Using the dead man as a ladder, she hoisted herself up. She peered over the edge of the nest.

A black witch-egg, the size of her fist, nestled amid moldering leaves.

She let out a low, cheerless whistle.

"Death already? I wasn't close to done."

A crow lighted on the branch above her. The bird sharpened her beak on the bark and smirked.

"Of course you'd know," Hecate said. "Go on then. Tell Upstart it's time. Just remember—nothing is what it seems in the Ninth."

Her familiar nodded and took to wing.

Wobbling on the dead cannibal's shoulders, the witch dropped her staff to the forest floor. She carefully retrieved the treasure from the nest. The corpse's sightless eyes fixed on the egg. She taunted him.

"It would've made a fine breakfast, yes. If your master had let you suck it dry. Pfft. I'd give a lot to be quit with him but my sand's run thin."

She jumped down, wincing at what once had been a trivial drop.

"No time for pain," she chastised herself. "Quick now. Call the troops to order, the battle's about to begin."

She plucked the Ratkipper's knife from the soil and wiped the dark loam on her dress. Her tiny face, stretched long and sharp, peered back from the polished steel.

"Old man, old man in the mirror, see me now, hear me here."

Her reflection remained unchanged.

"Come on, Hendiatrix. It's time."

She repeated the summoning spell. Nothing. She counted the day's hours in her head.

"Of course. Halfway twixt Sext and Nones. Feeding time in the Phrontistery. You're shoveling crumbs with the other monks, not scanning your mirror and making the Count."

She drove the shiv back in the dirt, all the way to the hilt.

"Feh to your belly, Oblate. You'll have to catch up later. Tho not with me. Not with me..."

She wrapped the egg in her shawl and cradled it to her belly. Picking her staff up, she peered through the woods behind her. A floating blue glow approached, relentless and slow.

Three Wardens were coming to collect the corpse. They would take it to the First Ward. As was their right. As was the Lady's will.

"Dustmen, Dustmen pass me by," she muttered, hastening away before they saw her, "today is not my day to die."

Three days, by and by, a dry voice added in her mind.

"Shush," she ordered the facts. There was no arguing with inevitability, but she did not have to pay it heed. Clucking tender nothings to her egg-bound daughter, the witch slipped through the forest and down the shattered path, away to home.

2

Six marionettes hung an upper room of an abandoned theatre in the Ninth Ward; a queen, a beggar, a gardener, a drunkard, a ragamuffin, and a clerk with a feather pen. The garish puppets were the size of full-grown women and men. They'd been crafted with exquisite detail. Above them, in the alcove of a clerestory window, a skull kept vigil.

Hecate's crow tapped at the glass. On the third tap, the pane fell in, shattering on the floor. The shards landed in the shape of an eye. The bird stepped atop the skull. She cawed a harsh message from her mistress.

"Upstart, shake the scenery!"

One of the marionettes—a plain and balding man with ink-stained hands and a secretarial mien—began to sway and click his limbs as though brushed by a gentle breeze.

There was no breeze.

The officious guignol's plaster face curled into a grin. He spoke:

"Oh witch, in thy orisons be all my sins remembered."

His strings snapped. When he landed, he was flesh and blood. He smirked. He brushed ages of dust from his shoulders. He frowned at the glass pattern of the eye on the floor. He swept it aside with one booted foot. He tapped his forehead to the skull in the window and bowed. With a tug on his hem, he addressed the rest of the marionettes.

"Step to, Canting Crew. The hour is short and there's work to do."

The rattle of pegs and slither of strings filled the backstage chamber; the symphony of liberated puppets. When the last of them had come to life, the crow winged backwards and vanished into the slate-grey sky.

3

A chicken-legged hut squatted amid the gravestones and tomb-vaults of the Sixth Ward. Its dirty clapboard walls had neither window nor door. Hecate called it hers, though she had never fully mastered its secrets.

"Izbushka, izbushka, your witch implores—open your mouth and show me the door!"

The battered plank walls rippled. Two windows and a door wrinkled into existence. It had taken decades just to ferret out the words to open the hut. She had never figured out how to control its legs. It tromped through the Wards at its own whim. Even Dedalus, the brilliant inventor, couldn't calculate a pattern to its path.

It didn't matter now.

Safe within, Hecate unwrapped her egg. It was already larger than when she had found it. She cleared a space on her bed, sweeping text-filled pages to the floor. She crumpled dozens of more loose sheaves into a makeshift nest, safe and warm. She patted the egg fondly. A shade of sadness dimmed her face as she considered her tiny home, packed with books and pages.

"I really wasn't close to done."

She shrugged the sorrow off her stooped back.

"Tisk-tosk. Sigh no more. Needs must when the Lady lashes." She tapped the egg shell. "And this time round I've learned a thing or two to share twixt me and you. Things I dared not set down till I knew the day of my death—the ghost of a whisper of a shadow of these secrets would be enough to end it all for everyone left in Osylum."

She fished a fistful of blank foolscap from beneath a flatiron by the fireplace. She plucked a feather pen from a shriveled gourd that had rolled into the corner some years ago. A cup of ink already sat on her writing desk, half-drunk that morning by accident instead of the tea next to it.

"Twill have to be enough. No time to make more ink—or tea, come to think of it. Time! It runs out. Where to? There's no out here in Osylum."

She tapped the enormous hourglass that dominated one corner of the hut thrice. With a grunt, she flipped it upside down. Three days' sand began to slip from top to bottom. Hooking a stool with her foot, she rested her hard hunks on soft wood. She dipped the quill. Driven by the hiss of minutes draining, she did not ponder where and how to begin. She dove heedless into the scritch-scratch of prose after a scant handful of dust had settled in the glass.

Dearest Daughter-Self,

I do not know if you will be me. My soul could settle in any new found body in Osylum, I suppose, and anyone's soul could settle in you. Whoever you will be, I can sneak you my

*words, under the Lady's Eye and past
the forgetting of death.
Words are magic, dearest, and that is
the first thing you should learn. Magic and realer than Real.
There are more words than things.*

She stopped. She read what she had written thus far.

"Pike! 'Tis more jammed and tattered than a Peripat's coat."

She balled her fist and struck her thigh. "Daft witch! Order your wits simple, so the wee newling girl can ken 'em easy! Don't pass on the gift of nonsense, she'll never escape with that."

It was easier said than done. Stuck and frustrated to find a clear way to say what needed to be said, the crone glared into an unseen distance. She savagely mouthed the feathery pen. Sand whispered relentless in the corner. At length she spat.

"Pah! The worst something's better than the best nothing. Save what you can in the three days before the Wardens show up to cart your corpse off for the Lady's will."

She wrote on without a second pause.

*Osylum. The world's a city full of
straying streets and death's the marketplace where each one meets. The
city has twelve walls—thirteen if you
count the sky. The birds know what
men never learn.
The walls girdle and split nine
Wards. Within the nine Wards are*

*everything that ever is and every-
thing that ever was and everything
that ever will be—or so the common
cant goes. 'Tis sure there is Nothing outside and Nothing below and
Nothing above and not a single door
nor road from the city to anywhere
else.*

And yet—

*There are words for things that are
not here; the sun, the moon, the stars,
the wind, the sea—so many words
scattered around this city hacked
in stone and scrawled on skin and
traced on frail leaves. And that's
what got me wondering, when I was
young as you will be. And wondering
led me to be as old as I am.*

*There is no memory now of those
things that were. Nor shall there be
memory in days to come of the things
that are now. A thick, half-chewed
leather-leafed book told me that after
I rescued it from a Ratkipper's mouth.
Why does no one remember?*

*Perhaps the Lady takes our memo-
ries for herself. Or the Wardens wash
them clean. Or they fly up into the
dark and suffocate. I haven't the time
to argue philosophy. We die and lose
our minds and are sent back to the
scattered bodies of this Prison City
none the wiser than when last we
walked or crawled or flew.*

So it is and so the Lady decrees it must

be.

That said, there's one more word, daughter mine, one more word I learned for things that no one sees. The most magic word of all, the word I learned last, the word that exists the least.

ESCAPE!

"What was, may yet again be."

Upstart said that to me. We had learned the word escape. He and me and Dedalus makes three. Maybe we'd learned it before—impossible to say how many times we had died and returned to Osylum-town. We learned it in this last life, he and I. And learned, cruel as it is true, that one life is not long enough to piece a plot together to get free.

There will never be enough time.

So we went our separate ways, the Player King and the Builder of Things and I. No one would know the whole of our plan. The Wardens would fade the whole city if they read a single jot or tittle of our wild design. Even now, even knowing these pages will dissolve into your brain, I cannot bring myself to write the truth of it. You'll learn when Upstart finds you and you find the oseovox. Dedalus is gone. He had a succession plan but he kept it to himself so he's out by my reckoning. Here I sit on the edge of forgetting and being forgotten. You grow in my

home to take my place. Lady's will,
you'll know no more than I did when
I stood unclad amid the wreck of my
own shell.

The crone snorted a rebellious laugh.

"Lady's will..."

Defiantly, Hecate poured out her life's wisdom across page after page as the three-day span slid away a grain at a time. The egg on the bed grew with every passing hour. It filled the whole of the crone's book-stuffed pallet. She paid it no mind—she would not sleep again. The swelling shell loomed in the bleary periphery of her vision. She ignored it. She wrote on and on, the disjointed, jangling fragments she'd hoarded over the course her long, long life. They were not sufficient in themselves, but coupled with the gift of her words they might prove enough.

With a scant double handful of sand in the glass, the hut lurched upwards. The witch pitched from her stool to the floor.

"No! Not now!"

The hut took off running on its chicken legs to its current occupant's final destination.

Hecate rolled around, tossed by the pitching floor. Every loose book in the tiny room scattered. The egg rocked slightly, but it had grown too heavy and lay too well-cradled in the mattress to fall.

"You ramshackle pile of kindling!" Hecate shouted and pounded the floorboards.

The shack loped on, indifferent. It was all she could do to hang on and not be jostled to a premature death. Through grimy windows, she caught flashes of the straying streets. Graves gave way to shop-fronts which in turn became wide lawns and rich estates. The hut scratched the ground of an over-grown folly garden. It settled into its new nest.

Old bones shrieking, the crone pulled herself upright. She leaned over the edge of her up-ended writing table. What she saw made her cry out in anguish.

The inkwell had emptied onto three-days' worth of pages, covering them all. Frantically, she blotted the split ink with her shawl. Ink spread faster than she could sop it up. The last drops glugged out of the well. She held a sodden mess of black-stained foolscap. Only scraps of words and cryptic fragments of phrases survived the inky onslaught.

Ink streaked her cheeks as she wiped away bitter tears. A lifetime's scheming, all but undone. A patchwork of blotted notes and piles and piles of other people's books would be all she could pass on to her successor.

A glimmer of hope, faint as a moonflower, shone in her eyes. One blank page had strayed from her desk, landing under the bed. She retrieved it. Not everything had been lost.

The last of the sand slithered through the glass.

"No use crying over spilt ink, dearest," she said to the egg.

Hecate riffled through the chaotic contents of her home. She seized a clear glass jar, filled with dried rosemary leaves. She shook it into a mortar made from a scrimshawed hip joint. She ground it up with a flint-gnawed thigh bone pestle.

"That's for remembrance. The Lady herself

spread her blue cloak over the plant while she rested which is why its flower is blue. You might learn that and you might not. Makes no mind for this."

Through the grimy window, the floating shape of a Warden drew near. Another two surely approached from angles unseen. A dry corner of her mind counted seconds while the rest of her flurried through the hut, gathering and mixing the rest of the ingredients.

"A ritual no one knows!" she crowed at last. "Polygonatum preserved in fermented tears!"

She squirted a full dropper of the milky liquid into the grey-green rosemary powder. The mixture swelled in volume several times over, frothing. She dissolved the pages in the mixture—spoiled as they were some dribs of knowledge might make it through.

The door opened.

The crone dodged out of the Wardens' line of sight. She snatched one last clean sheet of paper. She scrawled a single word:

ESCAPE

She tossed the page into the sludge. She drank the vial in a single gulp. Three Wardens arrayed themselves in a triangle in front of her hut. The hut knelt to them. Slipping down the slant of the floor, Hecate fell on the enormous black egg. Keeping her body between the shell and the Lady's servants, she spat the potion onto it.

"I give you my words," she whispered. "Pay them back with interest."

The slime seethed across the ebony surface. There was not enough to cover the whole egg. The sheen of white blotted the black shell.

The crone stepped away. Her shawl slipped from her back. She blinked bemusedly at the disarray of her surroundings. Her eyes were vacant, utterly lacking in intellect. Three short steps descended from the doorway to the ground. Senile and happy to wander, the witch toddled outside. She smiled at each of the Wardens in turn. Hecate laid down, curled into a ball, and died.

The floating blue-robed Wardens surrounded the body. It rose between them. They took it away to the First Ward. As was their right. As was the Lady's will.

The izbushka settled into the overgrowth of the abandoned garden. Wood-slat siding grew over its door and windows, sealing the mottled egg safe within.

4

T hree days passed.

On the third dusk, a magpie wove through Osylum's gloomy air. She darted past the garden gate. She soared over the hut. With perfect precision, she dove down the narrow clay chimney pipe.

Inside, the egg rocked back and forth. The magpie swept from the hearth and lighted on the shell. She tapped thrice, thrice more, and thrice a third time. The egg's see-saw motion increased, building and building till it reached the tipping point and upended. It crashed from the bed to the floor, sending the bird aflutter.

A spidery web of cracks shot through the mottled shell. A gentle tapping came from within. The magpie dropped down onto the egg and pecked several times. A single fleck of shell flicked to the worn boards of the hut floor. In an instant, the whole egg shattered, revealing the fledgling within.

A naked maid with wild midnight hair rose from a fetal crouch. Patches of grey down still fluffed from her skin. She blinked. She brushed shell-dust off her arms and legs. She puffed the last stray bit of down off the edge of her nose. She preened herself and whistled a little trill.

The magpie flapped atop a shelf. She perched on the pallid marble bust of a mad-eyed woman in a high-domed helm. She opened her mouth and spoke the fledgling's name in a delicate voice:

"Oneirotheria!"

The woman clapped her hands and laughed.

"Yes! Me!"

She reached up. The magpie hopped to her outstretched palm. The fledgling cradled her to her breast. The bird's heart beat in time with her own. The magpie became a part of her and vanished.

"Shivers and shakes, I am nude!"

With one light foot, the maid swept a path through the eggshell. She jerked her head this way and that.

She spotted a pure white linen dress of simple design, wadded up behind a pile of leather-bound handbooks. She wriggled into it. She snatched up her mother's shawl, shook the dust from it, and wrapped herself safe and warm. She gazed over the jumble of books and loose sheaves and scribbled lore. The wreckage of someone else's life waited for her to make it make sense. She smiled from her forehead to the soles of her bare feet; an improbable and enigmatic expression equal parts confusion and resolution.

"Here I am, off I go, so little time, so much to know!"

5

She'd scarce devoured three hundred pages, scattered amid a dozen half-books, when a growl from outside the hut interrupted her mind's churning flow. She pressed her ear to the rough plank wall. The sound, still indistinct, rose and fell with a peculiar rhythm. It reminded her of the skeleton behind the words, spoken by the voice in her own head, as she had silently read.

She realized she was the only one in the hut and that might not be the normal state of affairs.

Alone! That's what this is called. An old word for an old state with its sound unchanged through many mouths. Basic as can be. Is it bad? Is it good?

A welter of feelings crashed over her, each one rushing by too fast to put a word to it. Her mind tumbled in the maelstrom, surging between solitude and wild desire.

Whist. Who else in here? No one. Crumbs in cracks! I think I would like to see someone. Yes!

For the briefest moment, she caught a memory-glimpse of deep brown eyes reflecting her own tiny face and lips half-parted to kiss her own. The vision slipped away from her outstretched fingers.

She hopped to her feet. From the black spaces between the few bright islands in her brain, a useful rhyme swam into view. It sparkled with magic.

"Izbushka, izbushka, your witch implores—open your mouth and show me the door!"

The battered plank walls rippled. Two windows and a door wrinkled into existence. Oneirotheria laughed.

"Isn't that a delight?" A shadow of doubt clouded her face. "Is delight the right term?"

Atoms of words swirled in her brain, composing meanings out of fragments.

"Delight is not de- and -light. That would be darkening. The light is a late alteration to the pronunciation of -lecto which is to charm or please. Yes! I would delight in some company if there were some."

The hut did not respond. Oneirotheria danced through her brain to see if there were words to say to call forth other people. Instead, she found a cacophony of disjointed knowledge; fragments of countless facts, spells, customs, images, observations. None of them added up to a whole of anything.

How do I know all these things?

"Bad luck to bed down by the witch's house," a man's voice came through the window. He chewed his words with predator's teeth. Oneirotheria's belly grumbled in sympathy.

She dropped low and peeked over the window sill. The ghostly reflection of her black eyes stared back at her from the grimy glass pane. Beyond, five blurry figures in long, ragged red coats milled about.

"Luck is the thing with feathers," a woman's voice replied, calm as a dove in the nest. "This Stay is in the Second and Hecate's always been safe to us."

Hecate. A proper name that stopped at itself. The chaos in the hut had been hers, of that Oneirotheria felt sure.

Hecate peckaty, skull on a shelf—

The rest of the couplet dropped off a dark cliff in her brain.

The first speaker hunkered over a ring of kindling. With a click and snick he struck fire from stones.

"Safe? What about Platon's Oath? We still owe her more than I want to pay."

"We owe her because she saved us. Now hush. Here is where we stay."

It had the feel of an oft-repeated argument. The three other figures in the group moved about the grime-smeared scene, setting up camp. The woman, slight-stooped and soft-footed, stepped up to Oneirotheria's window. She gave no sign of seeing the crouched witch—perhaps the dirty was thicker on the other side of the glass. She made a circle of her left thumb and index finger. Extending the other three digits, she brought the circle to her left eye.

"Lady sees you, Hecate."

"Here-now!" Oneirotheria shouted. She leapt to the door, flung it open, and floated down three steps to the tangled garden beyond.

The grim-jawed man flung down his flint and tinder. He rolled between her and the woman. When he hit his feet, he had a blade in each hand. His teeth bared in a snarl. The others—two men and a woman—shouted alarm. They pressed their backs to the ivy-gnawed walls.

The woman folded her hands over one another. She turned with deliberate passivity towards Oneirotheria. The witch, still caught up in her enthusiasm, pranced up to her, heedless of the raggedy man's razors.

"I know the word for that hand sign! That's the apotrope!" she sang, mimicking the woman's gesture with both hands over both eyes. More linguistic brick-shards flew around her mind, assembling meaning as she spoke:

"Apotrope. From apotropaios. Apo- meaning from, away, and tropos meaning turning. Apotrope therefore a turning away."

She ruffled her hair. Feathers swirled in the gloomy air. She frowned.

"It's a greeting. No? Yes? A greeting by turning away? That hardly seems right."

"Back!" The knife man barked. He slashed the air a skin's-distance from her cheek.

"Philotech," the woman said in an even tone.

"I won't let her hurt you."

Ignoring the threat, Oneirotheria spun on her heel. It was the first time in her life she had been outside. She took in her surroundings—and was taken in by them in turn.

She stood in what once must have been a splendid bower garden. Now, caretakers long gone, a vicious vegetative struggle raged in the slowest motion. Wilted, hole-riddled blooms dotted gnarled swaths of greenery. Statues—chewed faceless by relentless vines—lined muddy trenches. A fountain glopped verdant scum into a basin. A dilapidated shed leaned precariously in one corner, the last remaining glass shard in its window frame reflecting the garden's wild chaos in flat grey tones.

A high wall enclosed the space, though scarce

a stone could be seen beneath the myriad plants who had claimed the mortar for their growth. A heavy sodden stink, commingled growth and decay, thickened the humid air. On the sole bare patch of the ruined wall, above a rusted iron gate, a swooping hand had written in charcoal:

In thy orisons be all my sins remembered

All of it crashed over Oneirotheria's awareness in a moment, unsorted and incomprehensible. Her flooded mind gasped. To stay afloat, she seized the word that had brought her rushing from her hut.

"Apotrope! Apotrope apotrope apotrope..."

She jumped from red-coat to baffled red-coat, slashing with questions sharp as the violent man's blades:

"Why say hello with turning away? What are you turning away? Is it literal or metaphorical? Does apotrope mean the fingers or the face or the fingers to the face?"

Her inquisitive circuit ended back at the calm woman with dove-grey eyes. "Who *are* you anyway?"

The man's shoulders—as broad as Oneirotheria was tall—hunched with barely contained force. "Back. Off."

"Philotech," the woman ordered, "leave the new foundling be. She is no danger to you—nor me," she interrupted his objection.

Tension still straining every muscle in his body, Philotech stepped to the side. A warning rumbled from his throat. The primal sound shivered Oneirotheria's belly, though with fear or thrill she could not say.

Is there a word that means both? Shush! Apotrope first. Every word else in the world next. Yes!

"Hecate is lost," the woman said. "Already I can feel her being forgotten. I find you in her place, knowing more than a foundling usually knows on her first day."

"I know so many words! How do I know so many words? And all the little pieces that make them up! They buzz around my face like gnats to be snapped, snapped, snapped. Gnats! Are there gnats in the world? And who *are* you?"

"We are the Peripats," the woman replied, as if that were sufficient.

"Peripats! Peri- meaning around, about, through, and -pat being pat-pat-pad-pad along, that is to say walking. So you walk around, about, and through. To and fro, up and down along the world, peripatpatp—"

The grey-eyed woman laid one hand lightly on Oneirotheria's forearm. The touch settled her darting brain—somewhat.

"I am Matron. I will guide you a little, on your path."

Matron let go of Oneirotheria's arm. The rush of thoughts returned. The witch hopped from foot to foot to keep her body busy while she tried to suss out what was happening around her.

"She's mad," Philotech said. "Let the city have her."

"When in doubt," Matron told her recalcitrant companion, "help a fellow out."

Fellow. Fee-low. Fee-lay, one who lays down a fee in part or whole, for or with another. A partner. Will these strangers be partners? In what? What is laid down? What's to be paid out? Prithee!

Oneirotheria realized her lips were moving to match her inner voice. She liked the trick. She could feel the words in her mouth and set them free, but there was no sound to distract those outside her mind. She resolved to do that henceforth whenever others were talking too slow.

Matron pointed to each of the other three Peripats in turn.

"Lucretius, Nomine, Orfeo," she said their names for the newling's benefit, "please prepare the Stay before Wardens come to feed."

The three returned to building a camp. Matron held Philotech's gaze till he bowed his head and joined the rest. He clicked sparks over tinder brush, but kept his eyes fixed on the witch and his leader. Seeing Oneirotheria still trying to learn everything at once, Matron pointed to the open hut door.

"Perhaps it would be easier to talk inside. Fewer things to distract you."

"There's wisdom in that. Wisdom... wit... witch... I'm a witch!" she cried and fluttered into her hut with Matron in her feathery wake.

6

Oneirotheria perched on the edge of her stool, quivering with barely contained curiosity. Only Matron's deliberate motion and the calm that clothed her like a cloak kept the witch from flying off in a dozen directions at once. The woman took a cross-legged seat and spread the long tails of her ruddy coat around her.

"The apotrope," she said, by way of beginning. She held up her left hand. She extended three of the fingers and joined the index and thumb in a circle. "Three fingers for three rules that govern all of Osylum and a circle for the Lady's eye which watches us all."

"Love we the Lady and fear we the Fade," Oneirotheria chanted.

Matron blinked, startled. "You know that song? Have you met others before this?"

Not trusting herself not to explode in a hurricane of speaking, Oneirotheria clenched her jaw. She sat on her hands. She shook her head.

"I've never met a foundling witch," Matron continued. "Hecate was already ancient when I was found, blank and naked in a brick gutter. Perhaps your kind know things from the very start."

That did not sound right to Oneirotheria. She

wanted to hear more though. So, with remarkable effort, she constrained herself to a noncommittal shrug. Sensing how precarious the witch's attention was, Matron waved away her own speculation. With her right hand, she pointed at each of the apotrope's extended fingers in turn.

"One: The Rule of Three. Everything that comes in three is complete and completion comes in threes. Two: The Rule of Circles. Everything that is circular is complete and completion comes in circles. Three: The Rule of No Escape—"

ESCAPE!

The word knocked the witch off her seat. It amplified in her mind, the command of a thousand thousand voices.

As she toppled, the magpie rose from her breast to her brain. By the time she reached the floor, her woman body had merged with the bird and transformed. Fleeing, she battered the window with flailing wings. She scratched the glass with delicate talons.

"Lady's grace!" Matron exclaimed. "I'd heard rumors."

The magpie ignored her. She beat away from the window. She ricocheted off the close walls. Matron ducked as she swept past to a rafter behind the chimney pipe. A black beak and one glittering eye peeked around the clay tube. The magpie whistled, low and querulous.

"Shoon... shoon," Matron cooed. She turned her palms up. She closed her eyes. She hummed five slow notes. She sang a soft contralto lullaby:

"One for silence, two for peace,
Three for a prison with no release,
Four know fear, but five know sleep,

Safe in the darkness, where the bad things creep."

Deep within the skittering magpie mind, Oneirotheria remembered her human half. By the time Matron's song finished, the bird had settled on the stool and turned back into a woman. She wistfully let her feathered other-self return to her heart's center. She knew the way back to that shape now. She promised herself she'd fly again.

"Better?" Matron asked.

"Yes."

"What happened?"

"I don't know. When you said—that word—it rang in my heart like all the bells in the city. Bells? How many bells are there? Why are there bells in the city? Do they ring? And how do I know that sound if I've only been here—how long have I been here?"

The jolting power of the word *escape* dissipated, borne away in fragments of a dozen questions. Matron remained unphased.

"How many days and nights do you remember so far?"

Oneirotheria thought about the rise and fall of light. She could not recall. "There were no windows until I decided to leave."

"Ah. Still, you must be hungry."

"Hungry! That's where this all began. I heard Philotech grumbling and my belly chimed in."

"It is nearly time for the Wardens to feed."

"Feed? That's a concerningly ambiguous verb."

Matron laughed. "I suppose it is. How is this: It is nearly time for the Wardens to feed us."

"To feed us to what?"

"Dear, you are a delight. The Feeding happens

three times a day. The Wardens go to the same places across the city and they provide food and drink in sufficient plates to keep us going till the next time."

"Wardens? Who or what are they? What gives them the right to decide when we eat?"

Matron put a finger to her lips. "Some questions are best not asked."

Oneirotheria wrinkled her face. "That sentence smells rotten as a Ratkipper's seasoning pit."

Matron blinked. "A Ratkipper's seasoning pit... Do you know what that saying means?"

"No, no and one more time no!" She shook out pale fingers. "I know so much more than I know!"

Agitation returned to the surface of her brain; peaks of knowledge and troughs of ignorance roiling.

"Never mind." Matron stood and beckoned her. "Come. Feeding time."

Just before they left the hut, Matron added: "Be wary of the Wardens. Take what they give without speaking. They will ask you a single question. They ask everyone the same question. Respond with the question in an answer form and you will be fine."

She had not sounded afraid till that moment. The quaver in her voice kept Oneirotheria's questions at bay. The witch filed the other woman's unexplained fear and vowed to have her curiosity sated, soon or late.

7

M atron led her crew through the garden gate, with the newling in tow. Beyond the ivy-wreathed archway lay a narrow cobbled alley. Ten paces to their left, the alley opened onto a broad piazza. Red-roofed arcades ran along all four sides, broken only by three streets leading out. The covered walkways fronted multiple connected buildings, accessible via alcoved doorways. The stucco structures were all three stories and several had balconies overlooking the plaza. A statue, hooded and hand-bound, stood vigil at the center of the open space, atop a white-streaked granite plinth.

Matron went to the stone man's feet and waited. The rest of the Peripats took up places around the square, lounging against pillars or sitting on curbs. They arranged themselves so as to cover every entrance by line of sight.

Oneirotheria stopped stock-still at the mouth of the alley. She turned her head upwards. The sky made a flat grey dome over the wide expanse. With slow steps, she circled to take it all in. As she stared, she became aware of a subtle ombre shading—the featureless hemisphere was a whisper greyer at the ring of the horizon, lightening to nigh-white at the zenith.

There are words for things that are not here; the sun, the moon, the stars. Whose voice is that? Not mine. My mind yes, the voice not mine. No sun no moon no stars no wind and the birds know what men never learn. Even the sky has walls in this prison town. My voice but not my words. I know neither what I am nor what I may be.

A warning whistle pricked her dusky bubble of thought.

"Tribunal coming," said the one Matron had called Orfeo.

The Peripats gathered beneath the statue, a tableau of ill-concealed tension. Bemused, Oneirotheria wandered their way. She'd scarce crossed half the span when three Wardens arrived.

They floated a full three handspans above the street. Empty air shimmered beneath them. Their feet—if they had feet—were concealed within the flowing hem of their vestments. The robes shone vibrant blue against the drab surroundings. Sinuous silver embroidery crawled along the silk, constantly in motion. Even if they had been standing, they would have been half again as tall as Philotech, who was the tallest Peripat by a head.

Their hands, pale yellow and desiccated, extended from trumpet sleeves. Their palms barely existed, but each of their three fingers was as long as Oneirotheria's forearm. Their faces too were jaundiced and mummified. Unbroken wrinkled skin covered where a mouth should be. Two narrow slits served as nostrils.

Two lidless eyes—flat and lifeless as dabs of black ink on a tattered page—stared across the plaza. Above them, at the peak of a triangle, sat a third eye. It was the Wardens' most human feature, lidded with smooth, living skin and trimmed by delicate lashes. It was currently closed. Above that, a crest of bone topped their heads with a crown of bleached and jagged blades.

Oneirotheria's feet moved of their own accord towards the Peripats. She could not look away from the Wardens, taking in every detail.

"They all look the same," she whispered.

"Hush," said Matron.

The Wardens wafted across the plaza. A polished steel bier hovered between them, borne on an invisible force. On it sat two troughs of steaming beige mush, two trays of hand-sized bread loaves, four pitchers of water, a stack of chipped brown clay bowls and matching cups, and a dun cloth box of pewter spoons. The smell from the mush set Oneirotheria's mouth to watering. The Peripats lined up in order of precedence. Matron motioned for the Foundling to take first place.

Reaching the base of the statue, the Wardens parted. They arrayed themselves so that Oneirotheria could only see two at a time—the third lurked forever just out of sight on the periphery. The bier continued its forward progress until it stopped just in front of her. As she picked up a bowl and spoon, the Wardens raised their left hand, palm up. An emotionless voice sounded in her mind.

"EVERYTHING IS AS IT SHOULD BE."

Startled, she squeaked and dropped the bowl. She cocked her head to the one side and the other, baffled by the eerie mental intrusion. Her lips parted, a flurry of questions dancing on her teeth. Matron gently tapped her arm.

Respond with the question in answer form, she remembered the grey-haired woman warning her.

The Warden had not asked her a question, though. It had been a statement. Almost a report of conditions.

Still, she tried responding as she'd been instructed:

"Everything is as it should be."

Apparently satisfied, the Wardens lowered their hands. The Peripats all sighed. The Wardens moved on to Matron. The grey-eyed woman nodded, as if she heard a question in her mind.

"Everything is as it should be," she softly replied.

On down the line of Peripats the peculiar litany concluded, question and response. Oneirotheria retrieved the bowl, took her fill, and moved aside. After everyone had their bread and mush, the Wardens and their tray drifted off. Everyone relaxed and began to eat.

"Why?" Oneirotheria asked everyone and no one.

"Why," Philotech growled derisively. "Why ask why?"

"Aha! You are metacurious!" she said. "Meta-being a way of going over whatever it's tacked on to."

Philotech rolled his eyes. He turned away. He hunched his shoulders over his bowl. He shoveled in mush like it was a grim duty instead of a meal.

Ignoring her cooling supper, Oneirotheria flung words into the growing gloom. "Why are you all afraid of them? Why do they feed you? Why do you take their food? Why do they talk in my mind without mouths and why are they so concerned that everything is as it should be? Everything!"

She waved her bowl round the plaza, spattering mush to the cobbles. "Everything? Should? Why those words? Why should *everything* be as it *should*?"

Matron raised a finger to her lips. "Why is the thing with feathers. Peace and eat."

Oneirotheria dropped hard to her haunches on the stone curb. Her mouth ate while her mind kept talking to itself and getting nowhere.

8

By the time her spoon scraped the bottom of the bowl, the sky was half as bright as it had been.

"What do I do now? Or is what also the thing with feathers?"

No one answered. The Peripats had all left while she'd been focused inwards. Their dishes were stacked neatly beneath the statue.

I suppose you went a-walking around. Peri and patting. Silly me to expect anything else. And me? I'm no Peripat. I'm—I don't know what I am. Well, whatever I am, it is not a walk-rounder. I have purpose. I don't know what it is.

She licked her spoon clean. She turned it over and over, watching her reflection swell and collapse, swell and collapse. A chant echoed from the vaulted darkness in her skull. She intoned the words aloud to the spoon.

"Old man, old man in the mirror, see me now, hear me here."

A tiny fish-eyed face replaced her reflection in the curved steel.

"Here-now!" She flung the spoon across the piazza. She immediately regretted the reaction. "Wait!"

She sprinted over to the glint in the cobbles. With relief, she saw the face was still there. A liver-spotted, tonsured old man in a rough wool robe of blue stared back at her, astonished. Behind him rose the rough stone walls of a cell, lit by sallow guttering light.

He said something she could not hear. She dropped to all fours for a closer look.

"Speak up!"

His mouth cut an irritable line. He spoke again, silently. His lips moved more than necessary. With effort, she read his words.

"The count's been over what it should be by six for nearly a sennet, and now this."

She ruffled feathers from her hair, indignant.

"I don't know what any of that means, but I'm sure I don't like being called 'now this.'"

"Did Hecate teach you the summoning spell?"

She grabbed the spoon. She fell back on her haunches. "Hecate! That's the name Matron used for whoever used to live in my little hut."

"Oh."

The monk's expression softened a little. Or gave way to relief. Oneirotheria couldn't quite tell.

"So she was one of the nine lost, three counts ago," he continued. "Which makes you one of the found to count tonight."

"Lost and found but nowhere to hide from you. Counts and counting but what for who?" The spoon trembled in her grasp. "How do you make so much nonsense with such tiny words?"

"New found and confused." With only his lips to read, she could not gauge his tone; pity or contempt. "The Oblates count the living and calculate the lost."

"Why?"

"So we can chant it to the Great Mirror for the Linnaea."

"Why?"

The monk shook his head. "Too many questions. How do you witches get me to talk so much?"

"I didn't do anything."

"You must have. Well it stops now. I'm not getting drawn in by another witch. My brothers would call me Hendiatrix the Heretic and shove me through the Phrontistery food slot for the Wardens to fade, if they knew everything I did for Hecate."

"What did you do?"

"Ask whoever taught you the spell. The one that lets us talk, even though that should be impossible. And tell whoever that was that I haven't seen an oseovox yet and won't ever and I'm through."

With that, he swept his robe over the scene, blocking his reflection. For a moment, the curved steel glowed blue, then Oneirotheria faced her reflection again.

Oseovox.

The word fluttered in her mind's black sky as fierce and fast as ESCAPE.

9

The sky was too dim to see very far down any of the streets off the plaza—even if she had known which of the three paths to take. She pondered. A melody of voices echoed down the garden alley. Twisting the spoon into her hair, she slipped on light feet towards the music.

Five shadows danced on the crumbling garden walls. Philotech's fire crackled. The Peripats stood in a pentagon around it, backs to the flame and faces to the gloaming. They chanted syllables, one per note.

"Lie, Mu, Na, Oh, Pay..."

From those five sounds they built a song. The flames rose and fell to their music. A dome of red light swelled over their camp, raised by their interwoven voices. Entranced, Oneirotheria paced the twilight perimeter. At the crescendo, the shell of light and music pressed against her. She ran her hands along it—a solid cool surface instead of fire-heated air. Coruscating scarlet tendrils trailed off her fingertips. Ripples distorted the Peripats' faces.

Their song ended.

"Here we stay till the day," Matron recited. "We have sung away the terrors that live in the night.

Nothing may cross the circle of our song. We will sleep safe."

"We will sleep safe," responded the others. "For we have sung together."

Oneirotheria pushed the crimson hemisphere of light. The night air held her out with invisible force.

"Well that's a handy trick," she said. "Is the magic in the words or the notes?"

Matron smiled.

"It's in the singers. The singers and the way they stand."

"Can I join you?"

"You do not need the safety of a Peripat's Stay. Your own little place will do."

In answer, the hut stood up. It scratched three deep furrows in the mouldering earth with one enormous taloned foot. It settled back down, a happy hen.

Matron climbed into her bedroll. She turned her back to the fire and closed her eyes. The others—save Philotech—followed suit. The gruff Peripat sat cross-legged. He stared at Oneirotheria, as if he did not trust his own magic to keep her outside the protective circle. He dragged a whetstone across one of his knives with a whining scrape.

"A different tune than singing down the dark," he growled. "Just as good against whatever comes."

Oneirotheria listened to the city. Silence, save for the skin-shivering sound of the Peripat's steel on stone.

"And what might come?"

Philotech grinned, his teeth just shy of fangs. "Just wait."

"You're afraid of me!" She hadn't known she was going to say that till she said it. She knew it was true nonetheless.

"Why should I be afraid? The Sung Circle could hold back even the Lady's Fog, if it came crawling at the end of the world."

"The Lady's Fog?"

He ignored the question. Instead, he scraped the stone once more across his knife. "I won't let you hurt any of us."

His body, she noted, only guarded Matron. So he didn't mean 'us' he meant 'her.'

Quick as she noticed the detail of his fear, she forgot it, remembering instead something the monk had said.

"Do you know what an oseovox is?"

He shook his head. "Your cant pads a madder path than an Abram-Man."

"I'm just trying to understand."

"Understand what?"

"Everything."

"That's a short street to a quick death."

A vision seized her. The light from the fire scribed bright words on the palette of the night.

Death's the marketplace where each one meets.

"Death. A very, very old word that one. So old it comes from nowhere. It's right next to fear on your tongue, Philotech. But not mine. Why am I not afraid?"

She whirled away from the wary Peripat's vigil. She considered her hut. Within its tiny confines waited pages and pages of knowledge, gathered by someone named Hecate. She could pore over them till her curiosity was as full as her belly after the Feed.

Yet...

She recoiled. The thought of four walls, trammeling her body and mind, made her chest tighten. The magpie grew uneasy. Oneirotheria did not disagree.

Whatever fragments Hecate had shored up had not been enough to save her. Besides, words would wait on a page. The world of the city, even in the dark, called to her. She could walk her own way out there, she hoped.

To where? Why is Philotech afraid and I am not? What's waiting out there in the dark? Esc—no. Mustn't even think that word or the bird will take to wing. Why do those two syllables shout so much louder than any other? Who is in my mind, if not me?

She spun back to Philotech, whose eyes had never left her.

"Too many questions," she said. "Too many thoughts. Too many words. Not enough things to go with the words. I can't sleep. Out to the straying streets."

With that, she left the baffled vagabond to the safety of his knives and fire.

10

Very quickly, Oneirotheria found herself in pitch dark. She trailed her left hand against a patchy stucco wall for guidance. Only that touch and the cool press of cobbles on her bare feet kept her from feeling like she floated in an endless void.

The sun... the moon... the stars... words for lights from above. There was no sun before and nothing now overhead. So why words for them? Did someone see a Peripat's fire and think 'that'd be nice up high and I'll call it the sun in the blue sky.' Blue? The sky was grey as cobblegrout when I ate the Warden's food.

Her thoughts whirled in the space around those three words: sun, moon, stars. Sun, moon, stars. Stars, moon, sun. Moon, stars, sun. Sun, stars, moon. Sun, moon, stars... After a while, the sounds uncoupled from sense. Did they mean anything? Had anything meant anything ever? Just a marching cadence of sing-song syllables. Left foot, *sun*. Right foot, *moon*. Left foot, *stars*. Right foot, *sun*... on and on and on.

Light suddenly flared around her. She blinked and shielded her eyes.

"Where did the darkness go?"

A four/four tip-tap tip-tap from the cobbles answered her. A brass creature with eight spindly legs scuttled along the sidewalk ahead of her. A blue-orange flame wavered from a burnished tube where its face would otherwise be. In the center of its back, a flat key slowly turned.

It had just left a bronze lamp pole, atop which a yellow light shone. It scurried straight on to the next post. Using a series of holes the precise diameter of its legs, the lamp-lighter climbed to the top. When its flame touched the spout atop the post brightness burst out. The spider nipped swiftly down.

Oneirotheria couldn't help but laugh at the delightful contraption.

"Clever!"

Oblivious to her enjoyment, the clockwork lamp-lighter finished its task. The street decently illuminated, it retreated towards a hole in the curb.

"Wait!"

She dashed after it. Just before it entered its hidey-hole, she snatched it up. She dropped it at once, as hot metal burned her fingers. She sucked on the hurt digits. The lamp-lighter landed on its back. Its key ground the stones, while its legs waved futilely. Its flame scorched a black patch on the street.

"When in doubt," Oneirotheria remembered Matron saying, "help a fellow out."

She wrapped her unburnt hand in the shawl. With a quick flip, she righted the flailing contraption. It crawled into the hole. A brass panel slid over the opening. She tapped it with a fingernail. No response.

"Thank you anyway," she said with a curtsy at the ground. She straightened up and looked around.

On one side of the street, a wall towered over her. The only break in the concrete expanse was a seamless brass slab—a gate, perhaps, though one with no obvious means of opening. The wall ran the entire length of the block, enclosing what must have been an enormous estate. Someone had scrawled swooping charcoal letters over the entry:

Double bosoms seem to wear one heart

Oneirotheria read the line aloud, in the hopes that would jar loose some sense from her jangling brain.

It did not.

A narrow tower rose behind the wall. The street lamps illuminated only its lower reaches. Presumably it continued into the darkness. High above, a single point of light twinkled blue.

That's not a star, I think.

She stroked the wall. Smooth concrete slipped under her hand. She'd never be able to climb over. Even if she could hoist herself up, jagged fragments of razor glass glittered on the top. Whoever lived behind that metal gate did not want visitors. No matter how many bosoms or hearts they might have.

"Fine and feh," she said and turned the other way.

A large garden park lay across from the compound. Unlike the unkept bower where her hut nested, someone tended this place crisp and neat. Crushed rock paths entered at precise intervals, between raised brick beds. Jumbled perfumes wafted across the way, interwoven with faint clicks and snips.

Rosemary for remembrance. Pansies, that's for thoughts.

Wait.

Once again, those aren't my words. Not like the Warden's question in my head, though. That was in the Warden's voice. It was my voice said those things about rosemary and pansies. Why is the voice in my mind saying someone else's words? Or is someone else using my mind's voice?

"Who are you?"

There was no reply inside nor out.

My rosemary's half-stripped and my pansies full of holes. Let's see if the garden has a gardener.

The crushed rock path caressed her bare feet, soft and chalky; a relief she hadn't known she needed. Padding hard cobbles had bruised her heels. Savoring the feeling, she strolled down a straight, narrow path. The streetlights receded. In their place, white flowers glowed on trellis vines, arched over each intersection of the gridded garden paths.

She plucked one. Its pale glow faded as soon as she severed it from the stem. She pressed it to her face, breathing in the elusive aroma of night secrets. When she exhaled, her breath re-ignited the cold flower's light. She held it in an open palm to illuminate her way.

Small things hopped in the plant beds. She leaned for a closer look. The pale flower-light broke into silver and gold flashes. Wee clockwork creatures busied themselves in the brush. Some trimmed dead leaves, others furrowed the earth, others spritzed water here and there. The sounds of dozens of tiny metal beasts swarmed around her... snip, drip, snick, scritch, tick tick tick tick...

"Poor safe Philotech," she murmured. "You're missing so much in your fear."

"Better to miss some things in fear than lose everything in folly," a man said behind her.

She turned. The moonflower lit him up, a scant six feet away. He wore a bramble-scarred leather coat over a rough wool shirt and trousers. Old earth stains streaked his clothes. Brown dirt caked his knuckles and nails, deep enough to grow roses in. The blade of the shovel he carried, however, was clean, sharp steel. As were the shears, hand rake, and trowel dangling from his workman's belt.

"Or so they say," he continued. His voice came from the back of his throat, thick as tree sap and every syllable flowed with slow insistence into the next. "They say all kind of things, though, don't they? Whoever they are."

"Whoever they are," she repeated.

"So you don't know? I'd've thought by now you'd know."

"Is this your garden?"

"No. This was Dedalus's plot, when he was alive. Now it belongs to the Linnaea." He pointed with his shovel in the direction of the walled compound. "They live behind that wall. They call it the Laboratory like it's one place, though it's a half-dozen buildings."

"You work for them?"

"I work for Upstart."

"Who does he work for?"

"You don't remember him?" He shook his head. "He's not going to like that."

"Why not?"

"I'm not sure. He doesn't tell me much beyond where to go and what to do." He tapped one pendulous earlobe. "But I listen. And I plant what I hear deep in my wits till it's blooming time. Right now I've sprouted a bud says you were supposed to remember Upstart. Maybe even remember me."

"I don't."

He circled finger and thumb over his eye; the apotrope. "I see you. Turnspade, at your service."

"I thought you worked for Upstart."

"He told me to find you and put myself at your service."

"Me?"

"Whoever you'd become, at any rate."

"I don't know what that means."

"His words. Not mine. Find whoever Hecate's become and serve that person well."

"You hear other people's words too? In your head? Their words, your voice?"

"Oh, if I had any doubts you was her, they're weeded clear by that mad cant. You're the witch, whether you remember or not."

He paused, concerned she might take offense and do something untoward. When she just stared at him, he continued: "No. He told me his own self."

"How did you find me?"

His thick fingers gently brushed the frail leaves of a hazel shrub. "I listened to the plants. They said a chicken-legged hut nested in a folly-plot in the Second."

He chuckled. "The man with the knives jumped and barked when I stepped through the gate."

"He's a fearful fox, isn't he?"

"With sharp steel teeth."

"Did he hurt you? Did you hurt him?"

"No on both counts. He puffed up and dared me to cross his singing line. I gave him my back. I rapped on your door and flashed the apotrope at your window. To be rid of me, he told me you'd wandered off."

"Then the plants told you I was here?"

"A third no. It takes a long time for green growing things to pay us much mind. I just took the shortest path a blind new-found woman might stumble down."

"That covers the how of finding me. Now. Why?"

Turnspade shrugged. His garden tools jingled. "Lady knows."

"And Upstart, presumably, who sent you."

The tools clinked again by way of reply. Oneirotheria made a decision.

"Take me to him."

"It's a long walk to the Ninth Ward. And dark for the most part."

"Snip me a switch to use for a torch," she ordered and plucked a dozen moonflowers to light their way.

11

Four blooms faded by the time the witch and the gardener came to the first gate. She fixed a fresh flower to her stick. She puffed it alight.

"They don't last long, do they?" she asked Turnspade.

"Neither does a single breath. And all of them together, well..." He spread his hands and waved into the night. "Seeds for the next breather, I suppose."

It was the first time he'd spoken since the Linnaea's garden, despite a steady peppering of Oneirotheria's questions. She eventually decided she didn't mind his noncommittal silence. Better than growled threats, or half-answers that doubled her questions.

"I shouldn't have wasted that blossom. Looks like candles up ahead, in a great arch, way at the end of the street." She stopped. "Candles. Lanterns, lamps, wicks, torches, fires, blazes, conflagrations, infernos... so many words for ways to get light. And still no sun nor moon nor stars."

He pointed at the flickering semicircle down the street.

"That's the gate to the Third. Don't worry about the smoke. It's not the Lady's Fog, just plain old smoke. Go straight through. Down the winding hill road you'll find a bramble plot surrounded by an iron gate. That's where I'll meet you."

"Why aren't you coming with?"

He made the apotrope over his left eye. "Lady sees us all. Best she not see us together at a gate."

With that, he slipped into a dim alley. His normally jingling tools, Oneirotheria noted, did not make a sound. He could be quiet as an owl over a mouse, it seemed, if it served him.

"Best she not see us..." she grumbled. "Like that means anything to me."

She marched towards the gate. Enormous wooden doors, three times her height, stood open. Beyond, a short tunnel passed through a thick stone wall. Dozens of unique gargoyles, carved into the soot-streaked archway, held sallow waxy candles over the passage. A haze of smoke seethed across the street, undulating with a sullen life of its own.

The wavering form of a Warden coalesced in the miasma. It floated forwards. She could not tell if it was one of the three she'd seen earlier, at feeding time, or a new one. It paused in the middle of the path. It folded its three fingered hands across its midriff. The trumpet sleeves of its blue robe continued to wave ever so slightly.

"*EVERYTHING IS AS IT SHOULD BE.*" The Warden's voice sounded in her mind, exactly the same as the last one. A statement of fact, reported as required.

"Every—ugh!"

Sickly candle-smoke choked her. A coughing fit wracked her shoulders. Doubled over hacking, she raised one hand in the apotrope gesture.

Apparently, that sufficed. The Warden drifted out of her way. She dashed hot tears from her eyes. Sipping shallow breaths to calm her spasming lungs, she shuffled through the portal between Wards.

The broad boulevards and spacious estates of the Second Ward gave way to claustrophobic chaos. The smoke from the gate persisted beyond, thickening as she went. Smudges smoldered on every corner, oozing incense fumes. Temples, ranging in size from a massive cathedral to a lean-to shrine barely tall enough for a waist-high votive statue, crowded the space. There was no rhyme nor reason to their placement. They were built in dozens of styles; high-vaulted stained glass windows soared above squat stone beehives, which shoved up beneath writhing carved plinths that leaned on stark granite shrines.

"Three for the temples that no one may fill," Oneirotheria chanted in an sing-song voice. It was a snatch of song she'd quoted earlier to Matron. Four stanzas for Nine Wards. The chorus went: "Love we the Lady and fear we the Fade..."

True to the lyric, every edifice in the Third stood empty. Most were near to falling over and a few had given way to age and gravity, collapsing in somber piles of stone, timber, and glass. The street was foot-worn, almost to the dirt below. When she strained her ears, she fancied she could hear echoes of mournful dirges but they vanished the moment she paid them heed.

The road wound down before her feet. She trudged until she came to Turnspade's bramble-plot. A rust-gnawed iron fence surrounded the tangle. When she pulled the lichgate to open it, it fell off its hinges. Startled, she jumped back. The wrought-iron shattered on the pavement with a CLANG that rang across the hills and valleys of the temple-thronged Ward. The peel receded and returned several times before its dying knell.

"Clearly not *everything* is as it should be," she quipped, and stepped into the churchyard.

A single labyrinthine path snaked round and back amid the thorn bushes, opening at last on a clearing. A marble weeping angel knelt at the center, her wings and lap making a bench. Not knowing how long Turnspade would be, Oneirotheria curled up on the stone seat.

The moonflower dwindled. She did not bother with another. The smoke provided dim light—perhaps from the spread glow of candles all over the Ward. For once, she couldn't manage to wonder. All her bits of curiosity drifted away into thick smog. The perfumed haze and oppressive architectural decay weighed down her brain. Exhausted by the relentless thoughts and skittering shock of her first full day alive, she closed her eyes.

12

She woke to a sky the color of dirty paper. Her index finger traced a word across it until she realized she was spelling 'escape'. She sat up.

"Yes! That!"

"What?" Turnspade's molasses voice asked.

Her burning eyes blinked the world back into shape. The incense haze still hung thick in the air. Brambles surrounded her. An angel cradled her in grief-bent wings. The gardener hunkered by the labyrinth arch, spade across his thighs. A line of dark red marred the rim of the shovel blade. A crumpled body leaned face-first into the thorn bush beside him.

"Planting corpses instead of flowers?"

"No need. Wardens will collect him. Their right. Lady's will."

"How do they know where to find him?"

Turnspade's tools clinked his ignorance. "Do you remember anything more?"

She introspected a moment.

"No. Still just islands in a black sea. At least the sea is calm." She snorted. "Words. Just words. Islands and seas don't mean anything in this flotsam city."

She went over to inspect the dead man. His

black fingernails were sharp as talons and his teeth had been filed to points. A dozen stains of dubious provenance decorated his threadbare breeches. All the smoky perfume in the Third Ward, balled up and crammed into her nostrils couldn't block the stink of him. It wasn't rot, either—he'd reeked that badly in life.

"Ratkipper," Turnspade said. "Sniffed you out while you slept."

"Why didn't you wake me up?"

"Why would I?"

She couldn't think of a good answer to that, so she returned to studying the corpse. A piece of skin, under-flesh still attached, wedged between his canine and incisor.

Human skin.

"Don't the Wardens feed Ratkippers too?"

"They do."

"So they're cannibals by choice."

Clink.

"Did he hurt you?"

"No."

"What was he doing here?"

"Not sure. They live in the Seventh Ward. Or in the sewers. Don't go elsewhere much. Unless Eschatos tells them to."

"Eschatos." She spat after saying the name. An ugly word, it sat on her tongue like ooze from an infected wound. "Who's that?"

"The Ratkippers worship him like the Lady's own priest. He holds court across town, though no one knows who gave him the right. Acts like he's a Warden with a voice."

"Do I—" she changed her question mid-thought. *Do I know him?* Instead she asked: "Does the Lady know him?"

"Who knows who the Lady knows?"

"Does he know me?"

"He knew the woman you used to be, before you withered and bloomed again, dressed in different petals."

"Does he really have authority like the Wardens?"

"I don't think so. Upstart says he's like a puppet with its hand up its own backside."

She snerked. "Colorful image. And it gets the point across."

"Upstart has a way with words."

Oneirotheria considered what to do next. She had not mis-spoken when she said the sea of unknown things in her brain had calmed. Whether it was sleep, growing familiarity with the world, or the soporific smog of the temple ward, the manic frenzy of her first day had abated—if only for the moment. A plan began to form from the fragments of yesterday.

"Upstart. We were going to see him last night. We should finished the trip."

Turnspade stood. Oneirotheria stepped towards the bramble arch. He blocked the way with his spade.

"One thing. If the Ratkippers take me on the way," he said, "the boss is in the theatre in the Ninth. Do you know where that is?"

"No."

He traced a fist-sized circle in the dirt. "First Ward. Lady's there, no need to go."

The Lady. There's a woman I have questions for.

Turnspade drew another circle around the first. He divided it in two. He pointed at the halves.

"Second. Third. Gates between them at either end."

"No gate to the First?"

He ignored the question. He dug a third circle around the first two and cut it in three. "Four, Five, and Six. Go to the gate from Three to Five—you'll know it by the lack of skulls. Don't take any other gate, Five's the fastest way."

He circumscribed the whole crude map one final time, and trisected the outermost circle. He only pointed to a single segment. "Nine here, from Five."

He held her gaze. "This is important: Nothing in the Ninth is what it seems to be. You'll be safe, just keep that in mind."

"I will. Once there, where do I go?"

"He'll know you're there. He'll send someone. Probably."

"Probably," she rolled the word in her mouth. "I like the way that word tastes. Wishful as a drop of honeysuckle and vanishing just as fast."

"Honeysuckle?"

"Oh, gardener, they don't have that here either?" She could picture the bloom, yellow-white and sweet, drooping from a bright green winding vine.

Clink.

"Remember the map," he said. "If you can."

"Lead the way," she replied, "so I won't have to."

13

H alfway down the switchback winding path,
Oneirotheria caught a whiff of Ratkipper.
The stench wormed out of the cloying temple perfume, an olfactory maggot. The stink thickened as
the labyrinth curved towards the outer brambles.
Turnspade choked his grip on the haft of his shovel.

"Be ready."

She clenched her fists. They were not particularly viable weapons. She snatched a trowel from
Turnspade's belt. He gave her a flat look. She
jabbed the air with the tiny tool. His face did not
change.

"What?"

"Are you sure you're a witch?"

The crack of brambles and a high-arcing hiss cut
off her reply.

A Ratkipper launched herself over the maze
wall. Blood dripped off her claws, pouring from
thorn-slashes down both arms. She snapped at
Oneirotheria as she pounced.

Turnspade's shovel caught the Ratkipper across
the cheek. The gardener's mud-caked boot kicked
her ribs at the same time. The force of the twin
blows knocked the airborne cannibal two meters

down the path. With a single step, Turnspade was on her.

The Ratkipper raised her head with a file-fanged grin. This one had no tongue. She hissed at the witch. Turnspade brought the flat of his shovel across her head several times, deliberate and methodical as tamping down earth.

The black sea of forgetfulness in Oneirotheria's brain froze solid in an instant. Inwardly, she traversed that chill crystalline expanse for what felt like aeons, trying to find a memory to explain the moment or provide a feeling fit for it. Outwardly, her eyes drifted from the violence to the trowel in her hand. Somewhere between the two, she heard herself say:

"I'm going to need a better weapon."

Turnspade finished his work. He strode past. As he did, he nudged her with his shoulder, jarring her out of the reverie.

"You're a witch," he said. "You alone are a better weapon than anything this city holds. Save the Fade."

"I don't know what that means," she said. She rushed to catch up, for he had begun to jog. "She would've eaten me six different ways before I could've punched her eye or raised a welt with this thing."

She flung the trowel into the brush. Turnspade grunted at the casual discard of his tool, but did not slow. She ran after, still in a space of icy, logical calm. She enumerated a train of reason.

"There's things I know, aren't there? Spells they call them. Incantations. Hexes. Craft, knowledge, witchery, on and on and on it goes. Too many words for just one thing. That's a change. It *is* all the same thing, isn't? Magic let us call it. And it is powerful, if your expectation is any—*whuff!*"

A Ratkipper's claw seized her ankle. She fell face-first on the path. The filthy clutch pulled her towards a burrow under the brambles. She twisted, kicked barefoot at the face in the hole. Turnspade kept running. By the time he realized she wasn't with him, Oneirotheria was already waist-deep in the labyrinth wall. He'd never reach her before she disappeared.

The Ratkipper couldn't wait till his prey was secured to start his feast. He sank his fangs into the witch's shin.

Pain shattered the ice in her brain. With a re-sounding crack, black inner spaces opened. Words floated to the surface. She kicked the Ratkipper's teeth loose. Palm flat on the ground, she chanted the magic.

"By oak and ash and thorn be broke and slashed and torn!"

The bramble-hedge closed in around the bur-rowing Ratkipper; a dozen seasons' growth in an instant. He screamed as the barbs stabbed his flesh. His nails dug into her calf. They tore great rents in her skin as she pulled her leg free with all her might. The hedge swallowed the canni-bal. The brambles thrashed. His shrieks reached a panicked pitch. Thorns pierced his heart and lungs and silence fell over the labyrinth again.

Turnspade helped Oneirotheria to her feet. He jerked his head at the thorn-patch whence the Ratkipper had vanished.

"See? Witch."

Rivulets of blood trickled from the bite and scratches on her legs. Turnspade pulled a leather pouch from his coat pocket. He fished around it, producing a bunched-up wad of moss.

"Gree—"

"—Greenbalm," she interrupted. "Curiously, that I know. And how to use it. There's no rhyme nor reason to my wits' store."

She took it from him. She dabbed it on the wounds, whispering nonsense syllables. The skin closed over, smooth and newly healed. She did not bother cleaning the swiftly drying blood. She offered the palliative back to the gardener. He pressed the pouch of plants into her hand.

"Keep them. No use to me."

She made a cursory inventory of the contents. She knew many magical uses for the oddments within. She added the remaining moonflowers to the pouch. She tied it to a loop on the waist of her dress. She led Turnspade the rest of the way through the maze.

A dozen Ratkippers waited in a half-circle around the exit. Whether they had heard the screams of their kin or they were less reckless or less hungry, Oneirotheria couldn't tell. Whichever, they did not immediately attack. They shifted nervously in place, each one was waiting for someone else to go first.

"Fly," Turnspade murmured to Oneirotheria.

She did not move. The danger might shake more loose in her brain and she didn't want to miss the chance.

"Suit yourself."

The gardener stepped ahead of her. He rested the blade of his shovel on his shoulder. It quivered with pent tension, ready to be unleashed. The Ratkippers sniffed.

"I don't want that one," one of them snarled.

"They talk?" Oneirotheria clapped her hands. "That's unexpected!"

"Me neither," growled another, ignoring the witch's incongruous glee. "Smells like wood and plaster. Be like eating a wall."

"Worse. Walls sometimes have bones in them," said a third.

"That one though," said the first. A knife-split tongue licked his filed fangs. "She would go down like a bird, all feathers and slippery meat and crunching bones."

A hungry moan started at one end of the cannibal semi-circle and rolled to the other. Their teeth chattered, filling the space with a wicked click-click-click.

Behind them, the shape of a Warden loomed in the incense haze. Oneirotheria laughed.

"Hey! You back there! Everything here is not as it should be!"

Turnspade lowered his weapon. His hoarse whisper was utterly unbelieving. "What are you thinking, witch?"

The Warden stepped into view.

Except—not a Warden.

The man who appeared wore a poor costume copy of a Warden's garb. Carved slivers of human bone, woven together with sinew, crowned his head. He bore the blue tattoo of a closed eye in the center of his brow. He'd grown the pale nails of his first two fingers and thumb as long as his forearm, in parody of the Warden's tridactylic hands. He even wore a blue trumpet-sleeved robe—a drab dye job on sack fabric, embroidered with crude-sewn thread instead of sinuous living silver.

He stood a handspan taller than the Ratkippers, but he did not float. The feral creatures bowed and scraped out of his way.

Oneirotheria knew his name.

Eschatos.

Somewhere in her lost memories, contempt howled at the sight of him.

He waggled his index fingernail at Turnspade.

"Marionette..." His voice was a purring match for the sickliest incense in the temple ward. "Marionette, tell Upstart no more of these foolish plays. The theatres are closed."

"Fly," Turnspade said again, his voice pitched just for Oneirotheria's ears.

"Where to? There's only one way out of a labyrinth," she replied, loud enough for all to hear. She shook her head, hoping it would jar a spell free. A few stray feathers fluttered from her wild hair.

"Hecate," the fake Warden smarmed. He didn't bother with an apotrope. "You've broken My Lady's rules, witch."

"My name is Oneirotheria."

"Your name is irrelevant."

"Oi!" she exclaimed. Of all the insults and threats facing her, that one landed hard as blasphemy.

"Irrelevant," he repeated. "You remember things from the other side of death. That's enough for the Fade."

"Step up," Turnspade said, "and I'll show you the other side of death."

Eschatos slowly turned his back. "Children, dispatch the puppet and soften the witch up for My Lady's Wardens."

"Fly," Turnspade ordered Oneirotheria a third

time. His shovel swept the first charging Ratkipper's legs. He spun the tool, a shield of swings holding the howling wildlings at bay. It would not last long.

"I won't leave you," she said.

"Go! Escape!"

That word, once more, shot through her. From a place before thought, the magpie rose and became her body. In bird form, she beat light wings against the heavy smog. She darted over the claws of wailing Ratkippers. She whirled, fluttering. She landed on a rain-melted gargoyle, safely out of reach. She whistled a mocking five-note tune.

Ignoring the Ratkippers surrounding him, Turnspade saluted her.

"Good. Go now. I'm done."

Suddenly, he collapsed, as if strings holding his limbs had been snipped. The ferals pounced. They tore into him. Pieces of plaster and wood flew across the church yard. Frustrated howls echoed from the baroque stones of the Third Ward.

Eschatos paced to where Turnspade had fallen. He nudged the fragments of a man-sized marionette. He drew himself up tall. He turned to the magpie on the church façade.

"You see? Your only allies are lifeless tools of a vile fool. Offer yourself up. Do not flee My Lady's law. You will only meet oblivion breathless and in fear."

A cannibal seized a scrap from the ground. She hurled it at the bird. The wooden hand that had held the gardener's spade smashed into a near-by gargoyle. Untouched, Oneirotheria hopped to a gutter spout. A volley of stones and rattling puppet parts peppered the church.

Seeing no reason to stay, she took to flight. Ratkippers scattered through the temples and shrines. Eschatos disappeared into the votive smoke.

14

Winging on instinct, Oneirotheria swerved through the Third Ward. The crumbling church facades meant nothing to a magpie.

Nor did the wall at the edge of the district.

She swooped over the high stone divider, the steady beat of her black-and-white vans unbroken. The roads beyond were neater and more concisely laid out than the haphazard snarl of the Third. Each street showed a different theme. Down one, every building fronted an anvil and forge pit. Along another, enormous ovens grew out of the back of squat bakeries. A third street showcased cobblers' benches in every shop window, along with signs picturing a dozen different styles of shoe—no actual footwear on display, however. On and on, in rows and columns, stores and trade shops ranged over gently undulating hills.

All were empty.

All had been empty for a long time.

None of that impressed itself on the magpie as she flew for the joy of flying. Somewhere deep in the feathered mind, Oneirotheria's consciousness catalogued the scenes—but the words never made it to her beak.

She landed on a signpost.

Bread Street, read the woman within the bird. Instead of speaking, she trilled a joyous dawn song. She preened herself. There was a moment of confusion and hesitancy—was she a witch who had become a magpie, or a magpie who foolishly wore a witch's body from time to time?

Before the question could be settled, she threw herself back on the clear morning air.

She darted through the ward. As the land sloped beneath her, she pulled hard upwards. The great empty gap widened. She stroked the sky, lifting herself higher and higher. The Fifth Ward gave way to the Eighth. A primal forest fed on the mortared stones around the district gate. Wild, dark trees thronged in a vast wood beyond. No light pierced the gloom they sullenly guarded.

Shunning yet another claustrophobic confine, Oneirotheria soared over the canopy. From that vantage she could see the barest traces of streets and buildings beneath the overgrowth. Unconsciously, she followed the roads, though there was no need. And then, awareness dropped away and she just flew.

An unknown time later, she reached the end of the city.

Automatically, her wings pulled up. She fluttered to a perch. Her claws scratched the top of a stone parapet. To one side, a wall wide enough for four humans to walk abreast hemmed in the Forest Ward. The trees leaned away from the wall, refusing to grow any closer than the width of a narrow house.

On the other side of the wall...

Nothing.

Just nothing.

A nothing so nothing that, had she been in speaking form and called out 'nothing', the void would've eaten the word from her mouth and been no less empty.

She whistled into the black. The notes stopped dead at the edge of the wall.

Can I touch it?

The magpie's wing stretched out.

Against Oneirotheria's will, the bird body refused to cross the line between something and nothing. She struggled to take control. She could not calm down enough to shake off the feathered form and stand as a woman again. At the border between being and nothingness, she hopped back and forth frenetically. Energy built within her, conflict between curiosity and avian instinct. At a tipping point, she shuddered. A single feather luffed from her twitching wing. It brushed the nothing.

It half-ceased to exist. The posterior vane, all the way down to the rachis, was simply gone. Excised without a trace.

Unbalanced, the rest of the feather spiraled away from nothing into the grasping fingers of undergrowth below.

Startled, Oneirotheria exploded into flight. She clawed air low above the parapet.

At the edge of the next Ward, she slowed her strokes. She glided between powerful downbeats. She pressed on, keeping the nothingness on her right and Osylum's city wall beneath her as guides. Eyes locked ahead, she didn't notice the character of the neighborhood on her left.

She passed two long Wards before finding herself once more on the edge of the forest. The nothing remained nothing the whole time. At each Ward, the buildings or trees did not approach the wall. The stone rampart rose three stories high, smooth as glass and impossible to climb.

Driven by an experimental instinct, she turned upward. Talons and belly inches from the void, she climbed. Gravity tugged at her. She shrugged it off.

The nothing curved above the town as much as around. It sat over the ruined city like a vast glass cloche, imprisoning a sullen collection of unwilling specimens. The grand dome glowed with greyish noon light from everywhere and nowhere.

At the peak of the bell jar, Oneirotheria's wings gave out. The air grew too thin to hold her up. Her lungs burned. Her beak snapped for breath. She flailed then fell. Tail over head she dropped towards the shattered landscape.

She did not give up.

Halfway to the ground, the air thickened enough to catch her wings. She strained every pinion to stop her spin. She stalled. She managed to slide into a circling glide. Hours of flight had left her wings too exhausted to do more than drift downwards at still-frightening speed. She spotted a high tower with a flashing blue light atop. Ruddering with the slightest tail feather movements, she edged her barely-controlled spiral towards it.

As she passed the observation tower's precipice, the wing-weary magpie gave way to the witch's woman form. Oneirotheria tumbled head-over-heels, skidded across white tiles and hit brass railing; a sharp stop a hair before a lethal drop. She huddled a moment in pile of bruises and hurt.

Then she laughed. Laughter hurt, so she laughed

harder, until at last she didn't hurt any more.

15

F rom the tower's top she could see nearly
the whole of the Second Ward. Immediately
across the street lay the garden where she'd met
Turnspade the night before. Beyond that, miniscule russet-coated Peripats convened in the statue
square. They waited for Wardens to arrive with
food. Oneirotheria paced the full circle of the
confines. Throughout the city, indistinct figures
gathered in small groups in open spaces. Wardens appeared. She never saw where they came
from—the snarl of streets may have blocked sight
of their passage, or they could have shimmered
into existence while she wasn't looking. No way to
tell from that height.

A clatter from below drew her attention. The
tower stood in the middle of a courtyard, surrounded on three sides by an interconnected
complex of buildings. The main door opened. A
large brass sphere, seated between two spoked
wheels, rolled into the courtyard. Unseen hands
closed the door behind it. With a grinding noise,
the seamless metal slab in the outer wall—that
had earlier frustrated Oneirotheria's attempts at
entry—slid open. The sphere trundled though it.
Wardens waited on the other side. Two clawed

arms extended from the creature's sides. They took something, presumably a tray, from the floating guards. Transaction complete, the machine rolled back inside and the Wardens drifted out of sight. The gate closed with a rattling squeal, sealing the compound again.

"The Linnaea," she said. The sound of words instead of bird-song pleased her ears, though she did not know what the name meant. "That's who Turnspade said lived here. Metal men? Why not? Important enough to have their meals delivered, anyway. Maybe they know a thing or two. Tu-whit, tu-whoo."

The magpie rose with her sing-song rhyme. Oneirotheria shook her feather-filled hair. "None of that. Witch now. Bird later."

To focus her mind on being human, she turned her attention to the immediate surroundings. White ceramic tiles covered the floor. An unbroken railing circumscribed the observation deck. In the very center, a glass-and-brass contraption stood on an elevated platform. It consisted of a long tube, mounted on a swivel post. The near end, just wide enough to peep through, pointed straight up. The far end, broader than her palm, pointed at the floor.

"Telescope! Tele meaning far and scope meaning see but for some reason far-seer was too common in the mouth, so that's what they called you."

She'd almost grown used to the knowing-without-knowing-how-she-knew. She continued inspecting the quaint construction in the center of the tower.

An angled steel table stood beside the platform. A small cushioned cradle stood waist-high, in line with the eyepiece of the telescope. It connected to a notched vertical bar. A crank on the side from the platform, with a series of gears, raised and lowered the cradle. A tiny person laying in it could see the whole vertical sweep of the telescope's view. Additionally, the entire platform could be moved by a second larger crank, allowing a full-circle vista of the city and sky.

Oneirotheria stepped up to the telescope. She moved the tube up-and-down. A semi-circular gauge on the support pole marked the vertical position with fine numbered hashes. Similar hashes circumscribed the platform, denoting the horizontal position.

She ran her fingers over the viewing cradle. The cushion felt soft and richly upholstered. It bore an impression, as of much use. She gave it a quick sniff. It smelled of delicate powder, masking the sour odor of skin.

Maybe not metal men.

On the table on her right, an enormous leather-bound book lay, open to roughly the middle. Miniscule neat handwriting covered half the page.

6 hours 19 minutes right ascension
14 degrees 22 minutes declination

No sighting

6 hours 19 minutes right ascension
14 degrees 23 minutes declination

No sighting

6 hours 19 minutes right ascension
14 degrees 58 minutes declination

No sighting

The odd notes ended there. Oneirotheria flipped backwards through the book. Hundreds of entries, painstakingly recorded in the same hand, filled it, all the way back to the first page. The numbers changed incrementally. They obviously came from the hashed numbers on the swivel-arm and platform. The right column remained the same from first to last.

"No sighting," she murmured. "No sun, moon, nor stars. Someone else noticed too, then?"

The sky shone bright as she'd seen it so far, though still a diffuse grey glow. She pointed the lens halfway to zenith. She squinted through the small end. Instead of sky, nothing leapt close. The same nothing that had severed half a feather at the edge of town. Oneirotheria cranked the platform round and round, tilted the telescope up and down. Everywhere the same. Nothing, nothing, and more nothing.

"No sighting," she repeated the notebook's refrain.

A smidge dizzy, she stepped away.

The only other object on the tower-top was a large lever. It angled out of the floor, across a long slot. For want of anything better to do, Oneirotheria pulled on it till it clunked into the opposite position. Vibrations thrummed through her bare feet. After a few seconds, a broad rectangular segment of the floor dropped six inches. The piece next to it sank a foot and the one next to that lowered

18 inches and so forth. A spiral staircase unfolded where the floor used to be. Only the telescope platform remained, atop a central core.

Heedless of danger and delighted at the cog-work display, Oneirotheria hopped the stairs two at a time into the Linnaea's Laboratory.

16

The air smelled of lemons and etched metal. The first noseful made her sneeze. Feathers flew from her tangled hair. A panel flapped opened in the frosted glass ceiling. A brass spider on a silver wire dropped to the floor. It clicked around randomly on the gleaming white tile floor, snipping with two flattened claws. It tip-tapped so fast that, even without apparent intention, it cleaned up the litter in seconds. It flipped on its back and, with a barely audible whirrr, wound itself back up the metal thread and into the ceiling. The panel snapped shut.

Oneirotheria surmised the stairs had ended below ground, because the hallway before her ran much longer than the diameter of the tower's base. Sconces of frosted glass provided light. Six brass doors broke the smooth walls at precise intervals; three on the left and two on the right. She tried the first. Locked. Delicious gold words labeled the doors. She could not help but read them aloud as she passed, trying and failing to open each one.

"Incubatorium... Pharmakon... Chirugia... Gazophylacium... Aeronauticia... I don't know any of these words! Whoever lives here must be the richest person in the city."

Thrilling with logophilic shivers, she made her way up the broad staircase at the far end of the hall.

The wonderful clean odor persisted on the ground floor, with hints of beeswax threading in. She entered a wide, bright foyer whose double-height windows somehow enhanced the light from outside. Four closed mahogany doors led out of the spacious chamber. A flight of marble stairs, with two iron tracks running parallel down the middle, ascended to an open second floor landing. She glanced behind her. The stairs down had the same iron tracks, spaced about double her hip-width apart.

"How odd," she murmured. She filed the new data far to the back of her long list of mysteries.

A brass spider, the size of her palm, clung to the doorframe beside her. A single rotating limb with a buff cloth at the end vigorously polished the rich red-whorled wood. That was the source of the sweet beeswax smell.

Floors, doors, fixtures, and furnishings glowed with depth and fullness. After a day and night and half a day again in the dingy city, the incongruity of this pristine manor dazed Oneirotheria. She felt like she'd stepped from a run-down theatre stage—cheap props and faded backdrops—into reality.

The sense of reality evaporated when she saw a long timber hull, held three hands off the floor by metal scaffolding. The bizarre structure dominated the center of the foyer, full six paces long.

"You're called a skiff! Or a dory," she whispered to the boat. She shook her head.

"How can that be right? How can there be words

that taste like salt and water and the up-and-down of a hard pull across surging waves, when I saw no sea in the city or around it big enough to fit you? You'd barely squeeze into the biggest fountain in the Second Ward, strange thing."

As décor it made very little sense either. Visitors through the front door would immediately be confronted by the prow, able to see little else of the mansion's splendor. It was not particularly fancy either. There was no figurehead and the hull paint, while free of fade and chips, was just a dull grey.

Curious, she climbed the scaffold like a ladder. The inside of the boat was as common as the outside. Warped planks laid cross-wise at regular intervals above a flat deck. A dark prow line, speckled with dried algae, curled next to the foremost foot brace. One oar hung under the starboard gunwale and the other under the port.

The rudder, made of brightest brass, did not match the rest of the craft. It hung off the stern from a gleaming tiller pole. The tiller could not be grabbed, however. It disappeared into a large ornate glass box, filled with gears. A crank jutted out of the bow-side of the box. The box's steel lid had a shallow circular depression, about the size of Oneirotheria's head.

"Here-now! Questions inside questions inside questions like all those gears inside gears! What possible—"

Distorted voices echoed across the foyer, interrupting her thought. She dropped to the marble floor. Head down and crouched, she crept towards the conversation. Halfway there, the fuzzy noises crystallized into a chant of nine voices.

"Oblate Isokolon, Ninth Ward, six hundred and

fifteen souls is the count," a man sang in a pure and steady tenor. A shakier tenor took up the melody.

"Oblate Thaumasmus, Eighth Ward, twelve souls is the count."

A querulous countertenor warbled next, followed by a series of nigh-identical velvet baritones.

"Oblate Hendiatrix, Seventh Ward, four thousand seven hundred and sixty four souls is the count."

"Oblate Zeugma, Sixth Ward, seven hundred souls is the count."

"Oblate Ekphrasis, Fifth Ward, nine thousand five hundred and ninety souls is the count."

"Oblate Diacaelox, Fourth Ward, three thousand one hundred and forty one souls is the count."

Oneirotheria reached the threshold. Not wanting to interrupt the scene before she understood it, she pressed one eye to the keyhole.

An enormous mirror dominated the far wall. In front of it, sat the room's sole visible occupant—a broad man draped in a voluminous wool cape. She could not see his face, however, because the mirror did not currently reflect the room. Instead, it showed a dark, candle-lined oratory with nine blue-robed old men.

She had seen one of these monks before, his face curving across her dinner spoon. And there he was, third from the left! She squeaked. Fortunately, the sound was covered by chanting:

"Oblate Graecismus, Third Ward, six hundred and twenty eight souls is the count."

Second monk from the right sang: "Oblate Barbarizein, Second Ward, two hundred and thirty-three souls is the count."

The last and oldest man in the group chanted in basso profundo: "Abbot Anaphora, First Ward, zero souls is the count."

All the monks voices intertwined in a celestial polyphony, much too elevated for such mundane lyrics:

"The total is nineteen thousand six hundred and eighty-three souls. Submitted by the Phrontistery Oblates in faith with the Lady's Grace to our benefactors the Linnaea at Sext. The memory of Dedalus be blessed."

The man watching them, with his back to Oneirotheria, raised his right hand in the apotrope. When he spoke, his voice cracked halfway through—his sentence started in a grown man's tone and ended in a high-pitched, almost infantile peep.

"The count remains higher than expected, though by five instead of six today."

The Abbot bowed. "Yes, my Lord."

"Are you certain you are not mistaken? This is the first time in my life the count has increased."

"My Lord, it is also the first time in my life. Yet it has gone up. We have seen what we have seen and counted what we sang."

"Very well. I do not understand the anomaly but what cannot be understood must still be accepted. Lady see you, Oblates."

The Oblates all bowed. "Lady sees us all."

Oneirotheria was so caught up in the monastery scene that she had forgotten that it was not actually the room she was peeking into. When the chapel flickered and was replaced by the reflection of a splendid ballroom, she yelped and fell over backwards. The high-vaulted foyer ceiling amplified her startled ERP! throughout the house.

17

The echoes of her own voice receded. She did not hear any hue and cry from behind the door. A vibration thrummed from the floor into her haunches. She felt no need to flee.

Let's see where this goes.

The thrum increased. It became sound. Above her, on the second floor landing, the brass sphere she'd seen from the tower-top rolled into view. Now that it was closer, she could see it was not a sphere but a many-sided polyhedron, suspended on two spoked wheels that were half again as tall as her. It picked up speed. When it reached the stairs, the creature steered towards the two iron rails embedded in the marble. The tracks enabled it to navigate the steps without a bump.

"Aha!" She scrambled to her feet. "So that's what those are for!"

She was so pleased at finally having a solved mystery that she felt no fear. This, despite the two threatening claws that had emerged from panels on the left and right of the creature's 60-sided body. An opening on the front revealed a carved metal face—or rather, she realized as it approached, not *one* face. Rather, a series of expressions clicked past the face-port with escalating intensity.

"Annoyance... irritation... pique... anger... rage...," she ticked off the various emotion-castings as they cranked by. "Oh! I'm not sure there's just one word for that one!" she exclaimed as the guardian's visage settled on something like homicidal battle madness.

The claws seized her upper arms.

"OW!"

She kicked the contraption. The pain in her bare toes distracted her from the pain in her arms. Several more panels opened around the polyhedron. Objects popped out. She recognized a boning knife and a pair of garden shears. The rest of the instruments were unfamiliar to her. She could guess their purpose well enough.

"Bird now, bird now, bird now!"

The sullen magpie refused to rise. Oneirotheria braced herself for maiming.

The ballroom door swung open. From within, the home's owner called out: "Cellarius, what is that disturbance? Come here."

Gears ground within Cellarius's body. The implements of destruction retracted. Its faces flipped until it wore a pewter mask of servile deference. Dragging Oneirotheria in an unrelenting grip, it wheeled into the ballroom.

"Here-now!" the witch exclaimed when she saw her host. "Are you singular or plural?"

It was the best she could do to phrase the query provoked by what she saw.

The Linnaea was (or were, depending on the appropriate grammar) a tall young man with euclid-edged features and intense brown eyes. He wore complex, baroque clothes. His thick black hair was sharply parted and slicked down. He held himself with aristocratic rigidity. He would not have looked out of place as a statue in a fancy plaza...

...except that half of a second, smaller body protruded out of his side—a homuncular vestige of a person, with a single pudgy arm and doughy infantile features. Wisps of down clung to his round head. Despite his cherubic face, the conjoined semi-twin's piercing intelligent eyes matched those of his full-grown counterpart. A thick leather harness supported the half-baby's underside, but he was otherwise nude.

Both of them dissected Oneirotheria with a scientific gaze.

"Who precisely are you," the man started to say, before the infant finished the sentence, "and how did you gain access to my sanctum?"

"Oh! That's why there was the cradle in the telescope!" Oneirotheria gleefully solved another minor mystery. "It was for you, little one!"

She tried to clap her hands, then winced when Cellarius's claws held her arms fast.

"The Laboratory is closed to all outsiders. I repeat: how did you get in?"

"Tu-whit, tu-whoo, I flew. How did you?"

"This seems improbable however, not impossible. The second anomaly in seven days."

She remembered something Hendiatrix had said that the Linnaea had just repeated. "The count was off, right? That's the first. What are you counting anyway? And can he—" she nudged on Cellarius's side with a heel, "—put me down before I bruise?"

"You might be dangerous or escape before I can—"

At the word 'escape' the magpie once again broke loose in Oneirotheria's breast. Cellarius's claws snapped shut on empty air, as her arms shrank to wings. Its faces rolled to a surprised mask. The Linnaea too gasped. She circled the room twice, batting against the walls. She darted across the center. She landed in the gleaming brass branches of a crystal chandelier.

Her curiosity was so heightened, however, that once free from the mechanical butler's grip, she easily shook off the bird form. She perched above her host and the now-stern-faced guardian. Sparkle-faceted leaves tinkled as the enormous gilt-branched fixture swayed under her weight. The ceiling bolts of the chandelier creaked but held.

"I suppose we both have a lot of questions," she said. "Can we be civil?"

Together, the Linnaea nodded. "Cellarius, fetch a ladder and refreshments for our guest."

18

O neirotheria followed the Linnaea out of the Mirror Room.

"Why do you have a boat in your front hall?" she could not help but ask.

"Please hold all questions until after refreshments."

They moved between her and the skiff, blocking her view. With small prods, they ushered her through the halls to a small mahogany-paneled study.

As they went, she noticed that her original impression of splendor was not entirely accurate. Closer examination revealed a make-do quality to the furnishings—as though a theory of style and wealth were at play that the actual materials could not quite live up to. This created a mishmash of not-entirely harmonious objects, like the chess board scattered with pieces from rithomachy that sat in the center of the study.

The Philosopher's Game, rithomachy was also called, her memories lectured in a detached tone. *While chess was for soldiers and kings. And now they're both partly here and partly not, between you and a pair of twins with one soul. Whist! Mad world.*

She perched in a high-backed leather chair

THE WITCH AND THE CITY

on one side of the board-table. The Linnaea eased into a similar seat—adjusted for their unique physique. Cellarius trundled in with a tray. She smelled the Warden's portion in one of the bowls. Tea, cakes, and fruits from the machine-tended garden across the street supplemented the bland mush. The butler set the refreshments on a credenza within her host's reach. It rocked back and forth on its wheels. It wore a mask of solicitous anticipation.

"Thank you, Cellarius, I will serve the guest myself."

The machine rolled away. As it passed her, its faces clicked through moods to a business-like neutrality.

"How many faces does he have in there?" she asked.

"Cellarius is capable of expressing three hundred and sixty different emotions."

"Clever! Did you build him?"

The Linnaea poured soft brown tea into a white porcelain cup, wreathed with a blue phoenix design. They passed it to Oneirotheria. The larger twin (in her mind, she dubbed him the Major) made up a plate of cakes and set it next to his brother. The smaller (whom she termed the Minor) daintily ate, while the Major assembled an assortment of treats for her.

"I did not build Cellarius. He found me in the Incubatorium when—"

"Incubatorium! One of those rooms downstairs. What's it used for?"

"I was still attempting to answer your first question. As I said, Cellarius found—"

"Found? Matron called me a Foundling. Is that where people come from? They're just found?"

"That is the correct terminology within Osylum, however—"

"Within Osylum? So there *is* an outside?"

"MADAM!"

The Major slammed his teacup on the side-table
hard enough to slop tea onto the inlaid board and
make the rithomachy pieces hop around the chess
grid. The Minor glared at her with infantile irritation. She held in her questions with a long, slow
sip of tea.

"Madam, I must insist on a more measured and courte-
ous mode of conversational proceeding. If you cannot
comport yourself in a linear and rigorous manner when
making inquiries then perhaps I should have Cellarius
show you the door."

"Sorry. It's just that I know a lot and I don't know
anything at all, if that makes sense."

"It does not. However, it is a place to start."

"Yes. Let's start there, then."

That mollified them. The Minor continued nib-
bling. The Major tented his fingers and closed
his eyes. Oneirotheria waited, not wanting to de-
rail her host's train of thought. The self-enforced
patience was more painful than Cellarius's claw
grip on her wrists. She pecked the plate clean of
cakes, fruit, seeds, and crumbs to distract herself.
Satiated with his own snack, the Minor drifted
off to sleep. His tiny wheeze intermingled with a
thoughtful hum from his twin and a slight squeak-
ing from Oneirotheria's chair as she vibrated in
place.

The soft sound of the Minor sleeping reminded
her of another word. Like 'sun,' 'moon,' and 'stars,'
she knew it meant a thing that did not exist in
Osylum. The word drifted from her lips without

her meaning to speak.

"Child..."

"Pardon?"

Downy, gentle words wafted across her brain and into the still air. "Children. Kinder. Kids. Juveniles. Infants. Babies..."

The Major lurched forward, waking his twin. The Minor frowned at her, like an angry old man.

"How do you know those words? Have you been in my library?"

Stifling a laugh at the Minor's tiny clenched fist, Oneirotheria shook her head.

"Then how?"

"I just know things. I told you that. Not everything. Some things. There's no pattern, at least not one I can patter out. Patter? Pitter? Pity..."

"There are no infants in Osylum. Everyone is Found as they are and as they remain. However, a number of the volumes in my Library speak, with illustrations, of processes like gestation, infancy, childhood, puberty, culminating in adulthood."

"And ending in death," she heard herself say. "There's a word Philotech didn't much like."

The Linnaea ignored that. They studied her intently. She twitched in her seat. They didn't have instruments pointed at her and tools dissecting her skin to middlemost innards, but it felt uncomfortably as though they wanted to.

"Am I correct in stating that you experience memories that antedate your present physical existence?"

"That's not the right way to say it. I know things from before I remember. Yes."

"Elaborate."

"So remembering. That's a thing with me in it. I remember earlier today, when Turnspade got taken apart by the Ratkippers."

The image swam unbidden into her mind—the gardener she'd thought was flesh and blood, turning into a puppet and the puppet pieces flying every which way from cannibals' teeth and claws.

"That's different than how I know the phrase 'rotten as a Ratkipper's seasoning pit.' That I just... know. It's there in my brain like knowing how to see two eyes, a nose, and a mouth as a face. Nobody teaches you these things, right?"

"There is a certain a priori knowledge implied by sensation. That much is logically ineluctable. However, said a priori knowledge is a rudimentary and necessary minimum, hardly rising to the level of colloquial expressions."

"But they're still all there! All these bits and pieces fly around in my head like a flock of starlings in a storm." She slapped the arm of her chair. "Storm! Why is there a word for storms when the sky is flat as a slate table?"

"Intriguing. It seems you have discovered the linguistic equivalent of one of my central mysteries. Why are there so many empty buildings in Osylum?"

Oneirotheria had a flash of inspiration.

"The count! That's what the spot-pates are counting for you. People!"

"Correct."

"The city is big and filled with places for people to be. When I was flying over it though, I barely saw anyone. And if the Oblates in the mirror are right, there are only..." she trailed off trying to remember the number.

"Nineteen thousand six hundred and eighty three souls," the Major said.

"Which is a big number but nowhere near as big as the number of buildings. And I've been to the edge of the city. There's no esc—" she caught herself before saying the word that triggered flight, "—No way in or out. So why build a town big enough for so many more?"

"My estimates range between one million and two million. There are a number of assumptions on which that is predi—"

"—that's fifty times as big as it needs to be," Oneirotheria interrupted, finishing the mental calculation.

"In the lowest end, yes. One hundred times too large at the upper end. Furthermore, the number of souls in the city is dwindling. Even with the anomalous extra few in the past four days, the general trend since the Phrontistery Oblates began reporting to me has been a decline."

"It never went up?"

"Never. Only down."

"Love we the Lady and fear we the Fade," Oneirotheria chanted.

It was the same snippet of song she'd sung for Matron. It confused her as much now as it had then.

"I have heard that doggerel sung in the streets, through my Teleotoion."

The Major pointed at a device in the corner, which consisted of a trumpet-shaped earpiece coming out of the wall and a complex panel of silver dials.

"What does it mean?"

"It is a counting song in which the Nine Wards of Osylum are numbered. 'One for the Lady who lives on a hill, Two for the rich folk in gilt array, and so forth...' Hardly pertinent to our discussion."

"The Lady!"

Oneirotheria hopped on the chair, heedless of her dirty feet on the silk upholstery.

"Madam, please compose yourself. We've much to discuss."

"I'm sure you do," she replied. "As for me, I'm going to find this Lady and shake some answers out of her."

"I cannot let you leave just yet."

He heaved to his feet with a quickness that caught her off guard. The Minor's single baby arm flailed as the Major sprinted to the study's only exit.

"Escape!" Oneirotheria cried and turned into a bird.

The magpie darted through the thick mahogany door right as the Major slammed it. Two voices shouted in unison: "Cellarius! Cellarius!"

Ignoring them, she wove through the pristine halls. She followed the flow of air till it led her through a half-open window in a privy chamber. From there it was a few quick flaps to glide over the Laboratory wall and through Osylum's straying streets.

19

Oneirotheria found herself thwarted at the border of the First Ward. A heavy mist filled the Lady's Estate, concealing any danger as well as the buildings and grounds. The magpie, driven by the instinct of self-preservation not to fly blind, shied away at the edge of the wall between the Wards, where the fog began. Piqued, the witch took back her woman's form.

I will learn to control you. Hear me, little bird?

Deep in her breast, the magpie trilled a mocking tune.

Feh.

She'd landed beneath a sign that read: *Liminal Boulevard*. Beneath it, on the cobbles, were scrawled the chalk words:

We know what we are but not what we may be

"That's only half true," she muttered to the unknown vandal. "And graffiti is rude. You never know who you're writing to."

Across the street, a smooth obsidian wall rose into mist. Next to her, a manor with a corbie-step roof half-slid awkwardly down the slant of the hill.

"Tu-whit tu-whoo, whither to? Or wither, too?

Mad language. Not only are there too many words but there are too few sounds to fit the words into." She shook herself. "You digress, witch. Find the gate and march through."

She foot-padded round the curve of the road. It was not a long street. It circumscribed the Second Ward's innermost edge. The black wall cut a sharp edge on her left. On her right, streets radiated steeply downhill at regular intervals, like bent wheel spokes. Rich yet unkept buildings tumbled away from the Lady's Ward—or, she saw in an inversion of perspective, the houses grasped upwards. Their owners had built as close to the fog-bound seat of power as they could yet found themselves forced by topography to lean away from what they wanted most.

What an odd story you tell yourself.

She reached the Lady's Gate in minutes.

Grey tendrils of fog caressed a featureless ebony archway; mist filled the passage beyond. Two Wardens flanked the entry. They folded their three-fingered hands in front of their knees. Their heads bowed. Their eyes were closed—all three of them. They bobbed ever so slightly up and down. Their movements matched the seething miasma.

They appeared unaware of her.

As she dithered about what to do next, three more Wardens approached, coming from the Second Ward. Between them floated a dead body. It was borne by the same invisible force that carried the tray of food during feeding time.

Tribunal coming, she heard the echo of the Peripat's voice.

The funeral procession sailed past her without acknowledgement. She recognized the body; the

Ratkipper who'd been devoured by a hedge, earlier that day. The one she had killed in self-defense. He no longer bled from the two dozen holes in his flesh.

The Tribunal and corpse passed under the arch and into the mist. Someone else's voice spoke in Oneirotheria's mind:

As is their right. As is the Lady's will.

"Dead man, dead man, I wonder what they do with you? Step to, step to. One, two, buckle my shoe," she quipped. She put one bare foot forward. She frowned at her dirty toes. "I really need to get some shoes."

"Keep walking at that gate and you won't need them," a wry voice said, behind her and slightly above. "Or feet."

Oneirotheria spun on her back heel.

A scrap-doll, the size of a full-grown woman, sat atop an estate wall. Her brilliant skin was a patchwork of plaids and paisleys and bright primary swatches in every angled shape. She looked stuffed and dumpy. Lumpy feet, shaped like wedge boots dangled beneath her. She leaned against a granite gate pillar. Her head cocked at an improbable angle—Oneirotheria felt sure her own neck would break if she tried to copy the gesture.

"Or hands or wings or head or brains or good red witchy blood," the stranger continued. She jerked her head upright. "You see, that's the Lady's Fog. No one who goes into it comes out—excepting of course Wardens. So they say."

"Who are they?"

The doll's shoulders bunched up in a parody of a shrug. "They. Them. Those 'uns. Other folk. Not me."

"What else to they say about that fog?"

"Strange things move within. And one day someone will break one too many rules and the end of the world will come. The Lady will breathe out and the fog will roll from the First Ward down to the Ninth and all the things inside will be free to move about and that'll be the last of Osylum."

"End the whole world? That's a lot of work for a little mist."

"I agree. That's why I said they said it, not me. Hup!"

The raggedy woman launched herself from the wall. A crazy-quilt robe with a cast-back hood fluttered around the odd bulges of her body as she fell. She collapsed in a heap on the stone sidewalk.

Oneirotheria rushed to her side. "Are you alright?"

Her face shoved into her torso, the doll mumbled something. Oneirotheria helped her to her feet. Her body felt like she was stuffed with wool. Improbably, the doll stood upright of her own accord and took a step back from the witch.

"That little pratfall? Barely a thing."

She lurched into a curtsy. Oneirotheria lunged to catch her—unnecessarily, as it turned out, for she wobbled out of the pose on her own. She made the apotrope with a thick-fingered glove.

"Ragpatch, at your service." Her black button eyes, dabbed with white paint for pupils, darted at the two slumbering Wardens across the street. "Lady sees us both, eh?"

"I'm Oneirotheria." She absently made the greeting gesture. "Sees us both? Does she?"

Ragpatch cawed a harsh laugh. It startled Oneirotheria. The Wardens continued floating, faces down-bent. "Oh yes, she does, she has, she will. Sees us right to death. Or worse than death, if you believe such a thing. Which I do. And so will you, before my task is through."

"At last," Oneirotheria replied, "someone who makes less sense than me."

The crimson stitches of the doll's mouth twitched.

"Sound and fury, strut and fret, how much madder can this town get?" She grew serious. "That's one of Upstart's lines."

"Upstart? The same one Turnspade worked for?"

"Worked you say? Poor Turnspade's past-tense now?"

"Yes. Or maybe no. He was a puppet. Ratkippers broke him into pieces and threw the pieces at me. I don't know what that means vis-à-vis life, death, and the grammatical proper tense."

"Your guess is as good as mine. Upstart knows. Maybe. If he doesn't, he'll make something up and it'll be too good to not call it true."

"Did he send you to find me? Are you a puppet too?"

"Yes and no. I mean, no and yes. Here's not the place to say things out loud." She lolled her head in the general direction of the still-impassive Wardens. "Let's limp a bit."

20

With a rolling gait, the patchwork woman led Oneirotheria through the Second Ward. Narrow streams of smoke trickled from a few of the resplendent sigogglin chimneys. Yellow lights glinted through one cracked bay window. She even heard the metallic pluck of harpsichord strings from the second floor of one townhome, though the musician was hidden behind thick black drapes. The same five note sequence trilled over and over, varying only in tempo. It reminded her of the Peripats' evensong.

Most of the mansions, however, showed no signs of life.

"Two hundred and thirty-three souls..." she mused.

"What was that?" Ragpatch asked, not breaking her stride.

"According to one of the Oblates, only two hundred and thirty-three people live in the Second Ward."

"The monks would know."

"Who are they? Or is that a secret we have to talk about someplace else?"

"Not at all. The Oblates are nine old men—always old men—who live locked up in the Phrontistery. It's a prison within the prison. They don't seem to mind. Feeble as they are, I guess it keeps them safe."

"How do they get in there?"

"It's where they're found. One ancient codger shuffles off and three days later, another spotty dodger wakes up in his cell."

Ragpatch pulled her hood over her head. She pressed her palms together. She did an extremely accurate impression of a querulous gerontion.

"Videmus te..." she chanted. "The brothers all gather round the new boy and shimmy him into the old boy's wooly robes and sing him the monkly cant of rules and regulations."

"How do you know that, if they're locked up in a monastery?"

Ragpatch laughed. Her hood flopped back. "Maybe I don't. Maybe I made it up. Upstart isn't the only mort who can make things up to fill the vasty void of things he doesn't know."

"Isn't it better to know things than make them up?"

"To be sure. But most things can't be known and a body has to get by somehow, right?"

Oneirotheria couldn't figure out how she felt about that. She let it be, reasoning aloud instead.

"So the Oblates count all the people in Osylum. They never leave the monastery. They can see through mirrors—" She remembered the spoon in the courtyard. "—Or any reflection. They must have mirrors in their cells and they spend all day staring at them."

Ragpatch tapped L-shaped swatch of crimson fabric where her nose should have been. "See? Now you're getting it. Make it up when you don't know. Maybe you'll be right."

"It's not the same."

"Suit yourself."

Irritated, Oneirotheria returned to the subject at hand. "How do the mirrors work?"

"Since you're persnickity about fiction, I won't make up an answer. However, I did hear Upstart and Hecate—she was you until a while ago—talk about it once. I was hanging in the green room, waiting for my next entrance. I don't think they knew I was only halfway asleep."

"Upstart knew Hecate?"

"Thick as thieves. For a bit. Then Eschatos—

"Eschatos! Why does he hate me?"

"That puritan? He wants to be the Lady's master from below, doling out his will under her name."

"What does that have to do with me?"

"If you wanted to be king of the sewer and you were a church-mouse, you'd hate the strongest rat the most, wouldn't you?"

"Are you calling me the strongest rat in a sewer?"

"No offense meant. Metaphors are more Up-start's gift than mine. Point is, Hecate flattened Eschatos's plans more than once—and a few of his Ratkippers besides. With no more effort than you'd take knocking me off a wall. So he hated her. And hate is a gift that carries over across lives when there's nowhere else for it to go."

"So what did he do to Upstart and Hecate?"

"He got onto what they were planning. Ran to the Wardens. Whatever play they had on the boards tiptoed up to the edge of drawing the Lady's Fog down on us all."

"The end of the world?" Oneirotheria said skeptically.

"Your words, not mine."

"The world's still here, so they didn't succeed."

"No. The boss went into hiding. Hecate kept in the open. Word went down somehow that the two of them were banned from meeting."

"Somehow?"

"Everyone knows the Lady's will. Nobody knows how we know it."

"I'm familiar with the feeling."

"There wasn't enough for the Wardens to fade anyone, so Hecate went on acting north-north-west even though she could tell a hawk from a handsaw."

"She pretended to be mad, with a plan."

"That's what I said."

"So what was the plan?"

"Don't know and I'm not clever enough to even make anything up. It was a good one I'm sure, knowing the boss was a part of its making." Abruptly, Ragpatch declared: "Dedalus, by the way."

It was the name Turnspade said when she'd asked who had owned the gardens. And the name that the Abbot blessed at the end of the monks' count. It hung in her dark memory, large and important, yet somehow totally disconnected from anything else.

"Dedalus? Dedalus what?"

"You'd asked how the mirrors work. Dedalus made them. He got a big one into the Phrontistery somehow, along with nine little ones for the monklets. They didn't always count, you see, those Oblates. Nothing is what it was, even if the Lady wants it to always be the same."

"Who was Dedalus?"

"An inventor. Clever as a talking clock. He crafted sets and scenes and sparkling effects that could take you to exactly where he wanted and you'd never know you weren't there. Upstart always claimed it was a playwright's words that mattered most, but he didn't complain when Dedalus made toys to bring his plays to life."

"Did he make the Linnaea?"

"Who knows? The mirrors are what matter to you now."

"Right. So? What else do you know?"

Ragpatch looped her thick finger and thumb and made the apotrope. She held it to one button eye. "'Lady sees,' you've heard people say. And that she does. The Wardens fly in whenever things aren't as they should be and take care of whoever's turning the sundial shadow widdershins. How do they know? 'The Lady sees' people say."

"Obviously she has people who tell other people who tell the Wardens. Like Eschatos and his Ratkippers. No mystery there."

"That'd be how I'd do it," Ragpatch agreed. "Hecate and Upstart though—they reckoned the number of rats and the number of Wardens and didn't like the total. According to their thinking, the Lady *had* to see things when there was no one around to see. So they wound Dedalus up and sent him after the problem, like a brass fly bouncing against window's glass, trying to find the crack open at the bottom."

"And Dedalus figured out it was mirrors? The Lady sees through mirrors?"

"Not just mirrors. Any reflection. I couldn't ken a lick of his mathematical cant, but the up and the down of it, near as I gathered from Upstart, was the notion that the Lady has a mirror before her throne and through it she can see the whole of Osylum's prison."

"Oh! And Dedalus figured out how the mirrors worked and built his own!"

Ragpatch nodded. "You're coiled tight and you tick quick, don't you?"

"But the Lady had to see that, right? Is that why he doesn't live in his house any more?"

"Aye. He didn't get the fade though. He gave Hecate the mirror cant book and set the Oblates on their task. Then, knowing the Wardens would be sweeping through his doors any minute, he shuffled off this mortal coil of his own choice."

"Why give the Oblates mirrors? Why have them count the people?"

"I don't know the why of the counting. Never heard of it till you told me. The story I'll tell is the Linnaea made that task up himself, after forgetting and being found. As to the monks and their mirrors, all I know is they were supposed to look for something."

The image of Hendiatrix's fish-eye face filled Oneirotheria's mind. His lips laboriously made out a word. *Oseovox.*

Oneirotheria repeated the word. A frisson crawled across her shoulders, delicious and forbidden.

Ragpatch hesitated. Her knit features wrinkled. They smoothed blank. "Oseowhat? Don't know the word any more than I—"

A sickly purr came from behind them.

"Hecate and the Upstart's puppet, plotting together in the open?"

21

The witch and the raggedy-doll spun on their heels. Eschatos had been following them—Oneirotheria had no idea how long. He clicked his long nails together. He ticked his tongue on his yellowed upper incisors.

"Very naughty, to flout our Lady's law. The witch and the Upstart are not allowed to meet. And the puppets are all Fade-bound by decree. The Wardens will want to know about this."

Oneirotheria rapidly scanned every alley and alcove. Not a Ratkipper in sight.

Ragpatch murmured: "The cannibals stay below the Second. Mostly. The rich won't have the riff-raff and they have the power to make that much so, at least."

Eschatos paced side-to-side, doing a poor imitation of the Warden's float. "True, true. I don't have those unpleasant servants to deal with you, doll."

Ragpatch emitted an enormous yawning sound. "So it's bore me to death then? Posture and pose, hissing like a basket of toothless snakes till I beg for the sleep from which no one wakes?"

Eschatos snarled.

Automatically, Oneirotheria's hands reached for

the belt pouch Turnspade had given her. She felt the prickly mesh of a birnam twig. If she threw it and hit him and spoke the right words, thorns would bind him in a cage—at least long enough for them to get a good distance away.

Before she could cast the spell, Eschatos's snarl turned to an unctuous grin. He looked past the two women. He made an apotrope over his right eye and swept his robes wide in a genuflection that took his face to the cobbles.

Two Wardens floated up the hill towards them. A third appeared behind Eschatos, closing at a good pace.

Ragpatch threw a soft arm around Oneirotheria's shoulder.

"Well, that's it for me," she said in a voice that just reached the witch's ear. "Watch careful what happens next. It'll put a fire under you if nothing else does. Get to the Ninth, where nothing is as it seems. Find the oseovox. Flee the Fade. Escape this mad place."

At the word 'escape' the magpie rose again. Oneirotheria clutched the birnam twig, driving it into her palm so the pain would keep her from changing.

"No," she whispered back. "Just tell them everything is as it should be. We'll be fine."

"That's the spirit," Ragpatch replied. "Sing that thought loud in your noisy half-full brain like a skull chanting the cant of days long gone. Everything is as it should be. For you, believe it true. Not so and never for me."

She capered between Oneirotheria and the two approaching Wardens. From the depths of his groveling bow, Eschatos cried out:

"She's one of Upstart's! And the woman is Hecate, who remembers her last life in defiance of the Lady's will!"

"Yes and no," Ragpatch quipped to the Wardens. She turned her head nearly full circle to face the one behind her. "Or no and yes."

All three Wardens stopped. Their third eyes—the most human feature on their alien faces—blinked slowly open. Instead of white, iris, and pupil, there was nothing.

Nothing.

The same nothing that Oneirotheria had seen at the city's outer wall. The nothing that domed the sky. That nothing now made three beams, centered on Ragpatch. When they struck the stuffed doll, she simply faded away. Ceased to exist. A smell, that Oneirotheria could only describe as new-made nothingness, filled the broad boulevard.

Eschatos chanted, his voice thick with religious ecstasy: "Love we the Lady and fear we the Fade."

The Wardens closed their third eye. They considered Oneirotheria.

"EVERYTHING IS AS IT SHOULD BE."

It took her a moment to register the voice in her head. The statement repeated a second time. The Wardens waited, as if for acknowledgment of their report.

"Yes!" she hastily replied, before they could speak a third time. "Everything is as it should be."

She did everything in her power to believe the lie.

Apparently satisfied, the triumvirate of Wardens floated past. Eschatos rose. He ran after them. He pawed the air behind them, imploring. He did not, however, approach more than five paces.

"No! No, wait! Everything is not as it should be. Didn't you hear me? That's Hecate, the witch who remembers! And there's more. The Phrontistery Oblates..."

The four figures passed out of earshot.

Oneirotheria went to where Ragpatch had stood. Not even a scrap of fabric had escaped the Fade.

The doll's sacrifice kindled no fire in her; only bitter cold certainty. Grim, crystalline glaciers jutted crookedly amid the frozen sea of her mind. Deep within them, clear images moved. Without emotion, Oneirotheria watched and rewatched the memory of Ragpatch's obliteration.

The Fade.

So. Those were her choices.

Escape.

Or oblivion.

There had been a million souls in Osylum once. Today the count stood at under twenty thousand. She now understood why.

How long did it take the Fade to erase that many people forever?

And how much longer till the count ticked down to nil?

It was inevitable. Time would grind the prison's inmates like grain in a mill, smaller, smaller, until even the dust disappeared. Whether she met her end tomorrow or after another thousand incarnations, some day she would step wrong and the Wardens' pitiless third eyes would open on a version of her.

Then what would all her questions mean? What would all this curiosity come to?

Nothing, nothing, nothing, nothing, nothing.

From the top of the hill, she gazed down on the crumbling city. She had stepped onto a bare stage late in the last act of a play. The scene was littered with corpses and the cast-off props of actors who had made their final exit long ago. If she did not escape, the curtain would fall on darkness and there would be no encore show.

A magpie rose from the frigid ocean of her thoughts. She clawed the empty sky, winging her way homeward to a witch's hut in a ruined folly garden.

22

Turnspade's advice notwithstanding, she did not seek out Upstart. To be safe, she avoided the entire Ninth Ward—where the puppet-gardener had told her to go.

It was not that she was afraid of Upstart, whoever he was. In fact, all evidence pointed to him as a former co-conspirator in whatever plot her prior incarnation had concocted. Hence a valuable ally against the Wardens and the Fade.

Which was precisely why she avoided him. The memories of Ragpatch vanishing from existence and the half-feather shorn by a razor of nothing remained vivid as the moment they'd happened. Eschatos's words and actions made it clear that Upstart's minions had been judged guilty already and subject to immediate obliteration the moment a Warden found them. The man himself was likely under the same sentence—and condemnation had a way of catching by contact.

Then too, the willingness with which he sent his servants to death and worse gave her pause. Perhaps he did know a way to escape and perhaps Hecate had helped him suss it out. But if he let Turnspade be torn apart by Ratkippers and Ragpatch face the Fade, she could not discount the possibility that sacrificing her was also a part of his plan.

Even if he were nothing but benevolent, his plan—his and Hecate's—expected her to remember him. As it stood, she had nothing but vague half-snatches of feelings, not even attached to a face. She strongly suspected that once she did re-connect with her erstwhile accomplice, whether she remembered him or no, a sequence of inexorable events would be kicked off that would end in freedom or complete destruction.

She wanted to be as ready for that as she could, not to flail into the middle of things like a fledgling still learning to use her wings.

She reckoned Upstart himself may have thought the same. At any rate, she did not meet another marionette and he made no effort to seek her out in person. The city was not so big nor populous that it would have been difficult to reach her—not if he had anything in the way of resources or cleverness. Very likely, she reasoned, after Ragpatch's Fade the puppet master had gone back into hiding.

Then, one grim afternoon amid the cenotaphs of the Sixth Ward, it occurred to her that his silence could mean the Wardens had caught up with him. The whole plot-across-lives might have failed before its penultimate phase.

"Tu-whit, tu-whoo," she whistled into an exhumed grave. "If that's true I'll come up with something better to do."

The weeping angels who were her only company did not disagree.

23

Days and months slipped by, whatever those words meant in a city without seasons or a sun.

Oneirotheria settled into her strange and fractured mental state. As she did, she became sure—and evidence and logic conspired to agree—the secret to escaping Osylum had to be hidden in her skull. It did not matter. Stubbornly, the blank spaces in her brain refused to fill. So she attacked the problem from a different direction.

She wandered.

She drifted through the city on instinct, avoiding any overt pattern or semblance of intention. Such a desultory walk-about would avoid the appearance of a deliberate conspiracy—giving Eschatos no fodder to run to the Wardens with.

She let curiosity be her only imperative. She ransacked houses and cathedrals for scraps of paper, catalogued broken images in picture windows, noted cryptic clips of graffiti that always made some glancing comment on the location that could only be understood after the fact. She gathered all these things and ruminated on them in her hut.

No matter how much she brooded, though, she

could find no order to the fragments that had survived in Osylum. Nothing spoke to her, everything she found was as random and isolated as her own store of memories.

She filled her mental gaps with new knowledge anyway, hoping that might dislodge old unknowns and send them floating to the surface. Or, perhaps, piling information into the deep ocean between islands of memory would eventually build bridges. She could link up the things she knew and finally make sense of herself and her fragmentary world.

For a while, she lingered around the Peripats. The group split up every morning after feeding. Each one of them roamed the Second Ward on private, individual purposes. She trailed Philotech—not because he was particularly interesting, but because his annoyance at being followed amused her. He spent his day hunting for pretty knick-knacks that he hid in the many pockets of his raggedy red coat.

She did not know why he bothered. He never took them out again.

At dusk the Peripats gathered and sang away the dark. Soon enough, Oneirotheria learned their song and system of music, though her voice never raised a glowing shield. The protective magic they created—as Matron had said when first she asked—lay in the singers, not the song.

The fifth dawn in the folly garden, the vagabonds decamped.

"A Stay," Matron told her without waiting to being asked, "is five nights in one place. No more. Then we move to the next Ward in the Octet."

"Octet? Not Nonet?"

Matron made the apotrope.

"You don't go to the First," Oneirotheria said, taking her meaning.

"We don't Stay in the First," Matron corrected.

"Stay, go—what's the difference?"

"You talk more than the last witch," Philotech growled. "Too much."

Matron touched his arm. Their eyes met and exchanged a conversation closed to the outside world.

"How do you know where to go next?" Oneirotheria asked Matron as they wended from Second to Fourth Ward.

"How is the thing with feathers."

"Pfft."

Leaving her izbushka in the garden, she trudged with them. They went from the Second to the Fourth to the Fifth to the Sixth. After the Sixth, they plodded towards the Ninth. Oneirotheria had no intention of following them the whole way, but she did ask Matron what that Ward was like.

"It isn't like anything," Matron replied. "That is to say, nothing is what it seems there. A place of appearances and effects, of glamers and mechanical illusions. Nothing is what it seems," she repeated for emphasis.

"I don't know what that means."

"It means," Philotech said, "you'll fit right in. The whole place is a gull-catcher's playground where fools set traps for more foolish fools and even the traps have little traps inside them and every escape is just—"

He did not finish the sentence. The magpie swerved out of the Peripats' path and beat wings hard away.

Thereafter, Oneirotheria wandered Osylum

alone, dancing the secret patterns laid down by intuition.

24

She encountered Eschatos more than a few times in her months-long walkabout. The would-be Warden flitted around the edges of her wandering. He never confronted her—as she grew in power, recalling more and more hexes, she could easily have dispatched him. He simply appear every now and then, lurking at a distance. Whenever she spotted him, he mockingly flashed her the apotrope, to say: *I'm watching. I'm always watching.*

Then, she noted, he prudently withdrew. Unless Wardens were present, in which case he would puff up with insolence. He'd loiter, wordlessly daring her to attack him and draw down her own annihilation.

She treated his cowardice and his bravado with the same dismissive contempt. She never let her guard down inwardly, but she did not display a whit of concern. She would not give him that satisfaction. Too, she hoped her flippant disregard for his self-appointed power would provoke *him* into attacking *her*. And so they maneuvered around one another in a rigid waltz of animosity.

Of his Ratkippers, she saw neither fang nor fingernail. Not even in the Seventh Ward where they supposedly lived. Like roaches scattering from a hobnail boot, they scuttled into the sewers at the mere whiff of the witch's approach. She could hear the hiss and scrabble of their flight like a susurrating wave sliding swiftly away beneath her feet.

Most of the other prisoners behaved similarly. Over nineteen thousand souls in the city, if the Oblate's count was correct, and the vast majority of them shunned her like a Warden's third eye.

As she un-forgot more and more of her former power, she saw the wisdom in their fear. A handful of importunate assaults early on proved to all that tearing a Ratkipper inside out with a hedge was the least of the witch-weapons at Oneirotheria's disposal.

25

The Linnaea did not fear her. Whether it was because their tick-tock tools were equal to her power or they simply too sheltered in their sanctuary to conceive of a superior force, she could never figure out. Not that she gave it much thought. As gruff and fussy as they were, she decided she liked them.

She visited from time to time. Never at regular intervals, never announced in advance, and always atop their telescope tower. She wanted to keep things cordial. They would have given much to capture her. Not out of ill will, of course, but curiosity—a sentiment she understood and appreciated well. Were she a geometric dissector of reality, she would have done the same to them.

Instead, both parties had to content themselves with conversations like the following:

The magpie lighted on the brass rail. Oneirotheria stepped down. The Linnaea—the Major taking notes and the Minor peeping through the telescope, nestled in his cradle—did not at first notice her arrival. She would watch them scan the sky a while. The Minor called out coordinates and the lack of anything to see and the Major repeated the observation and jotted it down. Eventually, boredom set in. She yawned theatrically with a little *yip!* at the end.

Without looking up from their work, the Linnaea said: "All guests should register with Cellarius. You are a guest. Therefore, you should register with Cellarius."

She had no intention of letting the brass butler get his claws on her.

"I don't know why you bother with this every night. Birds all know even the sky has walls."

Four eyes rolled at the non-sequitur.

"No witch follows simple rules. Oneirotheria is a witch. Therefore, Oneirotheria does not follow simple rules. Although whether that should be 'does not' or 'cannot' or 'chooses not to' or 'is constitutionally incapable of' or—"

She interrupted the tedious enumeration of modalities before it stretched on till dawn. "I brought you a present."

She rummaged around in her battered satchel. It had been the only item still hanging in a shop full of naked mannequins in the Fifth Ward. Its buckle was a silver crow, which was close enough to a magpie. Age lines spider-webbed the soft brown leather. It smelled of warm hands and hard work. It didn't hold as much as a Peripat's infinite coat, but it still fit a substantial supply of books, papers, ink vials, nibs, quills, and assorted witchments.

Best of all, it merged with her magpie form, just like her clothes and pouch. Most things she tried to carry fell away when she transformed. She hadn't solved the question of *why* that was. That didn't stop her from appreciating that it *was* that way.

The Linnaea descended the short step from the observation platform. By the time they joined her, she'd produced a rolled-up piece of vellum, tied round with a scarlet ribbon. She handed it over, hand trembling slightly with excitement she couldn't quite suppress.

Most of the scraps she'd found in Osylum had meant nothing; a collection of fragments tossed far from any context. This, however, had sent a shock of recognition up her arms and to the tips of her feather-littered hair.

"Find the oseovox," she'd heard Ragpatch's last words, as clear as if she'd been there. *"Flee the Fade. Escape this mad place."*

The page, torn raggedly from a bound volume, contained a diagram in rust-red ink. A skull in three-quarters profile dominated the crisp drawing. Several smaller, rotated versions of the same image surrounded it. Lines and curves were inscribed across the macabre object. Miniscule symbols buzzed around the skull. Whether the signs were mathematical, alchemical, astrological, phrenological, or the province of some other esoteric discipline, Oneirotheria had not been able to determine. It did not matter. What mattered was the single word that flowed from the bony jaw, as if the skull were speaking:

MEMORY

The instant the Linnaea saw the diagram, they rolled the page back up. Sweeping swiftly back to the platform, the Major whirled his cloak over the telescope and brass fittings. The Minor plucked several handkerchiefs from their pocket, handing them to his larger twin. In short order, they had covered every reflective surface in sight. Their voice dropped next door to silence. Even far above the straying streets they were not secure from being overheard.

"Do you know what this is?"

The oseovox.

She schooled herself to blank innocence. She wanted to see if they knew what she knew.

"I was hoping you could tell me."

"Where did you find this page? Was there a book attached to it?"

"No!" The question appalled her. However little she thought of the Lady's laws, Eschatos's demands, the Peripat's rituals, the Linnaea's courtesies, or any of the other myriad ridiculous rules her fellow inmates insisted on following, she still had standards. Pulling books apart affronted her to the last scruple.

"That's a shame. I would have given much for the rest."

"Well, there wasn't anything else."

The Linnaea flipped a switch on the telescope contraption. A brass seat unfolded. The Major sat, arranging the Minor in his cradle. "Start at the beginning."

Lacking her own chair, Oneirotheria settled cross-legged on the chilly tile floor.

"Scrivener Street in the Fifth is short and not special. Row houses with corbie-step gables. Shingles over the doors with nibs and pens and swooping cursive. Windows displaying paper in every size. I needed writing tools so I thought I'd scav up some there. I discovered one of the houses—and only one—was sealed."

"I find it hard to believe you let a locked door stop you, given your disregard for my security."

She loftily ignored the jab. "I didn't say locked.

I said sealed. I only noticed it because someone had scrawled some graffiti across the front of the building. That drew my att—"

"—what did it say? Every detail may be important."

"It was the last rowhouse on a block. In charcoal, someone had written 'Come not within these doors; within this roof.'"

"Within this roof what?"

"Nothing. The bar of the 'f' dragged down the side of the house, like the graffitist almost got caught and had to run away before finishing. It doesn't really matter, I'm sure. The only reason I mention it is, because of the words, I paid more attention to that door. Which is why I noticed the Lady's Eye sigil pressed across the door and jamb."

She recognized the Major's expression. He was sorting through books in his mind's library. She let him search.

"The Lady's Eye sigil is not a term I have come across."

She made the apotrope.

"A closed eye spanning the gap twixt entry and building. If you try to cross it... fwwwttt..." She flung the apotrope fingers out, to indicate annihilation. "I saw a careless budge in the Fourth crack a window sealed with that sign. Soon as his crowbar jimmied into the latch, there was a blue flash. When I could see again, he'd gone the way of nothing, sure as if a Warden had been there in person to Fade him clean."

"So you found a building where someone warned you not to enter and the Lady's own power sealed against intrusion? Naturally, you had to get inside."

"Naturally. Nothing interesting is out in the open, is it? Scavvers picked the easy places clean long afore I hatched."

They did not reply. She continued her narrative.

"Every window on the place and all three doors, back, side, and front were sealed the same way. The roof-thatch though... that had a number of convenient holes."

"What did you find within?"

She reached out and tapped the diagram in the Major's hand. "Just that. That and enough dust to choke every Ratkipper in the Seventh."

That was not true. A scrap of crazy-quilt fabric had hung, torn, on the ragged edge of largest hole the thatch. A line of lumpy, staggering footprints traversed the dust, from just beneath the hole to the page and back. There was dust under the page and not much on top, which suggested Ragpatch had placed it, rather than coming across it.

Oneirotheria concealed those details. She only trusted the Linnaea so far and there was no value—yet at least—in telling them about Upstart. She'd already figured out who the anomalous six (now four) souls in Osylum were, that the Oblates had fussed about. If they or the Linnaea didn't know about Upstart and his puppet crew, well, maybe they shouldn't.

The twins settled into a cogitative pose. They stared at the diagram. They murmured inaudible arcana back and forth, Major to Minor, Minor to Major. Oneirotheria held her peace as long as she could—by now she saw some value in letting them plod through their paces.

After minutes or hours or days of waiting (subjective time played tricks and she still did not idle well), she hopped to her feet. She whistled a jaunty tarantelle as she danced whirling steps round the edge of the tower-top. She came to rest leaning over the Major's shoulder, opposite his homuncular twin.

"Well? What *is* it?"

"This is an ancient technology called an oseovox. The word means 'bone voice', a fact I am sure you will find inordinately gratifying."

"I do!"

"The Lady and the Wardens have forbidden even speaking about this technology. I did not think they existed. There are many records of things that do not now exist and likely never did, regardless of the Lady's proscriptions."

"What does it do? How does it work?" She could not conceal the eagerness in her voice, even though such vulnerability put her at a disadvantage. She *had* given them a gift, but they could easily decide sharing their knowledge required more offerings.

As luck would have it, they were just as eager—if more controlled in manner—to discuss the topic.

"These lines here are wires of precious metals, alloyed in precise ratios. When a dying person exhales their last, the theory is that breath holds the person's memories, all they are or were or could be. If they die in proximity to a skull prepared according to this diagram, the weave of wires captures that breath and with it, everything that person knew. The oseovox then could give voice to all that knowledge."

Oneirotheria fell back. Had it not been for the brass railing, she would have tumbled to her doom.

"Here-now," she whispered.

"Indeed. I need more time to verify the accuracy of this drawing, but if it is a viable technology—"

"Then oseovoxes could exist. And if they can

exist, they remember everything about what the city used to be. What happened before it was what it is and how it got this way. Why there are words for things that aren't there and houses for people who don't exist and—"

She clapped her hands over her mouth to hold the last thought inside.

And the way out.

The Linnaea rolled up the vellum page. Thinking more slowly, they had not yet made the dangerous leap she instantly had.

"Correct. The knowledge contained within such a thing could be of inestimable value to my research. If there is even one oseovox, we should make every effort to find it."

She lowered shaking hands. She clutched her skirt to hide the tremor. She smoothed the surface of her churning brain with a few deep breaths. It would have been easier to turn into a magpie and back a dozen times in a second than keep a casual face, but somehow she managed.

"If only you knew someone who could scan the city through mirrors..."

The sky was pale by the time the ensuing argument ended.

The twins did not want to share the possible existence of an oseovox with the Phrontistery Oblates—such knowledge, they insisted, was best kept in as few minds as possible. Nor did they want to take time away from the monks' primary project of counting the number of living people in Osylum every day.

Oneirotheria tried to persuade them finding the talking skull would answer the question as well as relentless bean-counting, and in less time. She even considered revealing that her predecessor had already illicitly suborned Hendiatrix for the search, so the secret was in the open already. However, the jealousness with which they guarded their resources led her to hold her tongue.

In the end, the only concession she could wrangle from them was to have the Oblates make note of any bones they saw during their usual cycle of spying. Since the Wardens collected all bodies within hours of death (and disposed of them in an as-yet unknown fashion), any skulls casually laying around would have to be candidates for oseovoxhood.

That suggestion prompted her to spend several minutes debating herself aloud as to whether it should be 'oseovoxhood,' 'oseovoxery,' 'oseovoxness,' or 'oseovoxcivity.' Each had its merits. The Linnaea—frustrated by the relentless digression—cut her short.

"If I agreed with your proposition, will you cease your pointless nattering over terminology?"

"Deal," she said. "Oseovoxhood."

The matter settled, she flew away.

26

Her izbushka had nested in the Second before she had hatched. It showed no signs of wanting to hike up its chicken legs to wander elsewhere. She could not dredge up how to control it from her missing memories. So, regardless of where she wandered or how long, she always returned to the ruined garden eventually.

As she sailed over the Feeding Plaza, she spotted a Warden floating through one of the broad arcades on the perimeter. She wouldn't have given it a second thought, except Philotech skulked next to it. And then she caught the flash of silk-slippered feet beneath the "Warden's" pale blue robes.

Eschatos.

That merited a course change. Focused on one another, neither man had noticed her. She swerved above their line of sight, glided to a stop on the slant red-tiled roof, and transformed back into Oneirotheria. Stepping as lightly as she could, she crept to the edge and shadowed the two men from above. She strained to give shape to their murmured voices.

"The rats whisper that the witch walked with you for a while. Is that true?"

"Not by my will. Nothing to run to your Wardens about, smudge."

Eschatos's voice gave no sign of irritation at the insult. "Of course not. Were you to flout my Lady's laws, it would hardly behoove me to talk with you, would it?"

"Last time you came to my kind, it wasn't to talk. You and your lickshits tried to kills us all. Or do you think I didn't know about that because I wasn't yet found?"

"A misunderstanding, I'm sure."

"And Hecate crushed half of the kippers to raw meat over it."

Irritation edged Eschatos's smarm. "Let's say the witch tarried near you then."

"Why do you care? It's your fault we owe her a debt anyway."

"Ah, so Matron made sure you knew the story of Platon's Oath."

There was a hiss of steel on leather and the whuff of a man hitting a wall. "Say her name again, smudge, and I'll open that third eye in your face."

"And who will watch over her when you're food for rats?" Eschatos squeaked. "Or do you think I come unprotected?"

Reflexively, Oneirotheria scanned the plaza. A pair of red eyes glittered deep behind a broken sewer grate across the way. Likely several more Ratkippers hunkered in the filth out of sight. It was only the second time she'd seen them this far away from their slum.

When Eschatos next spoke, he sounded as if Philotech had let him go. "That is a more fitting way to treat one who comes to you as a friend."

"Spit your wits quick and be done. The stink of

you brings my breakfast up."

The witch stifled a giggle. She did enjoy Philotech's street cant insults.

"My dear, I came to you to say this and only this. The Lady sees everything, but some things she needs her servants to see for her. Whatever the witch is doing will be the doom of anyone too close to her. You and I aren't so different, Peripat. You're a rough beast in rags, but you love your lady as much as I love Mine."

Philotech growled. His knife scraped along the stone wall.

"And if you would walk with her forever, you need to keep her safe."

"So what then? Kill the witch?"

Eschatos laughed, a forced and false sound. "Oh wouldn't that be a thing? No, dear, no. I've watched you kill a time or two, when the Lady willed it. You don't have the blade to take a witch's blood."

"So what then?" Philotech repeated.

"Just watch. I'll find you when I want to know what you've seen."

With that, Eschatos emerged from the arcade into the plaza. Oneirotheria flattened herself to the terra cotta tiles. He languorously turned. He made the apotrope to Philotech.

"Lady sees us all, Peripat. And She judges."

With that, he swept away across the plaza. The eyes in the sewers receded in his imperious wake. Philotech's heavy boots stomped in the opposite direction. Oneirotheria clung to the slant roof. She did not follow either man. She lost track of time, trying to glean what the unusual scene might mean.

27

Moonvines wound around the izbushka's slender ceiling beams, rooted in thatch mud. Their flowers slowly brightened as the light outside faded. Curled on a pallet of books and pages, Oneirotheria blinked awake. She grunted in frustration. A day's sleep—to make up for the missed night's rest—had provided no clarity.

That Eschatos had asked Philotech to spy on her made sense. The Peripats wandered the most widely of any of Osylum's inmates. They saw as much of the city as the mirror-gazing monks. Maybe more. She herself had considered recruiting them to find the oseovox. However, she didn't know what their stance was on ancient forbidden lore, nor if they desired escape from Osylum's nothingness.

It wasn't the kind of question one could simply ask, even as a witch with a reputation for being mad.

Too, she doubted that Matron would agree to something so improper. The red-coats' followed their own many incomprehensible rules with rigid obsession. In her weeks wandering with them, Oneirotheria had counted over six hundred separate commandments they had to tick off. She couldn't find any spare room in a pile of imperatives that big to sneak in a quick side job.

Somehow Eschatos found a crack...

Her stomach growled. She growled back. She rummaged around the chaos for leftovers—the Wardens weren't the only source of food in Osylum, just the most convenient.

As she pieced together a plate of farrow-seed cake, dried apple, and wilted mugwort salad (courtesy of the Linnaea's garden), she muttered to herself. Overhearing her words helped sort them out.

"Yes. He found a way—or he thought he found a way, anyway—to get Philotech to tack on one more task to his chores. Who gives them their commandments anyway? No. Not a helpful question."

She mulled a bite of cake. Dry as a crone's bones. She coughed on a stuck crumb and couldn't stop hacking. She spotted a cup of antique tea, precariously balanced on the edge of the clay oven. She washed her throat clear, scarcely noticing the tea contained a significant quantity of ink.

That explained the quill sticking out of the cup.

"Ahem," she said, composing herself again. A word bobbed to the surface of her brain. "Love?"

Yes. Love.

The magpie fluttered under her left breast, almost the way it did at the word 'escape'; close but with a subtly difference cadence.

"Shush," she told the bird. "I was just thinking of something Eschatos said."

'You're a rough beast in rags, but you love your lady as much as I love Mine.'

"Love we the Lady and fear we the Fade," she

sang in a soft and cracking voice. "That's the only time I hear that word. And I don't think it means anything there—or maybe in that spot it means something different. Or maybe it's just there for the alliteration. Poets. Feh."

She smiled around a bite of mugwort. She did not really mean the 'feh'. She loved poetry—such fragments as she'd found—but poets didn't use words to *mean* things so much as to *do* things. It could be very confusing, and language was enough of an impediment to communication as it was.

Regardless, Eschatos hadn't been using it as part of a ritual formula.

He'd meant something by it. Meant... something. What?

Love.

It wasn't one of those words for something that didn't exist; like sun, moon, stars. There was something behind it and that something was in Osylum.

Did Eschatos love the Lady? If that was love, Oneirotheria wanted no part of it—a cloying, clinging, possessive affection that alternated between groveling and demand. It made her skin crawl just thinking about it.

"He said he did."

She swigged the dregs of the inky tea. She set the cup on the empty plate and, with a slight rattle, returned both to the oven-top.

"He says a lot of things. Even if he does, that verb's at best a homophone to how Philotech feels about Matron."

She'd watched Philotech enough to know he felt about the Peripat's leader. He treated her differently than the other three wanderers. He reached out when she stumbled. He twitched at any threat to her, real or imagined. Every night, he watched her sleeping until his own sleep forced his eyes shut. Every morning he reluctantly let her stray on her own path, because she insisted.

"Maybe that's love, but there's fear in it," she said to the moonflowers. "More fear than anything else, I'd bet, if the Linnaea could measure that kind of thing. So that's Eschatos's leverage. Philotech's fear."

She sifted through her memories—the ones since she'd hatched—to see if she'd heard the word 'love' out of anyone else in Osylum.

"It's not a Ratkipper feeling. Hunger and fear and the lust to kill are the only three emotions in those mort's hearts. And everyone else? Fear is in everyone. So much fear. Except me."

That startled her to her feet. She'd never given it thought. All her fellow inmates ran on some measure of fear. Matron feared the Wardens. Hendiatrix feared to talk to her. Upstart's puppets—the two she'd met—feared things they would not name for new-found her. Nameless dozens feared her.

Even the Linnaea harbored fear—why else hide behind walls, guarded by locks and traps and tick-tock soldiers, if you weren't afraid of what lay beyond?

She did not fear.

The closest she'd gotten to afraid was the unease she'd felt in front of the Lady's fog. That had not been fear, though. Not precisely. Revisiting the moment, she thought what had stopped her was, strangely enough, a sense she could only call 'not yet, not yet.' As if deciding to take one road instead of another because the former was a better path to... somewhere... than the latter.

An uncomfortable realization coalesced. In her vague, impulse-driven wanderings, she'd just been following rules laid down by someone else for their own purpose long ago.

"Ugh," she said. "I'm no better than a Peripat."

While others ran on fear or (dubiously) love, she'd been flailing around the city on instinct. But what if instinct were nothing more than strings from a long-dead puppeteer? Could she trust the suggestions that rose from the dark gaps in her memory? Whose purpose was she really fulfilling?

Who lay at the center of the lost world within?

Another question slashed across those brooding speculations and when she asked it aloud, the words in her own voice swept away every other thought, like farrow crumbs brushed from the tabletop to the floor.

"Do *I* love anyone?"

Her heart raced. Her face flushed. Her belly grew warm, then hot. Her hands trembled in search of something to hold. A frisson slithered from the soles of her feet to the crown of her skull. A vision of two faces raced unbidden into her mind's eye; a mud-smudged gardener and laughing crazy-quilt doll. The quiver she felt was not for them, though. The love—if it was love—strained past the puppets to clutch at the invisible, unknown hand who twitched their strings.

Upstart.

As swiftly as it had seized her, the feeling fled. Only a vague after-sensation lingered, like sharp ink left on her tongue after the taste of sweet tea dissipated.

"Cack 'n' pike," she cursed, still breathless. "I guess I'm off to the Ninth."

She did not move.

Paradoxically, it was the strength of the impulse to go that checked her. Her feathers were still ruffled by the realization that what she called instinct might well be someone else's intention. Given that, she trusted the unexpected surge of attraction for the unknown Upstart about as much as she trusted a Ratkipper to guard her while she slept.

"Maybe Hecate loved you," she said, "whoever you are. Maybe by her lights you were worth it. Well, I'm not she and she's not me."

She could think of one person who might have seen her previous incarnation and the hidden puppeteer together. One monk huddled in his cell, spying on the town, might be able shed some light on that aspect of her past. While Hendiatrix had refused to answer her call since that first day, maybe the Linnaea's latest change of orders would make him more amenable.

There was no way to contact him here, though. She didn't keep a mirror to preen herself, that wasn't who she was. And she'd removed every reflective surface from her hut soon after learning about the Oblates' power. She kept the windows shuttered so the grimy panes wouldn't show her face. Her plate and cup were scuffed clay instead of porcelain that might carry the ghost of a reflection. She'd even tossed the spoon in which she'd first seen Hendiatrix's fish-bowled face—it was too small for a decent conversation anyway.

Even when she had nothing to hide, she still wanted a space free from someone else's eyes.

28

O f the five dozen public houses in the Fifth Ward, Oneirotheria picked one at random. Perhaps not at random—she liked the sign. It was the only pub with a bird out front. That had originally drawn her to it, when she'd strayed these streets with the Peripats months ago. The cracked shingle that hung over the front door still bore the faint, faded paint-traces of a scarlet eagle, carrying an infant by his swaddling. Where once wrought-iron letters naming the place had hung, now were only broken-off spikes and a bare brick wall, on which a by-now-familiar hand had scribbled:

A great reckoning in a little room

The window panes had been painted black. Still, she knew from previous exploration there was a long mirror inside. As in many of the other taverns in the ward, the glass hung behind the bar. Why people would want to hunker on sullen stools and stare themselves into oblivion, she did not know.

By a moonflower's light, she checked the door for a Lady's Eye. It had not been sealed the last time she'd been here, but why be careless?

It remained safe—from the Fade at least. It opened with a creak that echoed down the street. She slipped inside. She bolted the door with a thunk.

The pub was lit. A fire kindled from broken stool legs crackled in the hearth. Fat-wicked lamps hung at regular intervals above booths and along the bar. The mirror doubled the gleam, giving the entire room a cheery ambiance she'd never experienced in Osylum.

No one sat at the bar. She checked the four booths; likewise empty. A cramped corner housing a billiards table and dartboard was also unoccupied. A wrought-iron circular staircase led to a door on the second floor. Before she went to investigate that, she heard a low drone from behind the bar. There was a majestic snort, followed by an indistinct grumble. The drone resumed.

Oneirotheria picked up a cue. She didn't want a fight. And she certainly did not need a mere stick as a weapon. The sight of her brandishing it might, however, give someone pause before launching at her. On light feet, she crept to the bar. She peered over the top.

A man in a rumpled coat and pants, well-stained with a variety of dubious liquids, lay on his back on the floor. He'd propped his head on one wooden pony keg and his feet on another. He cradled a third keg in his arms. Its bung was popped and the contents half-drunk. Small spurts of ale slopped forth every time the sleeper stirred. A brown puddle of it surrounded him, its odor rising sharp and rancid.

"The one place in all the city..." Oneirotheria muttered. She was irritated. She wanted a private conversation with Hendiatrix. There were other bar mirrors in the Fifth, but none as well preserved. She jabbed the man in the short ribs with the sharp tip of the cue. He lurched bolt upright.

"Tosspot a-yer service!" His breath roiled over Oneirotheria, forcing her to take a step back and gag.

He groaned. He pulled himself standing. Lacking the structural support to maintain the position, he leaned heavily on the counter. He smacked his lips. His face wrinkled at the taste of his own mouth. Two blood-shot eyes tried to go their separate ways before gradually deciding to cooperate. He squinted in Oneirotheria's general direction.

"Bugger me dry with a handful of hops," he slurred. "It's you. Now I have to do my job."

"Don't bother on my account."

"'S no bother."

With slow, deliberate, inebriated movements, he righted the two empty kegs. He squatted next to them. He paused for several deep, steadying breaths. He stacked one atop the other. He sat down, balancing on the makeshift stool like an overstuffed pigeon on an undersized fence post. He circled his index finger and thumb and waved them in a perfunctory greeting.

"Lady sees, et cetera," he said. "It's been a long sail on an ocean of ale to toss me on your shore. The captain said you'd stolen the dinghy and paddled off on your own. I told him if anyone were adrift in the smaller ship, 'twas us. Made no mind, we still had to tack our own way clear without charts or buoys, he said. And I said—"

"Oy! Sail? Captain? Ocean? Your patter's as bad as the Abram-Man's gutter cant. Make more sense!"

The drunk drew himself up, indignant. He raised a finger and pointed it at her. Baffled by the trembling digit's appearance at the end of his hand, he stared at it. Impatient, Oneirotheria goaded him again with the billiard cue. His gaze wavered back her way.

"Tosspot. Is that your name?"

"I'm borrowing it for a while."

She wracked her vocabulary. "Captain? Caput means head, but you're talking about a person. So, metonymy for your leader?"

Tosspot tapped the side of his bulbous nose. His skin looked badly painted by a child with fingers daubed in crimson and purple ink.

Oneirotheria lowered her stick. "Upstart."

Tosspot did not disagree.

"How many of you *are* there?"

"Counting were never my strongest suit. Anything higher than three barrels makes my head spin."

She snorted. He held up a trembling hand.

"Peace, peace. We have a theme song, the Canting Crew do. I've not sung it since the last time I sang it, but I'll do my best."

He drew himself up. In a rough and haggard tenor, he croaked:

"Upstart shake the scenery
Pigeonfoot pull the plague
Ragpatch peel your sock off
And show a player's leg!
Turnspade tear the tickets
Tosspot heave a sigh
Wailenweave pluck their heartstrings
And play them till they die!"

The last note cracked. Tosspot, true to the song, heaved a sigh. Tears glinted in his eyes. He cleared his throat. He hopped off his barrel-stool.

"It was a much longer song once. Those were brighter days," he mumbled. "And now we're four."

He picked up a keg. He tipped it to his lips. The beer had all slopped out on the floor as he slept. He dropped it wistfully.

"Brighter days," he repeated.

"Four of you. That matches—what I'd guessed," she changed what she'd been about to say. *Matches the extra numbers in the count.*

She still didn't know how much Upstart and his crew knew about the Linnaea or the Oblates. And, fluttering feelings aside, she had no particular reason to trust them.

Tosspot roared, slamming a hand on the bar. "Yes! We were never many, but we could raise a ruckus like we was hundreds. We could fit you a scene of a battle of two vast armies or sit you in the middle of a busy city and you'd swear you'd been there, trampled by every foot in the mob. My specialties were soldiers and clowns with the occasional lover thrown in when the play called for more than Turnspade's good face."

"You're actors?"

"The very best."

She thought about that. Tosspot shuffled around the bar. He flopped down in a red leather booth.

"Good witch, have you any brew? I'm dry as the Ninth Ward river."

She slid in across from him. She handed him a flask from her satchel. He unscrewed the cap and sniffed. He urped.

"Is that water?"

"Tea."

"Smells like the underside of Pigeonfoot's fingernails."

"Drink it. It'll wake you up."

Melodramatically, he pinched his nose. He squirted several generous swigs from the skin. He handed it back to her. She took a sip and put it away. His eyes cleared up almost at once.

"Painfully effective," he said. "The blissful haze is lifting. What's in it?"

"Witch stuff."

He smirked. "Hecate was clever too and never gave away more than she got."

She ignored that. "Actors. The grand plan relied on actors?"

"Who better?"

"In what conceivable way?"

His hand resting on the table, covered by his body, Tosspot made the apotrope. Three fingers pointed to the mirror behind the bar. He leaned his chin on his other hand, shielding his lips from reflection. She did the same—hiding the ensuing conversation from any lip-readers who might be peeping through the glass.

"Who better," Tosspot continued, "when everyone is watching, than someone who can be anyone? Lady knows, we are not who we are. None of us."

"It's all a show?"

"It is. Until it isn't. Take my meaning?"

"Are any of you real? Upstart? Is he real?"

"There's a question for philosophers. I'm just a player, strutting and fretting between drunken sprees."

"You said, when you first woke up, you had to do

your job. What did you mean?"

"Right! Thank you for the reminder. After Turnspade got smashed to bits and Ragpatch—" He cleared his throat. He took a moment to compose himself. "When you failed to go straight to the Ninth, the skipper figured one of two things. You didn't remember who you were or you did remember and decided to turncoat."

"'Either way, Tosspot,' he told me, 'the heavy black curtain of nothing is rolling towards us. Faster if it's on the wings of a treacherous witch than a forgetful one, but rolling all the same.'"

"I'm not a traitor," Oneirotheria interrupted.

"Many's the Judas who called himself James," Tosspot replied. "Or so the captain said in one of his fouler moods. Don't ask me what it meant or I'll never finish the story."

"Please, just go on."

"'If she won't escape with me in the flesh, I'll have to carry her in my heart and on my lips—'" Tosspot interrupted himself. "By that, he meant to tell your story, once he got on the other side of Osylum's walls."

"So there is an 'other side'!"

"Another question for philosophers. Tinkers and tick-tock men breathe heavy about it back and forth."

"And you?"

"My suggestion was we scav up whatever brew still bubbled in this ruined burgh and drink till we didn't care about oblivion."

"Which is what you were doing when I found you."

"It was. Though not by orders. The skipper gave me a task. It was just happiness that I found those wooden friends while searching for a thing."

He glanced at the mirror. Not even trusting his hand in front of his mouth to hide him from any prying eyes, he did not speak the word aloud. He sketched a skull in the dust on the mug-gnawed oak tabletop. He swept it clean immediately.

The oseovox.

"I've been looking too," Oneirotheria said, soft as she could.

"HA!" Tosspot cried. "Looking! That's the best thing I've heard since my first gurgle of beer! You're still with us, then? Even if it brings the Lady's Fog and the end of the world?"

"That's a question for philosophers," she replied.

He shook his head ruefully. "Taste of my own backwash. Well, say what you will, I'm counting you on our stage."

"Where did you find the kegs?" She didn't really care about that, but it would tell her where he thought the oseovox *might* be.

"In the cellar of this fine house, of course."

"Show me."

He slid out of the booth. She followed him behind the bar. He moved much more steadily now. His eyes were keen and unclouded. He rolled aside the keg he'd been using as a pillow. Beneath it was a trapdoor. With a grunt, he heaved it open. With a flourish and a bow, he waved at the ladder descending into darkness.

"After you, good witch."

She scampered nimbly down. No sooner had her foot touched the cold limestone floor, than Tosspot slammed the trapdoor shut. She hurled herself up the ladder, only to be met by a solid THUNK as he bolted the door. She heard him dragging several heavy pieces of furniture over it, for good measure. She punched the ceiling hatch, knowing it would bloody her knuckles. The howling pain matched her fury at being so easily duped.

"Lady?" his voice came muffled from above.

She did not deign to reply.

"I reckon you're angry. That's proper enough. But I'm one puppet who's not going the way of Turnspade. Or Ragpatch. People get hurt around you. Maybe you're with us and maybe not. Not for me to say. You just stay there till I get the skipper here to sort it out."

Creaking bootfalls receded. The pub door opened with a faint chime. It closed with a boom.

29

She fumed in the musty dark. She replayed the conversation with Tosspot over and over. She picked apart every detail; how had she missed his betrayal?

He said he was an actor. 'We are not who we are.' He as much as told you not to believe a thing he said or pretended to feel. So why did you hop down the first hole he pointed you at?

Parsing his words, his face, his voice, his gestures got her nowhere. He was too consummate a performer to pinpoint the tell of his deception. She took a different tack. She turned her memory's eye to herself. That proved more fruitful.

'If she won't escape with me in the flesh, I'll have to carry her in my heart and on my lips.' He told me that Upstart said that and I flushed foot-to-cheek. I squirmed in my seat. I imagined kisses and more. Even after that puppet explained he meant only to tell my story—ah! But that was a lie. Tosspot played me by revealing Upstart loved Hecate, lips and heart. Somehow, deep down below where I do my thinking, there's a piece of me that reacts like one beloved. And that short-cuts my smarter parts.

Well no more of that. Harden your heart, witch.

Love's a pile of seeds on sticky lime, waiting to trap an unwary bird.

She still had her satchel. By feel, she found a wilted moonflower inside. She pressed it to her lips. The warmth of her life revived the bloom. She placed it in a hanging lantern.

Warped and filthy racks lined the walls. The cradles varied in size, from demi bottles all the way to full barrels. She could see white drag marks along the stone floor, where Tosspot had pulled his three kegs to the ladder. She rapped a couple of the others with her knuckles. Empty. None of the bottle racks were occupied.

In addition to the bar stores, the cramped room contained several extra stools, a booth bench in dire need of re-upholstering, rusting piles of taps and tools, a well-chewed roll of carpet, and a large rectangular object draped with a dingy canvas sheet. She tugged the covering off, revealing a full-length standing mirror, trimmed with flaking gilt pine.

"Now that's a thing I can work with."

She placed the moonflower in an empty hanging sconce. She straightened the canted mirror. She closed her eyes and dredged through her brain for a phrase. When she found it, she chanted aloud:

"Old man, old man in the mirror, see me now, hear me here."

She opened her eyes. A liver-spotted, tonsured old man in a rough wool robe of blue glared at her from the glass. His rheumy eyes wavered between fear and anger. He was backed by the rough stone walls of a cell and lit by sallow guttering light.

"Hendiatrix!" she cried, moving her lips in exaggerated curves around the syllables of his name, to make it easier for him to read her speech.

"Witch," he replied. "I've been expecting your face. Ever since the Linnaea asked us to keep an eye out for bones. That had to have been your doing. Another way to find... it."

"That's not immediately important."

"It's going to get us all faded."

Impatient, she waved away his fear. "Stop. I need your help right now. To escape."

He startled. He repeated the last word.

"Not from the city," she said. "Just a little minor matter of being locked in a pub house basement."

"Step back," he said. His face had gone flat. "Turn the mirror all the way around. Let me see where you are."

She did as he asked. After a full circle, his expression changed. He shook his head, a mix of disbelief and admiration.

"When you see me where you've never seen..." he said.

"What?"

"It was something Hecate said to me. Late in the game, when she taught me something—something blasphemous. 'When you see me where you've never seen, use this spell to set me free.' And now, here you are. Someplace my glass has never shown me, asking for escape. How did she know?"

"She—I—she probably told you a lot of things. You just remember the ones that happen. It's a common trick."

He shook his head. "Do you know how long it's been since I've seen someplace new? The week I was found in the Phrontistery, that's when."

Above her, she heard the tavern door creak.

"No more time. Whatever she told to do, do it

146

now."

His lips barely twitched. She could only make out the word 'Lady'. He set his shoulders. He moved towards the mirror, filling up the silver.

Above her, she heard Tosspot. "This way, Skipper. I've got her bottled up below decks."

A muffled voice replied.

"Aye-aye!" Tosspot cried.

The scrape of furniture and kegs told her the drunkard was uncovering the trap.

"Hurry," she said to Hendiatrix.

The monk's cell in the mirror was empty. Baffled, Oneirotheria moved side to side, trying to look past the gilt edges of the glass. She even checked the back. The monk really had left her.

BOOM!

A keg hit the boards above her head. By the sounds of it, Tosspot had slipped.

"Care, drunken coxcomb," chastised the second voice, "break the floor and she'll fly free afore we trade words."

The sound of it tugged deep within her. She flushed all over again, confused and eager and leery at the same time. She turned her face up the ladder. Tosspot slowed his uncovering of the trapdoor, but did not stop.

Mind racing, she catalogued the hexes at her disposal. She didn't care if she hurt Tosspot—he deserved as much for tricking her into a trap. His boss on the other hand... She couldn't sort herself on him. She furiously flipped between plans for attack and defense, between spells lethal and those merely inconvenient.

"Lady fade you," she muttered at the absent oblate. "Never rely on a monk to do a witch's wo—YURK!"

Two arms reached out of the mirror. Hands seized her shoulders. The last thing she saw as Hendiatrix pulled her into the glass was a flare of light from the upper room as the hatch flung open wide.

30

Oneirotheria stood in darkness behind the mirror. As if she had gone suddenly deaf, the sound of Tosspot's clumsy clamoring cut off. Instead, the faintest lapping—like beer in a cask—came from every direction. The hands released her.

"Blasphemy," muttered a cracked and querulous voice.

A glowing rectangle sliced the space in front of her. Through it, she could see the cellar. Silently, the drunkard clomped down the ladder. He looked around. He scratched his head. He swayed in place—clearly he'd found a tipple or three on his way to fetch his boss. He staggered towards her, seemingly unaware that she watched him. She tried to take a step back. A pungent, bony body blocked her.

"Careful," Hendiatrix said, not bothering to whisper. "The island is only as large as the reflection laid out flat."

Tosspot gave no sign of having heard the monk. He shuffled to the edge of the portal, disappearing. He reappeared a short time later on the other side. Oneirotheria realized he must have walked around the mirror. Still massaging his greasy crown, as if his hand could knead sense into his head, he turned his back to her. He said something up the ladder—she could tell he was talking by how his ears waggled.

Upstart must have replied. Tosspot nodded. He made one quick circuit of the empty wine and keg racks, checking for any dram he might have missed on his first go-round. He found nothing. Dejected, he crawled back up the pub. The hatch slammed shut. The rectangle dimmed. The moon-flower faded in the lantern. Gloom shrouded the cellar.

She turned to Hendiatrix. She had not expected him to be as short he was—he barely came up to her chin. Shadows etched his face into caverns and crags. He grimaced at her with carious teeth.

She made a quick survey of her immediate surroundings. They stood on a deep grey trapezoid. It stretched, like a shadow cast from the mirror-portal to as far as the mirror reflected the cellar. The ground was a soft, barely perceptible substance that was neither earth nor wood nor stone; pressed to describe it, the best she could come up with was 'matter's afterthought'. Outside the three-dimensional trapezoid, everything was black. Not the complete void of the edge of Osylum; somehow she sensed that it ebbed and flowed, like water in an unlit world.

"Where are we?"

"Somewhere impossible to be."

"You use that word often and incorrectly."

"Somewhere the Phrontistery's Order of Law says is impossible to get to, anyway."

"But *where*? This isn't your cell. And it's not behind the mirror—at least not in the same way part of the cellar is behind the mirror."

"This," he said, pointing at the solid space beneath their feet, "is the Reflected. And that," he waved at the vast lapping ocean afore, behind, above, and below, "is the Unreflected."

Her eyes adjusted to the low light. She gazed across the space. Above her, she saw a thin slice of bright light. If she leaned her head back, she could widen the slice. Within, she saw a narrow projection of the pub's first floor.

"Oh! That's the mirror upstairs, isn't it?"

Hendiatrix grunted.

"Can we get to it?"

"Why?"

"Why not?!"

Not waiting for him to reply, she launched herself off the sharp edge of the Reflected island. At once, she plunged over her head. She sank rapidly. Instinctively, she kicked. She clawed at what felt like warm and slightly salty water. She churned in a direction she hoped was up.

Her head broke clear. She gulped a breath. She circled her hands and feet to try to stay afloat. Hendiatrix still stood on the grey island, an incongruous angle below and leftwards of her. He dove upwards and began to paddle.

However it was that up and down worked in this place, it was not the customary fashion.

With clumsy strokes—half flying, half crawling—she pulled herself through the gentle waves towards the bright slice of the pub's mirror. All around her, the Unreflected lapped. It tugged at her body in ways that did not match the tidal ebb and flow. She couldn't spare the thought to wonder about that. It was all she could do to keep her head up.

The white line lengthened and rotated as she drew near—opening up as it did. In a shift of perspective, she realized it was she who was turning, not the line. The random waves ordered themselves to aid her flailing strokes with regular forward pulses. She heaved herself ashore, beneath the reflected image of the bar and stools. Moments later, Hendiatrix joined her.

She found herself dry. Whatever liquid filled the Unreflected, it did not behave like water. She stood. The ground here was that same dull tone as the first island, though a lighter shade due to the increased illumination through the wider aperture to the world.

Oneirotheria peered through to the world beyond. To her disappointment, Upstart had already left the pub. Tosspot, in animated theatrical soliloquy, puttered around the room. He sucked the bones of the last keg dry. He turned the wick-lamps off one by one. He dowsed the cheery fire with a large pail of ashes, scraping it to a low red glow. He unflapped himself and urinated into the hearth to kill the coals. There was a brief flash from the door as he left.

She could barely make out the common room now. However, she was sure she could see more of it from this strange vantage than she would have been able, had she stood in the unlit room itself.

"There's always a little light for the mirror to drink up," Hendiatrix explained before she could ask. "Nothing is ever completely dark. Except the edge of town."

"Except the edge of town..."

"At least that's how it works when we scan the

mirrors in our cells. It's my first time here." He made the apotrope. "Lady's will, may it be the last."

"You keep acting like this is the worst thing anyone could do," she said. "It really doesn't seem that bad. Convenient, even."

"It's forbidden," he intoned in a voice etched in stone.

Weeks with the Peripats had taught her the folly of arguing someone out of their commandments. And the less of a reason they had for doing them ('we've always done it this way' being in her mind, a historical observation, not a reason for behavior), the harder they clung to them. This was likely as true of Oblates as Peripats. She let it go.

"Where do we go now?"

He pointed a knobby finger at the bar. She shook her head.

"If I were them, I'd be waiting, one outside and one on the roof. For at least an hour. I wouldn't trust that I hadn't managed to hide somewhere."

"I can't stay here that long," Hendiatrix said.

"So? Go then. There's nothing here to worry about. There *is* nothing here to worry about, is there?"

His craggy voice rasped, sepulchral.

"Who can say? Knowledge of the Unreflected is anathema."

"Yet here we are. This Hecate, whoever she—I—was, must have been very persuasive."

The monk scowled. His face darkened.

"She was as demanding as the Lady on her throne." Hearing himself, he shook his head. "No. That isn't right. She didn't demand. She just had a way of saying what you were going to do before you did it. As though she were describing the past instead of the future. Before you knew it, you were doing what she said you were going to do."

"She told you to rescue me from a pub basement?"

"Not specifically."

Oneirotheria sat, cross-legged. "Tell me the story."

"I have to get back before Matins."

"Matins... The third hour past midnight, right? By my reckoning, you've got two hours left, less time to swim."

He hesitated.

"Please?" she asked. "I know you'll miss the sleep, but I really want to know."

"Death and forgetting has changed you," he said. He sat facing her. "The crone I knew never said please."

"It's a perfectly good word. Might as well give it some air."

Hendiatrix stared over her left shoulder, into the Unreflected. "It was halfway between Nones and Vespers when Hecate first hijacked my mirror..."

31

Ratkippers were dying by the dozen the afternoon Hecate took over my mirror, *the monk told the witch.* Some squabble among themselves. I don't know what they were fighting over; I did not care. My office was to count the quick and the dead in the Seventh.

Using the mirror in your cell?

Yes.

At first, I thought a Warden floated into the blood-walled alley. When he stepped over a red creek, trickling into the sewer, I realized it was that beadle who played dress up—we'd all seen him, except the Abbot who watches the First.

Eschatos.

Is that his name? It doesn't matter to the story.

Sorry.

Another word Hecate never said.

I added him to the count as quick, with his stone close to the pile of the dead. The only thing Ratkippers kill faster than their own are others.

Him, though, they did not touch. They stopped their murder, some still holding one another's throats. They bared fangs. He raised a single hand in the apotrope. I did not expect that. I was too taken aback to read his lips.

Whatever he said, they bowed and scraped at his silk hem.

I confess, at this point, I stopped the count. That's not explicitly forbidden, even though Anaphora orders penance if we spend too much time gawking. Stealing a sight now and then, who can blame us? The cells are cold and the count never-ending.

I picked an image with better vantage—I think it was a half-shattered window on the upper floor. I couldn't see his face clearly because of the multiple refractions. He waved his hands. The Ratkippers followed them, like a flame following the wind's fingers.

Fascinating, I remember thinking.

That's when my dark glass took on a mind of its own. The scene lurched. It jumped to another place and another and another... the images rushed by so fast I almost vomited. I closed my eyes. I prayed to the Lady this was not my end—I don't know why, it felt like this might be death.

When I opened my eyes again, Hecate's face filled my mirror. I read her lips.

"It worked," she said. She nodded, as though there had been no question. She pulled away from the frame. She hunkered back on bony haunches. A book lay open across her thighs. I could make out a sketch of a monk and a glass, with lines running between them and symbols. A column of text explained the picture. The print was too small for me to read.

I had seen her once before.

In the Seventh. The Fist of Peripats was walking to their next stay. Ratkippers surrounded them, out of the sewers and alleys. They circled, outnumbered. I was already adding five more stones to the dead pile when a nearby building aged a thousand years in a blink. The foundation gave way. The walls fell outwards, crushing eight Kippers in a blink. Before I could count that, seven others exploded in a hail of stones.

The crone stepped out of the cloud of dust. A crow rode her shoulder. She made the apotrope at the old man leading the Peripats. They palavered for a while. I couldn't see their lips from any angle. Something was decided, that much was clear. Everyone went their separate ways. Fifteen more in the Dead pile.

I didn't see her again, till she seized my mirror that night.

"Who are you?" I mouthed.

"Hecate peckaty, my black hen," she replied, "scratching the earth in a fox's den."

That was how she talked. Nonsense and riddles mostly. Maybe it made sense to her. Maybe she left out half of what she meant to say—her cant was like a building missing most of its walls. You could see it had been something once, but what, no one could say.

"You're an Oblate," she went on. "Huddled in the Phrontistery, seeing the world through a glass darkly."

I nodded. I was still shocked that someone could take over my mirror. It wasn't till later I remembered the Phrontistery Order and how it was forbidden to talk that way.

"Your name?"

"Hendiatrix."

"Fair enough. Hendiatrix, look closely."

She pulled out a skull made of folded paper. Her

fingers lodge up inside it, working its jaw.

"This is what's beneath our skin. I need you to find one, made of bone instead of paper. Somewhere in the city. It's called an oseovox. If you tell anyone about it, the Wardens will fade you and all your brothers."

Her face didn't change at all when she said that. She might as well have been giving me instructions on how to boil tea or build a fire—risking the Fade was that common to her. Only later did I learn what an oseovox was. The Wardens wouldn't stop at the Phrontistery if they thought knowledge from the ancient days was clattering freely around the city.

That was all she had to say. She snapped her fingers. The mirror showed my own face again, pale and sweating bullets. I prayed and took control of the reflections again. Like a mindless puppet, I cycled through the Seventh Ward count. I do not remember anything until the Evening Chant for Dedalus.

Dedalus?

He came before the Linnaea.

That night was the night Dedalus died. We sang the count. Instead of thanking us, as he usually did, he held up a sign that said the word STOP. The mirror in the Audience Chamber was the only mirror I knew through which voices carried—but Dedalus's throat was too feeble to be heard by any save one with his ear pressed right against his lips.

Abbot Anaphora held the Chantry Mirror on the Laboratory, instead of letting it go dark. I remember the rest of us muttered at the irregularity, which drew a sharp look and, later, harsh penance.

Dedalus had always been small, with weak limbs

and a crook-back. By that time, though, he'd withered to nearly nothing. He lived in a shell of metal, with many arms of brass. Treaded belts beneath enabled him to move. Wheels within wheels controlled the machine, giving him strength to build and delicacy of touch.

He rolled towards the glass. With two claws, he reached out and pulled it from the wall. You've seen the Great Mirror—the weight would crush any three of us. His metal arms did not even shake. He carried it out of his Audience Chamber.

It was the first and only time any of us would see the Laboratory. It wasn't forbidden, just a courtesy to our patron that we avoided spying on it. He seemed to know we'd be curious and so took care to linger the mirror over his sundry marvels so we could admire them.

I most remember the big wood thing in the foyer—I don't know why.

"It's called a skiff," Oneirotheria couldn't help but interrupt.

"You could call it the Abbot's pants for all that means," he snapped, *"let me finish my story."*

The rest of his inventions had a flash and gleam to them. Yet this was the thing he lingered over it for longer than anything else. It looked like half a giant water barrel to me, except for that glass box of gears with the metal flap under it. That looked prime Dedalus, complicated and coiled up with power.

It didn't do anything though. Just hung there in its skeleton frame. But the way he looked at it... like it was the master build of his life. So that... skiff... stuck with me, even though I couldn't tell you about a single other of the magical contraptions he showed us that night.

The tour ended in a room called Incubatorium. Dedalus rested the Audience Mirror against a wall. He rolled into view. Beside him, an enormous glass cylinder—twice as wide as my cell—rose from floor to ceiling. Glass tubes and metal wires ran from it in a dizzying tangle. Worse than the alleys in the Seventh. The giant tube itself was filled with a transparent yellow liquid. A figure floated suspended in that. A naked man, with a second, tiny man protruding from his side. Their eyes were closed and they gave no signs of life.

Dedalus held up a six foot by six foot board, covered in iron cubes. Each cube bore a single raised letter. He tapped a button on the side of the board. The letters moved in tracks.

THESE ARE THE LINNAEA. TEACH THEM WHEN THEY ARE FOUND. THE EXPERIMENT MUST CONTINUE.

Anaphora bowed.

"Yes, patron. We will teach. We will serve. The experiment will continue."

Somehow, though this ritual had never happened before, we all knew to echo the Abbot's words.

Dedalus shook the board again. I told myself it was my imagination that he was looking right at me, when the letters shifted to read:

IF THE WITCH ASKS, SERVE.

That broke Anaphora's obedience. For the only time in my memory, he lost control.

"No!" he cried. He clapped his hands over his mouth. That night, we would hear the wet slash and grunt of him flogging himself for hours. Any one of us would've done the same. The Lady's own law said witches walked alone.

Dedalus did not even notice the offense. He hoisted the mirror back up and returned us all to the Audience Chamber. He hung it back in its proper spot. Cellarius rolled in behind him. Of all its myriad faces, the machine wore grim resolve.

I THOUGHT I WOULD HAVE MORE TIME.

The doorway behind him framed three Wardens. Their third eyes began to open. We all dropped, quailing and wailing, face-down to the floor. I alone looked up. I saw Cellarius driving a spike through the center of Dedalus's mechanical shell. His frail body twitched. I couldn't believe how much blood could come out of such a tiny form. The Wardens' Fading eyes closed. Cellarius peeled back the layers of its master's exoskeleton. Dedalus's corpse floated out. The Wardens carried it away to the First Ward. As is their right. As is the Lady's will.

We mourned for three days. We covered all the mirrors with black cloth and did not count. We chanted prayers from the office of the dead, which we all had to read from long-neglected breviaries because none of us knew them. We'd all seen hundreds—thousands—of deaths, but our task had not been to grieve.

My mind chased itself in circles, trying to make sense of Hecate's appearance, Dedalus's death, and his last command, which, no matter how much I tried to convince myself, I knew was aimed right at me. And the circumstances—the Wardens had been coming to fade him. The penalty for the worst crimes. We were his servants. What did that make us guilty of? Every whisper of the city through the high barred windows sounded like

Wardens coming to obliterate us all.

After three days, the Abbot's bell called us to the Chantry. He called up the Laboratory in the great mirror. Cellarius waited for us. It cradled the vat-grown bodies Dedalus had shown us. They were wrapped in a fine red silk robe. The machine placed them gently in their special-made chair, its face a mask of maternal devotion. Their eyes opened. They took their first foundling breath.

"Hello," the Abbot said. "Welcome. You are the Linnaea. We are your loyal Phrontistery Oblates..."

With that, he began the long task of instructing the foundlings on everything we knew; everything Dedalus had taught us. They devoured the knowledge like Ratkippers gorging on a corpse after a seven day forced fast.

That night, after the long and short and narrow and wide of my story, is the part you wanted to know. Ten minutes before Nocturn, I felt someone pluck my ear. I woke wide in an instant. A low glow came from my mirror. Shielding it with my body, so no one would see under the crack of the door, I peered within. Hecate waited.

"Dedalus is dead," I told her before she could speak.

"Just dead?"

I knew what she meant. "Cellarius killed him before the Wardens could fade."

She sucked her gums. "No point scraping a yolk back into a broken egg. Better than nothing."

"What does that mean? What does any of it mean? Why are we doing this? Why am I looking for a skull and why did Dedalus tell me to serve you and why did they fade him?"

There were a dozen more questions following

that one. I couldn't control myself. They fell out of me fast as I could form the words. Hecate just waited. When I ran out of breath, she went on like nothing had broken her cant.

"I'm going to teach you something. You won't like it. You'll learn it anyway. And, when you see me where you've never seen, use this spell to set me free."

Then she read to me, from that same book. I think Dedalus had written it and given it to her. I don't think she stole it. It doesn't matter. Once I realized what she was teaching me, I tried to pull away.

"Why didn't you?" Oneirotheria asked, having been silent a very long time for her.

She had power. Maybe it was witch-work. Maybe it was just her. Abbot Anaphora at his most Abbotish couldn't match her for command. I'm not sure even Dedalus could. I couldn't look away, however she did it.

What did she teach you?

How to enter the mirror. How to find the Reflected behind the reflection and become part of it. And though I did not leave the island behind my cell's mirror that night or any other till this one, she made sure I knew how to find all the other islands in the ocean of the Unreflected. All those points of light... every mirror in Osylum... surrounded by a shell of nothing, beyond which no one can go.

Tell me how.

I can't.

"Why? Is it forbidden?" She could not keep the derision from her voice.

No. You don't forbid what is impossible anyway. I couldn't teach you to do this any more than you could teach me to turn into a bird. If Hecate could have done it herself, she would have. She made clear how little she wanted to depend on me—on anyone—for whatever her plan was. Oh, how often she made that clear.

It took many nights for me to learn how to step into the Reflected. Once I had the trick down, she repeated her order. "When you see me where you've never seen, use this spell to set me free."

We never spoke of it again.

32

The monk's face faded into the Unreflected around them. He fell silent. With a startle, Oneirotheria remembered where they were. She glanced into the pub. Still empty.

At least as far as the mirror showed.

"We can get anywhere from here," she said, to herself.

Hendiatrix puffed dismissively.

"No, we can!" The thought flared in her brain. "Anywhere there's a reflection, we can go!"

With only the dim of the bar mirror to light them, the Oblate looked like an insubstantial shadow among shadows. She could not read his expression. His voice was the whisper of a midnight bat, slipping by her ears almost unheard.

"Look around."

Her eyes now adjusted, she gaze above—or was it below? Direction seemed arbitrary here. In every direction, thousands of tiny lights twinkled. Each one must be a reflection.

"Stars... constellations... galaxies...," she murmured. "No, that's not what those are. Just what they are like. Never any stars in Osylum."

"Look between them. And behind them. All that distance. And past the edge of town? Nothing."

"How do you know that, if you've never been?"

"I can see. The lights stop. No reflections beyond the city, no where to go. Swim till you die."

"You can't know that for sure."

He did not argue.

"There. That is my mirror. That is where I must go, before Matins."

"That's in hours and hours from now."

"No."

She felt the rough wool of his shoulder pressed up against her elbow. A hand clutched her arm.

"You must go now. Back to the city."

"I don't want—"

He pushed her with force belying his size. Caught off guard, she stumbled towards the grey opening into Osylum. Before she could right herself, he shoved again. She tumbled out of the mirror, onto her hand and knees. Without the Reflected's gathered light, she crawled in pitch darkness.

"Wait—"

"Please," the Oblate's ruined voice begged from above her, "do not ask me to do this again. Forget me. Forget all of this. Just serve the Lady and let that be enough."

"Pike that!"

The night did not reply.

By the time she'd lit a moonflower, Hendiatrix was gone. Doubtless swimming the Unreflected to get back to his tiny cell.

"Coward!"

She grabbed the closest mug and threw it hard in his direction—taking care even in her anger not to actually smash the mirror.

"Serve the Lady," she growled contemptuously.

"Let that be enough."

She paced the floor to calm herself. The tide of fury ebbed across her brain. In its wake, she found abundant rocks and pools of new-revealed knowledge. She had learned a great many things that night. Her skin prickled with delight. Her fingers twitched. She could not wait to return home to catalogue the facts and observations; caress them with loving mental fingers and sort them into dozens of meaningful orders.

She did not know what would come of it.

It might be magnificent.

Oh. It will be magnificent.

33

H ecate (so Hendiatrix said) had a tome that taught her how to call him up. He thought it had been written by Dedalus. That made sense, if Ragpatch had been right that it was Dedalus who built the Oblates' mirrors.

So. That was the first thing. If she could find that, maybe she could teach herself to step into the Reflected. She wouldn't need a musty old monk. The twinkle of a thousand thousand mirror-lights beckoned... and the vastness beyond them, that might come to an end in a reflection of somewhere outside the prison.

If I can make it before the Fade.

Back in her izbushka, she considered the chaos of books and scraps and scribbled-over loose pages. She had not read them all—not yet. She had not been at the task long and Hecate, she reckoned, had amassed all of it over a long, long life.

It did not help that no discernible system organized the material. Once, beneath a bed frame in the Third, she'd found a clear glass globe filled with water and sparkling chaff. When she shook it, the glitter whirled over a woodland scene. It settled in random drifts.

Hecate's collection looked exactly like a giant hand had seized the hut and shaken it wildly. Overwhelmingly disordered.

"Well you useless pile of wild dross," she addressed the daunting mess with good-natured annoyance, "better start anywhere than dither nowhere, I suppose."

She dropped cross-legged to the floor. She snatched up the nearest book.

A TREATISE ON PLUMBING embossed the plain brown leather cover. No author given. The frontispiece displayed a city—perhaps Osylum, though the woodcut was generic enough to be anywhere. Beneath the buildings snaked a tangle of tubes. A river ran in one end and out the other. Stamped over the image she read faded red curlicue letters: O.P.L.

"Intriguing..."

Forgetting she was looking for Dedalus's book about mirrors, she quickly absorbed herself in the plumbing treatise. It was crammed full of figures and diagrams, calculations of the ideal length to drop ratio, arguments about optimal diameters... and just when things were getting most interesting, the pages ended.

"What? No!"

She shook the book. Nothing extra fell out. She cracked it open. Along the inner spine, tiny worm-like threads testified of torn-out pages. The last third the book—starting just before a chapter on Urban Waste Removal—had been removed.

"Cack," she said. "Literally and metaphorically. I was interested in that. Oh well. I'll file you under 'P' for unfinished."

She made to toss the book back on the pile, then

caught it at the last minute.

"I'll save you for the Linnaea. They'll love your numbers and lines. And maybe they can glean some new clues on the city's proper size. All the toilet holes must add up to a number of cheeks, divide by two and tu-whit tu-whoo!"

She set the plumbing treatise next to her. She went on to the next volume.

The cover was discretely blank. In lieu of a title, the first page bore a picture of a man with scales for skin, clinging to the side of a wall. He looked down at another scurrilously dressed man who had small horns on his forehead, goat legs, and a pointed tail. The sketch had been stamped O.P.L. with the same red font as the *Treatise on Plumbing*.

What followed was a titillating and explicit picaresque poem about the roguish adventures of two men named Timeo Danaos and Dona Ferentes. They were thieves and grifters and lovers. They ran cons and ransacked marks and pleasured each other in an unnamed city that, like the plumbing frontispiece, could have been Osylum but could as well have been anywhere.

That much was clear. Frustratingly, Oneirotheria had a hard time following the thread of the story proper. She found herself lost time and again, having to backtrack. Nothing resolved itself. Timeo and Dona would be in grave danger on one page only to be midway through plotting a new heist on the next.

Eventually, flaws in the meter and rhyme helped her figure out the problem. Stanzas would break incorrectly, or the end rhyme on the bottom of one page would be different on the top of the next, or the count of feet would not quite add up.

She was reading correctly. It was simply that a great many pages had been excised. The book was not numbered, so there was no clear jump between, say, page 65 and page 69. And the missing pages had been razored out singly, in pairs, or at most three at a time—too few to immediately notice.

That's a relief. I thought I was getting stupid.

Curious, she flipped back through the novel. She noted the breaks in text, along with what remained on either side. They were not random. Every time Timeo Danaos or Dona Ferentes was trapped in a seemingly impossible predicament, someone had removed the pages describing how they escaped.

"Bastard," she cursed the unknown censor. "Butcher and bastard."

Had she known who the vandal was, she would have drubbed them unconscious with the heavy book and possibly not stopped there. Osylum seethed and reeked with violence, but this assault on words churned the witch's guts.

After a few more choice bitten-off profanities, she set the tawdry tale aside for later. Not all of the techniques of pleasure described within were pertinent to her. However, there were a few intriguing activities she could see modifying for her own circumstances. She wondered if Hecate had played such sport with Upstart...

Gracious, it is warm in here, and without so much as a smudge in the stove.

After a small break to regain her concentration, she resumed perusing the cacophony of texts. She worked for hours. The pattern persisted across every volume. All of the books bore the rusty O. P.L. stamp. All had pages missing.

Someone had objected to something in those gaps.

And no sign of Dedalus's book of mirror wisdom.

34

H er head swam from reading and a few missed meals. Wan light struggled through the shutter slats. It took her a minute to figure out whether it was dawn or dusk. Outside the city struggled to wake.

"Lady!" she exclaimed. She stretched every limb to their furthest extent. Joints popped. Her belly grumbled. Haunches complaining, she pushed herself off the floor. "Breakfast time."

By chance, the Peripats stood waiting in the plaza. Matron saw her first and made the apotrope.

"Lady sees you, Oneirotheria."

With a perfunctory wave of pinched fingers, she returned the gesture. "Yes, yes. All of us. Seeing and seen. Are the Wardens here yet?"

Across the cobbles, Philotech whistled. "Tribunal coming."

Tedious pleasantries exchanged with the Lady's servants (whom once again she assured everything was as it should be), Oneirotheria grabbed a bowl. She was scraping the clay bottom before the Peripats had even sat themselves and started. She dangled the spoon between her fingers. She contemplated the stretched-out red-coated reflections, hunched over and grimly shoveling gruel. She wondered if the Linnaea had anything extra to eat this morning. She could trade them a *Treatise on Plumbing.*

"Plumbing!" she snapped her fingers. "O.P.L.!"

The five Peripats raised wary eyes. She hopped up. She danced across the plaza, down the alley, and up the three steps of her chicken-legged hut.

Moments later, she re-emerged into the folly garden, carrying the treatise. Philotech loomed in the iron-gated archway. He'd followed her alone. His enormous arms crossed over his broad chest. Above his head, faded graffiti still read:

In thy orisons be all my sins remembered

He spoke without greeting. "What are you doing?"

She held up the censored book. "Just grabbing a thing."

"That's not what I meant."

"It's what you said."

"What are you doing?" he repeated.

"Are we going to go in circles?"

"What are you doing?" he asked a third time. "With everything. What's your grift?"

"Oh. That."

A growl that could grind gravel worked its way out of his throat.

She shrugged. "I don't know. Not exactly."

"I don't believe you."

"What you believe or do not believe is largely irrelevant." That struck her. Fluttering laughter stirred dust on the rose petals. "I suppose that's true for all of us, isn't it?"

He spat an insult like a fly from a mouthful of

porridge. "Bedlam mort."

"Oh, now there's a word to wonder at. Bedlam, I mean. The contraction of a contracting place that doesn't exist here, does it? See? If I don't know *how* I know that, *how* can I know what I'm doing?"

"STOP!"

He punched the brick wall. The force of the blow would've broken her fist, yet he didn't even flinch. She stifled a giggle. All his bluster and strength couldn't catch her if she took to wing. Nor stop her from any of a half-dozen hexes that would flip his pebble to the Dead pile afore he could cross the space between them.

She did not want that, though. The Peripats, with their forced wandering, had uses for her yet. So she schooled her face to contrition and spoke as plain as she could for his simple brain.

"I am sorry. I went to get this book because I thought Matron might be able to answer a question about it."

"Don't—"

She remembered his protective fear. She hastily added: "—Or any of the rest of you. It is the sort of thing any one of you might have seen padding around town."

He held out a hand. She opened the book to the frontispiece. She came to his side, careful to present only slow and threatless motions—for his safety, not her own.

"Here."

She pointed to the three-letter stamp.

"Have you ever seen anything that looks like this?"

"Matron hasn't. Don't trouble her with such foolishness." He said that quickly and she was sure he lied. She did not say anything. After a beat, he went on. "I have. Deep in the Eighth Ward wood."

"What was a book doing in the forest?"

"Not on a book. On a door. Over a door. Those letters in stone on the archway. Not cut in. Pushed out. And some animal pushed out of the rock too. I don't know what kind."

"Can you take me there?"

Matron's voice called down the alley. "Philotech?"

"Here."

"Time to wander. Where will you walk?"

He hesitated. Matron beckoned him again.

"He's with me!" Oneirotheria shouted.

Startled expression on her face, the lead Peripat joined them.

"Truly?" She directed her question to Philotech.

Oneirotheria nodded, eyes the picture of innocence. Philotech shifted his shoulders, as if his coat were suddenly three sizes too small. Matron placed a hand on his forearm. Oneirotheria marveled at how that instantly relaxed his nigh-perpetual hair trigger vigilance.

"Just remember," Matron said softly, "Platon's Oath."

On tip-toes, she kissed Philotech's whisker-bristled cheeks. She gave Oneirotheria a farewell apotrope.

"Keep him safe."

"I will."

After she left, Oneirotheria frowned. "Platon's Oath?"

Philotech's gaze still hung on the emptiness of Matron's passage. "An old story."

"Tell me."

"Let's walk." He strode quick. She caught up, two steps for each of his one.

"You can do both. I believe in you."

"What you believe or do not believe is... whatever it was you said before."

"Largely irrelevant. But it's a long way to the Eighth..."

He shook his head. "You won't give up will you?"

"It's not what I do."

"Platon. He led the Peripats two people before Matron. The lead goes through the names."

"Lucretius, Matron, Nomine, Orfeo, Philotech," she named the current five. "So Platon was before your time and between him and Matron, someone with an L name set the route for your walkabout?"

"Before my time. And before Matron's. Like I said. Old story."

"How long does a Peripat live, generally speaking?"

"Lady knows. Do you want the tale or no?"

"I do."

"Platon led the way. The Stay was in the Seventh. Ratkippers must've sussed out the path in advance. They set an ambush. So many of them jumped out. The Fist was sure dead. Maybe newlings would all be found at once. Maybe not. Wouldn't matter. Newlings don't know a thing. The path would be lost and the rules with it. No more Peripats. Not proper ones anyway."

"Oh!" Oneirotheria remembered something Hendiatrix had said. "Hecate rescued them all!"

Philotech lurched to a stop. He turned on her.

"You already know?"

"Someone told me."

"Who?"

She glanced at the windows around. Their grimy panes reflected her and Philotech's ghosts. "No one important."

"Not one of us."

"No."

He did not seem to believe her. He resumed walking, though.

"If you already knew the story, why make me tell it?"

"I didn't know that I knew it. And I didn't know about the Oath part. Was that what she and he talked about after she crushed the 'kippers under a building?"

"Yes. The Five owed her their lives. That's a debt that outlasts the Funeral Tribunal. Platon swore we're be quit with the witch, one life at a time. However long it took. Hecate made good on that promise four times. Four deaths in her service. The first was his own. Two leaders and a new witch later, we still owe one."

"You don't like that."

"I don't like being held to a dead man's promise."

"But you will be?"

"It's what Matron wants." An unspoken 'unless' hung after his words.

Unless I need her life? I don't think all the rules in the city will hold you to that oath then. Well, may it not come to that.

They passed through the gate to the Fourth under a gloomy pall. To head off brooding speculation that might make Philotech reconsider guiding her, Oneirotheria peppered him with frivolous questions about the humble tenements that lined the winding roads of the Ward. She offered a few tidbits of her own—trivia she'd picked up pecking around the past few months. In time, the witch and wanderer even managed a reasonable imitation of convivial conversation.

As they padded through the straying streets, neither of them mentioned Eschatos nor his efforts to recruit Philotech as his spy.

35

A single Warden guarded the gate between the Fourth and Eighth. Oneirotheria and Philotech shared a glance.

What do you think that means?

The Wardens always watched the transitions in pairs. Here, however, the right-hand post stood empty. The lone watcher floated as usual, hands crossed and eyes downcast, but it lacked a partner. They proceeded anyway. It did not challenge them. Averting their gaze, they passed beneath the simple, functional brick arch that ended the Common Ward.

Philotech's nose twitched as they approached the other side. He stopped, tensing.

"Fade."

Oneirotheria sniffed. A green and pulpy smell wafted down the passage. She caught whiffs of new-made nothingness winding through it. The same lack-smell had filled the air after Ragpatch's obliteration.

"We can't turn back," she said. "Nothing would look more guilty than that."

"Just remember: Platon promised a life for a life. Just a life. You face the Fade on your own."

"Fair enough."

She led him, three steps ahead, to the other side.

Just before the exit, a Warden's silhouette drifted into view. It moved past them without acknowledgement. She noted the third eye was closed. Philotech relaxed a hair—as much as he ever did.

There was no gate proper in the Eighth. Empty iron hinges twisted off the stones. Oneirotheria pictured a twelve-span door being ripped away. *How much force would that take?*

"The Linnaea would know."

Philotech grunted. "Know what?"

"Never mind. I said the inside part outside."

It was not merely the hinges that were wrecked. The entire archway appeared gnawed away. The arch-stones hung ragged and, in some cases, torn back several layers-worth of rock. Oneirotheria touched an edge with a finger. Smooth. In places, grown over with spotted red lichen. This was not recent damage.

"Did it happen all at once?" she wondered. "Or over a very long time?"

"How would anyone know that?"

"I don't know. But I do know that no one would ever know anything, if someone didn't ask a question first."

"Let's just go."

The forest did not start immediately at the wall. A broad clearing—about the size of the statue plaza in the Second—opened in an semi-circle at the entrance. Here, the smell of the Fade lingered strongest. A cursory examination revealed why.

Every branch that had encroached on the clearing, every root and vine of undergrowth had been neatly severed.

"Why would they fade the forest?"

"Why is the thing with feathers," he quoted Matron. "Let's just go."

"Peace!" she said. "I can't believe *I* have to tell someone *else* to be patient. Give me space to study."

He stomped along the edge of the clearing, looking for a way in.

"It doesn't mean anything. Nothing the Wardens do means anything, except nothing."

"Everything means something," she countered. "To someone. And this might mean something to me."

She knew she didn't have to argue with him. He wouldn't have come with her if he didn't intend to stay with her. So she ignored his pacing and examined the scene.

The clearing extended ten paces to either side of the gate and thirty paces out. Beyond that, the forest grew hard against the wall. Branches pressed against the stone. There was not the same evidence of vegetative destruction that she'd seen on the gate area.

The trees had tried to force an exit.

She recalled the aerial view of the Ward; a thick canopy, all-but-concealing the traces of roads and buildings.

"How long has this forest been here?"

"Longer than me. Longer than Matron. It's older than stories."

"That could be old. Or young. No one remembers anything before they're found. Except me and I don't remember much."

He shifted in his boots. Her casual admission of such an extreme transgression apparently made him nervous. She ignored it. She waved at the trees.

"Where did it come from?"

"Don't know. No one says."

"Did people just let it grow like this? The Wardens wouldn't let it take ages to ruin a gate and *then* fade it. Besides, look here."

She pointed at a branch. Its growth tapered midway at a perfect edge. From that grew a much thinner branch. That reached towards the wall, then ended abruptly.

"What?"

"It looks like it was snipped here at the thick part and then tried to regrow from the core as the thinner stick. The Wardens regularly cut this back."

Out of nowhere, she wondered if Turnspade had ever been put back together. If he even could be put back together. She preferred his gardening touch to the Warden's depredations.

"So? The Wardens keep a passage open. People have to come and go. The trees are vicious. Some of them."

The twisted iron hinges—thick as her wrist—made that clear.

She stared into the brooding wood. She knelt down. She touched a root. Her skin pricked. Power hunkered in this Forest Ward. It coursed from her palm to her spine. Deep, strong power that resented being hemmed in and pent up by Wardens and walls.

"I understand," she murmured.

"Do you? Good. Let's go then."

It was the third time he'd said that. There wasn't much more to be learned anyway. No sense taxing his good will any more than necessary. She motioned him to proceed.

He made one more pass of the perimeter. He stopped. She waited. He did not move.

"The piking path I took. It's gone. Since last Eight Stay."

"How long ago—"

"—it was the last Stay before the Second. This Second."

She thought about that. She calculated arboreal growth rates like she was the Linnaea. She idly whistled a five note round. She realized it was the Peripat's night-time song. She chuckled. Philotech's face hardened.

"I can't take you where you want to go."

"The world's a city full of straying streets," she chanted. "You're telling me one isn't as good as another to get to where we're going?"

"Not if the trees don't want us there."

"Self-important piffle! The trees don't care about us." She patted the acrid bark of a tanner's oak. "Isn't that right?"

Leaves rustled across the wood.

There was no breeze.

"See?"

"This is a bad idea. We'll get lost."

"The surest way to get found is to get lost first."

"You won't let it go?"

Menace bristled his tone. She had learned to read that as a sign of fear. She danced across the clearing. Imitating Matron, she rested one small hand on his thick forearm. He stiffened. A low growl rolled around in his chest, like granite in a slow grinder.

"Agreed. That was awkward. If you don't mind

..."

She withdrew the hand. In what she hoped was a soothing tone, she continued.

"Matron told me to keep you safe. I said I will. Do you know anyone who could keep you safer?"

"Anyone. I'd be safer standing next to any other berk in the city."

Her irritated cry erupted through the canopy.

"Fine! Go back to the Second and walk you little circles. I'm going in there to see things I've never seen. I think. In this version of me. You know what I mean..."

Trailing off, she scanned the forest.

"There are three openings. Of course there are three. This one looks to have been a road once. Here-now!"

She ducked between two rhododendrons. Canted cobblestones—broken by roots—led her on. A few minutes in, she smiled. The crash of an oversized Peripat, thrashing down the path, followed behind.

36

P hilotech had not been wrong.

They got lost.

What had, at first, seemed a clear enough path disappeared after ten minutes. They back-tracked for five minutes, only to discover the narrow track they'd taken was also gone. Undeterred, Oneirotheria dove through a gap between two brooding willows. Philotech followed, shoving branches aside and cursing. When forward progress that direction failed, she veered off another angle. And on and on, their trail making a mad scribble on a featureless map.

"Oh hush," she scolded the grumbling Peripat after an hour of trudging through the brush. "Yes, we don't know where we are or where we're going. But it's all the same to me and the Ward is only so big. We'll find a wall sooner or later and with it, a way around."

"It's not what we'll find you should fear." Philotech snapped a sapling in half. "It's what will find us."

Why did you even come here in the first place, she wondered, *if it makes you so afraid?*

She did not want to bicker so she left the question unasked.

"This is stupid," she said. "Crawling around like wood mice. Let me get a higher view."

She shook out her arms.

"Wait!"

He lunged and seized her before she could turn into a bird. Shocked at his own effrontery, he flung her wrist away like a hot iron. A dozen expressions flashed across his face, each trampling the next too quickly for her to read. She cocked her head. She whistled a quizzical tune.

He composed himself.

"If you fly away, you may not come back. You may not find me. This is a Ward where you walk by twos and threes."

"Aha!" she cried. "Matron *was* here with you. She saw the O.P.L. building too."

His flushed brow confirmed her leap of logic. She brushed aside his discomfort.

"No worries. She's safe in the Second and you're here with me."

"I am here with you."

She leaned against a post oak. She craned her neck.

"We still could use an aerial view. Boost me up."

Despite the fact that he had just laid hands on her, he was not eager to do so again. She motioned for him to interlace his hands, which he did. She stepped up. Her fingers curled in the hollow of the tree fork. Bracing her bare toes on rough bark, she pulled herself halfway up.

"One good shove," she ordered. Broad hands cupped her backside. She could feel his discomfort through her haunches. It made her laugh. "Come on, hurly-burly. Shove!"

He launched her upwards, nearly through the V-shaped split in the trunk. She caught herself. She balanced. She glanced back.

"Hop into the fork. You're tall enough to not need a hand. You'll be safe off the ground and able to keep eyes on me all the way to the crown."

Not waiting for him, she reached to the nearest branch and began to climb.

A strange illusion overcame her. Instead of shards of bark, her hands and feet pushed into slack flesh stretched over a frame of bone. Her joints ached. Her fingers crooked and her hips creaked. Her muscles strained to lift her and every effort throbbed. The crisp leaves blurred. Breath whistled from a half-blocked nose. An old woman, she scaled a tower of corpses towards an astigmatically obscured destination.

I've done this before. I was alone then. These are the pearls that were his eyes. Here-now. I wasn't done yet. Upstart shake the scenery. To your scattered bodies go. Always someone else's words to fit my thoughts. And now another body to fit my soul. Here-now.

In a heartbeat she was herself again. Young and lithe, she skipped up the side of the old oak. She checked over her shoulder. Philotech had hoisted himself to the crotch of the tree. He did not seem possessed by any eerie visions. He was trying to watch her and the ground and the surrounds all at the same time.

"Just you and me and the Lady makes three," she called back, in an effort to lighten his mood. And her own. The fleeting experience of being old and mounting corpses clung to the edge of her brain; cobwebs on a cold grave stone.

She pushed her head through the canopy. After the gloom of the wood, the perpetually grey sky of Osylum gave a welcome shine. She basked a moment. The moment passed. The city's dinge returned. Shifting her feet with tiny movements on the slender branch, she rotated a full circle to get her bearings.

She floated in an undifferentiated sea of dark green and brown. On the far grey horizon, she saw the ramparts of Osylum's outer wall. A short distance away, the trees ringed an oblong lake. At the center of the flat slate-colored water, a low circular island rose, like a glazed hazel iris contemplating the tedious sky. A ruined temple of white marble stood at the center of the island.

Oneirotheria checked between her feet. The V of the post oak's main two trunks aligned with the direction of the lake; the thicker trunk was the leading edge. One more quick circuit, jerking her head both ways, confirmed the water and temple were the only landmarks in view. She scampered down, bouncing past Philotech. She pointed.

"This way."

He followed without question.

She was just beginning to suspect she had picked the wrong side of the oak when she plunged through a thicket, over a short bluff, and nearly toppled into water. Philotech grabbed her satchel. She dangled at an angle over placid grey-green lake. He hooked her waist with his free arm. Effortlessly, he lifted her back to stable land. He held her only as long as he had to; he was still uncomfortable with any touch. She nodded.

"Thank you."

"What?"

"Thank you," she repeated, louder.

"I heard you. Just—never mind."

"You've never heard a witch say thank you?"

"Not words I thought Hecate knew."

"I wonder if I know things she did not. I know things she did, somehow. It stands to reason I would have gathered a few of my own."

The loamy soil of the forest gave way to the pebbled path a hand-span from the water. Tiny licks of water lapped white pebbles, like the Minor's tongue dabbing a saucer of milky tea. Oneirotheria pointed across the lake.

"There. A bridge. Or part of one anyway."

Philotech kept himself between her and the water as they followed the shore. She was sure-footed, but appreciated his solidity to lean against now and again, when the overgrown path canted too sharply down. The shore cut a regular circle. It reminded her of the dilapidated fountain in the folly garden, built large.

"Someone made this on purpose, every bit as sure as any house."

"Why bother?"

"I don't know. We all get plenty of water from the Wardens and the dribble-drip through public pipes. It's not a cistern or septic tank."

...the sea—so many words scattered around this city hacked in stone and scrawled on skin...

"What?"

She had not realized the memory had fallen out of her mouth aloud. She shook her head to say 'never mind.' Philotech seemed glad enough to comply.

They reached the erstwhile bridge. It stretched five paces over the lake. Delicate rails of carved marble ended in random cracks. The pavers too were marble and ended just as abruptly. The island lay fifty or so paces beyond. Oneirotheria and Philotech stood side by side underneath an intricately wrought iron arch at the bridge entrance. Rust drops fell on them from time to time. They ignored them; a common enough occurrence in Osylum.

Philotech shook his head at the distant temple. "That's not where I saw the letters from your books."

A disturbance on the water near the side of the bridge caught Oneirotheria's eye. She bent down. A small craft, woven from twigs with a broad maple sail, bobbed on the lake. Another listed a few feet away, and another and another. A dozen miniature sailboats drifted across the surface. The ripples of their wake led back to the island.

"Don't touch them," Philotech barked.

She had already lifted one out. She held it up, turned it this way and that. It was cunningly made. The hull was wound of willow twigs, watertight and curved. A hawthorn spike pierced the maple leaf top and bottom to make a full-bellied sail—purely decorative.

Never any wind in Osylum.

"Listen," Oneirotheria said. Soft soprano syllables sang over the water.

"Full fathom five thy father lies;
Of his bones are coral made;
Those are pearls that were his eyes:
Nothing of him that doth fade
But doth suffer a sea-change
Into something rich and strange..."

"I've heard that song," Oneirotheria murmured. "There was a stage and a woman in see-through silk. She wore lace wings. So many people crowded round but no one made a sound, save her song. No. None of that is my memory, but I remember reading it in a book..."

Philotech snatched the boat out of her hand. He threw it hard as he could over the water. It dashed on distant rocks.

"Wake the pike up!" he shouted. His hands raised, as if he were considering shaking her. He settled for jabbing an angry finger at the isle. "That—whatever that is—is not to be messed with."

Her voice could have frozen the whole lake.

"Says who?"

By his sputter, that was not a response he reckoned on. She pressed the advantage.

"You live your life by these rules and underneath them all there's only fear. Fear and fear and more fear, pulling you this way and that, and you don't even know who's holding the strings. So much fear there's nothing left of you to be lost when you die.

"Here are your choices, Peripat. Stay on this bridge. Turn around and go back to the Second to pad around until the Stay moves to the next ward in the order. Or splash some water on that turning-burgundy face and shake some courage out of that endless-pocket coat of yours and follow me."

She had not intended to be so imperious but she had had enough of his recalcitrance. She fixed him with a flat, aristocratic stare—in no way diminished by being only a hair over half his height and a quarter his girth. He could not outmatch her gaze. He glanced down and away, towards the tiny armada.

"Good choice," she said. "Whoever's over there may know where that O.P.L. building is. And if she doesn't, she may know other things."

She strode to the end of the broken bridge. "Let's walk on water."

37

It had been a figure of speech. None of the hexes nor spells that lingered in her amnesiac brain actually imparted the ability to walk on water. She unslung her satchel. She untied the pouch from her belt. She sat and took stock of what she had and what might be of use, while Philotech paced up and down the marble jetty.

The easiest solution was to turn into a magpie and fly over. However, though she had not used the words 'I promise' in guaranteeing Philotech's safety, she felt as bound to try as if she had sworn on everything that mattered. And, while she did not share his fear of the forest, prudence suggested leaving him alone and lost did not qualify as 'protecting him'.

She rolled a prickly birnam twig twist fingers and thumb. *This little charm will cage him. The cage might float across the water with me atop. Or it might sink and hold him underwater till he drowned. That would settle the ledger of Platon's Oath. Not worth it.*

She balanced a warm tube of fire-fennel on her index fingers. She had three of them, hollow reeds with the ends sealed with tar. When exposed to the air, they would release an enormous heat for such little things.

Not enough to boil the lake, I don't think. And the steam would probably scald us both skinless.

"How deep do you think it is, at its deepest?"

"Five fathoms," Philotech replied, quoting the mysterious singer across the lake. "Whatever the pike a fathom is."

"Was that a joke?" She checked his expression. "It *was*. I wouldn't have believed you had it in you."

He ignored her. He studied the trees.

She cradled a pile of snowdrops in her palm. Even without invoking their power, they chilled her skin.

From fire to ice. You'll harden the blood in someone's heart and turn their skin frosty blue. Eyes wide cracked. Breath in little flecks on brittle lips.

Ice floats, right? I could just freeze Philotech and tip him over and... ah, but thawing him out on the other side. That would be the trouble. Next!

She jiggled a gurgling vial of black henbane. One drop, flicked in the eye or mouth, would cause vomiting. The whole vial would poison everything living in the lake, like as not.

Here-now. I have a great many terrible tricks packed away in this little pouch. Is there nothing pleasant in my arsenal?

"Witch?"

She quickly gathered up everything she knew was too violent to be useful. That left precious little. She traced the curves of a bryony root—a vegetable mimic of her own body's shape. Properly coaxed by invocation, it would form her twin, indistinguishable from her appearance, though mindless.

Useless, useless, useless. One of me with my tat-

tered faculties can't figure this out, what's a second brainless plant going to do?

All that remained was some chamomile for calm, licorice root for flavor, and a few moon-flowers. She swept the benign herbs back into the pouch and re-tied it to her waist. She did not bother with the satchel—the result would be the same.

"Witch?" Philotech repeated with increased urgency.

Lost in trying to solve the problem, Oneirotheria tapped one of the bobbing sailboats.

It would take forever to tip over enough trees to make one of these big enough to carry us.

"Wait!" she said. "The Linnaea have that skiff in their foyer... I wonder if we could nip over and slip it out without asking..."

"What's a skif—URK!" the Peripat shouted.

CRACK!

Oneirotheria snapped out of her reverie. While she'd been thinking, the trees had closed ranks along the shore. A wall of branches hemmed them in. Worse, they had begun moving up the bridge. Roots splintered the rock, decay accelerated out of pace.

Philotech lay on his back, with a tendril of oak wrapped round his ankle. He slashed at it with a dagger in each hand and kicked with his free boot. Blood-red sap covered his leg and arms, but the root held tight. It dragged him towards the seething trees.

"Eat a witch, drink her blood—" Oneirotheria incanted. *No! That will only save me!*

She leapt forward. She drew her flint witch-blade. She let memory's voice move her lips in an incantation of force. With both hands and the full weight of her body, she drove the knife through the grasping root. Weighted by magic, it pierced the bark, wood, and clear through to the stone below. She released the blade, leaving the animate oak pinned to the bridge. For a moment.

The tendril round Philotech's ankle went slack. He hacked it clear. She hauled him back. The tree swayed, furious. Flecks of flint splintered off her knife. Behind the oak, the rest of the wood leaned hard towards the frail humans on the broken bridge.

"That won't hold it long," he said.

"Long enough."

In the still eye of her roiling mind-storm, she marveled at how useful danger was for clarifying a problem. She ducked under the satchel strap and seized Philotech's wrist.

"This way!"

She charged towards the water. Her left hand dipped into her pouch. She fished out a pinch of snowdrops. As a weapon, it would freeze blood in veins, but she hoped it could serve a different turn. She flung it with the proper words across the churning lake.

White ice spread beneath them as they sprinted off the edge. Here and there, like insects in amber, aquatic plants hung suspended. They had been lashing upwards to meet their shore-bound kin and tear the intruders in two. Instead, Oneirotheria and Philotech slipped and slid across a new-made glacier.

With a bright flash, the oak shattered her flint knife. Root and branch, it advanced up the rimy marble. As it passed, the bridge crumbled to pebbles. The wrought-iron arch and rails crumpled like paper toys. The work of centuries passed in seconds. The forest reclaimed the span.

Philotech and Oneirotheria ran. It took another two handfuls of snowdrops—all she had—to flash-freeze a path across the raging water to within six paces of shore. Full speed, they launched themselves over the gap. Pondweed and brittle water nymph lashed the soles of their feet. The ice split behind them, dissolved. With a roar, the water tossed and frothed. They landed face-down on the island. Blood and breath roared in her ears. She checked for Philotech and winked when she caught him checking for her.

As suddenly as it had risen, the animate storm of trees stopped. The water flattened like glass. Silence hung over the lake. The still scene would have made a pleasant sylvan painting, if it hadn't just tried to murder them.

"Hark, hark," sang a lilting voice above them. "The witch-dogs bark!"

"Pike," Philotech sighed into the sand.

38

A woman in a grass-stained shift beckoned them with a muddy hand. A circlet of willow branches wreathed her head. Wings—leaf feathers on a twig frame—dangled crookedly from a harness on her shoulders. Burs dotted her sagging hose. Her light-weight slippers had once been white, but now were the color of earth. She stood at the top of mossy granite stairs, framed by two vine-nibbled marble columns.

"Welcome," she said in a high and noble tone. "I am Wailenweave."

She laughed. In tones as low and common as street patter, she continued: "'Welcome' I say, like it were my place. It's all the Lady's, innit?"

Oneirotheria pushed herself standing. Philotech hulked behind her.

"Oh stop," she whispered. "Put a smile on or at least try to look less stabby."

She skipped up the crooked steps. "You said something about witch-dogs."

"Did I? Sure I must have meant watch-dogs."

"What's the difference?"

"Watch-dogs watch. Witch-dogs witch. Which barks the question: who witches the watch or watches the witch?"

Wailenweave held up a thin branch. With a few quick twists, she fashioned a credible hound and offered it to Oneirotheria with a curtsy. "Switch dog."

"Mad..." rumbled Philotech.

"You think everyone's mad," Oneirotheria snapped back.

"Everyone is mad. Except me and Matron. And I'm on the edge for following you."

She ignored him. She took the switch-dog from Wailenweave. "Thank you. It's lovely."

"I done me best. Never seen a dog outside pictures."

"No dogs in Osylum either..."

"Love we the Lady and fear we the Fade," the woman trilled. She bowed theatrically and swept a long trailing hand along the ground, towards the temple behind her. In her affected noble accent, she asked: "Will you sit with me while I work?"

The building consisted of only three walls. There was no evidence that a fourth had existed—no extra stones or corner angles. A line of free-standing columns along the portico supported nothing, serving no apparent purpose. An overhang along the back wall covered about a quarter of the space. The rest of the structure was open to the sky. In the center of a mosaic floor, the woman had piled up driftwood and leaves.

"Make yourselves whatever you wish," she said.

She plonked her haunches on a worn rock stool beside the materials. She plucked out a fistful of vines and supple twigs. She twisted the gunwale of another boat and began twining the hull.

Philotech leaned against a column. He positioned himself so he could watch the shore and the temple. He produced yet another dagger (having dropped two during the pell mell sprint across the ice). He cleaned his nails, slowly and with more attention to detail than was warranted.

Oneirotheria perched on a backless obsidian chair. It had been carved to look as though it had grown from the raised black plinth on which it sat.

"How did you get here?" she asked. "Those wings don't look too effective."

"I walked. Right across the bridge, when there was a bridge."

"How long ago was that?"

"Don't know. I fell asleep. When I woke up, the park was gone, the trees were there, and the bridge had fallen down."

"The temple too?"

"No. They built it broken."

"Why?"

"Lady knows."

Philotech interjected. "Wait. You say you've been here since before the forest ate the Eighth Ward?"

"I don't know about the Eighth Ward. This used to be the Lady's Park. Fields and glass houses and places to play as far as you could walk. Pretty as could be, if I remember right. Which, remembering? Who knows if I do that?"

The Peripat's next questions dropped heavy with dark insinuation. "How have you survived? What do you eat?"

Oneirotheria answered before Wailenweave could. "She doesn't need to."

The other woman kept her eyes on her twig-work.

"I'm right, aren't I?" Oneirotheria said.

"Everyone eats something," Philotech said. "Or someone."

"Puppets don't."

Wailenweave's fingers fumbled. Twigs sprung out in all directions. "Well that's bungled to damnation. No fixing it neither."

She snapped the craft and tossed it over her shoulder. She started another. Undeterred, Oneirotheria went on.

"You're one of Upstart's."

"Fine, fine. And if I am? What gave it away?"

"You're actors," Oneirotheria replied. "No matter what part you're playing, you're always playing a part."

"Sound and fury, strut and fret," Wailenweave sang, "play the part another set, till the Lady herself forgets..."

"Also, Tosspot told me your name. He had a little song."

"That drunken ass!"

"So. How did you really get here? And why did Upstart send you?"

"I told you."

Oneirotheria pursed her lips skeptically.

"No, truth! I was wandering in the Lady's Park one day. I was watching a witch."

"Hecate?"

"Her name was Marrigan if you must know. She's got her own song too."

The actor cleared her throat.

"Marrigan, Marrigan, here again, there again, how does your garden grow? With vicious trees and wispy bees and corpses all in a row."

She took three winsome bows, blowing kisses to an imaginary crowd.

Oneirotheria glanced at Philotech. *Marrigan? Know her?* He shook his head slightly. Wailenweave went on:

"'Twas she taught me to weave sticks. I couldn't make them move like she could, a-course." She bobbed a half-finished boat, in a miniature, hand-made storm. "Only in my mind."

"She could make sticks move?"

"She had a way. She didn't that day. That day, she weren't there to amuse me. Those was her words. 'I am not here to amuse you, poppet.' Like I'd ever asked her for that."

"So what was she there for?"

"A different form of trees. Pounded flat and scribbled on."

"Books?!" Oneirotheria couldn't keep the excitement out of her voice. "Are there books in these woods?"

"I told you, they wasn't woods then." She gazed into the distance and crooned: "'Woulds and shoulds and coulds,' the Abram-Man wails, naked in his barrow of air...'"

Wailenweave trailed off. "I forget the rest of the words. I must have been a long time on this island."

"Before that," Oneirotheria said. "Go back to before that, when there were books."

"A big building full of them. On the bluff over yon, so to look out over the pond. Osylum's Park Library they called it, because that's what it was.

"O.P.L.!" Oneirotheria cried, remembering the stamp on every book in her hut.

"Aye. Of course, most of the books were gone by then."

"Wait, most of the books were gone by then? Was this before or after the city turned into a prison?"

"The city's always been a prison."

"That can't be true."

"You sound like her. Marrigan, I mean. She said things like that. Just as sure as you. And where is she now and where am I?"

"What was she looking for in the library?"

"Words, milady."

"What kind of words?"

"The kind that were not amusing to the likes of me."

"So you wandered off."

"I danced among the shelves till Marrigan cursed me to leave. I lingered on the shore picking rushes for a while. I wove a crown of pussy-willows and I sang a song about love and I dove into the warm pond and swam till my dress dragged me down. I woke in the mud with Upstart lifting my head.

"'Quick now,' he said to me, 'to the isle and sleep till trouble's past.'"

"What did he mean 'trouble'?"

"The kind that floats but not on water."

"Wardens," snarled Philotech.

Wailenweave tapped the center of her forehead. "Now you see, now you don't."

"Did you see them?" Oneirotheria asked.

"Not at first. I ran across the bridge, still sopping wet. I hid behind a column. I heard Upstart and Marrigan shouting at one another. I only caught torn bits and pieces of their fight—I can weave it into this much of a story: She were going to make magic to tear the wall down and he were saying that would flood us all with nothing."

Oneirotheria leapt from the obsidian throne.

"What kind of magic? The nothing—that sur-rounds the city? Was she going to break the city wall? How could she even do that? And why would the nothing flood in, if it doesn't already do that?!"

Wailenweave held up a maple leaf as a frail shield against the barrage of questions. "Peace, peace. I told you, I couldn't hear most of what they said. I don't know more than what I told you, truth times truth."

Oneirotheria sat back down. She gazed at the false broken columns. "Sorry. Of course you don't. No one knows anything but scraps about anything. Even me."

"They were still railing against one another when the first Warden came down the white chalk path to the pond. My throat sealed near shut. I forced one warning note through it. And then, I fell asleep. When I woke, the forest were every-where."

"Marrigan raised it..." Oneirotheria said to her-self.

"I don't know. It wasn't the end of the world be-cause the Lady's Fog hadn't rolled over the water. I went back to sleep and dozed ever since. I rouse now and then. I gather flotsam from the shore. I make toys the way Marrigan taught me to."

"Upstart escaped," Oneirotheria said. "If you were wondering."

"Somehow I knew that. He is the moon and we the stars—we sleep and wake together."

The sun, the moon, the stars... echoed across Oneirotheria's brain. Wailenweave continued:

"Thank you for caring enough to tell me all the same. Care is rare in a witch."

"So I've heard." Oneirotheria stared past

Wailenweave and Philotech. Even the jagged edges of the broken bridge were gone. "Was the library near the bridge?"

"If the isle were a dial and the bridge noon, you'd find the library at three."

Oneirotheria oriented herself. She peered across the water, wishing she had the Linnaea's telescope. After a minute, she fancied she could make out squared edges of brownstone amid the dendritic chaos. It could well be a building.

"Wisp," Philotech said from right behind her. She had not noticed his approach.

"What?"

He pointed with his stiletto. A small white flicker danced in the depths of the ruined library.

"Little lights in the trees. They lead you where no one wants to go."

A snippet of rhyme tripped off her tongue. She shouted across the lake: "Little wisp, little wisp, if wisp ye be, show yourself and come to me."

The light stayed where it was. As she watched, she realized it had a regular cadence—like a reflection, swinging back and forth, visible only from her angle at intermittent points. Her own image, stretched long and rippled, stretched before her.

Old man, old man in the mirror ...

"It's time to go," she said. "Wailenweave, will you come with?"

"There's not enough driftwood to carry me, let alone three."

"We're not taking a boat."

"How then?" Philotech asked.

"We'll swim," she said, "but not the way you think."

39

P hilotech was silent the whole journey.

He said nothing when she squatted on the shore and called Hendiatrix out of the still reflection. He merely watched as she wheedled, bartered, badgered, and eventually commanded the old monk to pull the three of them under the water. He passively allowed her to link him to herself, the Oblate, and Wailenweave by a length of vine.

Wordlessly, he helped stroke towards the next Reflected island. He stepped through the plane of Reflection to the real world when Hendiatrix ordered him, making no argument. And, when at last they stood in a high-vaulted hall beneath a single crystal shard (all that remained of a once enormous chandelier), he simply stared at her, as stony and pensive as the gargoyles that lined the walls.

For her part, Wailenweave babbled fragments of nautical chanteys—verses about the sea and ships and wind and waves that had place neither in nothing-bound Osylum, nor in the vast ocean of the Unreflected.

Hendiatrix did not emerge. He herded them out

of the Reflected and left them there.

Oneirotheria bounced on her heels. It was too dim to see more than a few paces away. The missing pages—and who knew what other books—must be in this dark cathedral of knowledge.

"A moonflower won't do," she said. She rummaged in her satchel blindly. Her fingers closed on the warm tube of fire-fennel. She flicked the tar cap off with her thumb. She commanded the flame, taking care to point it straight up, so as not to burn any books. A bright green flare illuminated the room, clear as day.

"No..."

Row upon row of shelves stood empty. Lecterns, cabinets, writing desks—all bare as a beggar's larder. A layer of dust one knuckle deep covered it all.

No...

Bas relief letters carved over the entrance read Osylum Park Library. Beneath that, the seal bore the letters O.P.L. Across them, the insolent graffitist had scrawled:

Fear not; 'tis empty of all things but grief

Oneirotheria's howl echoed off the cavernous ceiling like a hundred Ratkippers denied human flesh.

"Pike! Pike and plague and pox and coxcomb dangle and hell and whores and..." Spitting her entire lexicon of curses, Oneirotheria ran up and down the stacks, searching frantically for any scrap.

Nothing remained.

She seized Wailenweave by the shoulders.

"Do you swear there were books here?"

"I—"

"SWEAR!"

"Lady's Hands, I swear there was books all over. 'Twas half full when I was a younger puppet and got bored and left an angry witch to her business here."

"Half full? You call this half full?" She drew back her hand to slap the other woman.

Philotech caught her wrist. He did not seem as uncomfortable about touching her as before.

"Peace," he said. "It's not her fault."

Oneirotheria shook her arm free. He was, of course, right. It in no way reduced her desire to slap someone. She took aim with a vicious kick at a lectern but spun away at the last second. She'd no desire to break a toe for a tempest that would pass. She did throw a stray brickbat at a gargoyle and chip his smug face.

"I suppose," she said through gritted teeth, "I'm no worse off than I was this morning. Nothing lost except what I had hoped for, which didn't exist to begin with."

"That's the spirit! And you have me now, off my lonely exile," Wailenweave chirped.

Philotech stepped away from defending her. "Now if she slaps you it *is* your fault."

Oneirotheria did not react. She hooked a scissor-chair with her ankle and dragged it over. She sat. She sighed.

"I am tired. It has been a long day."

"Shoon, shule, shoon," Wailenweave sang in a soothing tone.

She moved behind the witch. She ran her fingers

through Oneirotheria's tangled black hair, gently smoothing it. She massaged her scalp and neck and shoulders.

"Lulla, lulla, lullaby... never harm, nor spell nor charm, come our lovely little witch nigh; So, good-night, with lullaby..."

Oneirotheria's blinks grew longer and longer. Eyes closed, she murmured, "You're going back to Upstart once I'm asleep aren't you?"

"Shoon shule shoon..."

"That's what I thought. Tell him... tell him I set the Linnaea to find the oseovox... I remember some things... I don't remember him..."

"Lulla lulla lullaby..."

"...oh and tell him enough puppets..."

Her lips stopped moving and she spoke the last dream-like words only in thought, before the blank of sleep fell over her brain.

Tell him I want to see him.

Tell him I want to escape.

Tell him this time we'll make it.

40

She woke wrapped in a comfortable musky smell. Eyes still closed, she declined full consciousness. She burrowed deep into the woolen odor. Warm and rough, it lay heavy over her whole body, snuggling her in a profoundly sensual space. She'd never experienced such a thing. The only word she could find for it was the small and inadequate 'pleasant'.

"It's light out now," Philotech said.

The day intruded. She sat up. Pale colors dappled the floor, cast from picture windows. Philotech's coat, which he'd draped over her as a blanket, slipped off her chest. At some point she'd been relocated from the chair to the floor. She winced, stiff from sleeping on cold stone.

"Still no books, I take it?"

He plucked his coat from her lap. He shrugged it on his broad shoulders. "No books. And you were right. Wailenweave left as soon as you fell asleep. I didn't bother stopping her."

"No point." Using the edge of a pen-scarred oak table, she pulled herself standing. She stretched. She shook her body, head to feet. Her soreness sloughed off like molted feathers.

"Were you up all night?"

"Someone had to watch. We didn't have five to sing out the dark."

"Will they miss you?"

"With four they can survive the night in the Second. It's safer there. Mostly."

"Thank you. For staying and guarding me."

He asked the next question quickly—whether because he was afraid of her reaction or because he did not want the answer, she could not tell.

"Are you Hecate?"

"No!" She thought about it. "Or yes. Maybe? I have her memories. Some of them. But I also have my own. Are we just the sum of our memories? Tosspot would call that a question for philosophers. I think I'm going to insist on no. No, I am not Hecate. Unless it turns out I am."

"But you *do* remember things. From before you—or she—died."

"Yes."

"What was it like? Dying?"

Oneirotheria searched within. She found nothing.

"I'm sorry. I don't know. That bit's gone, if it ever was. Like all the pages in the books, tore out and taken away."

He leaned forward, bristling with insistent urgency. "But there is something? Before and after? Some piece of—us—that keeps going into the next life?"

"I—I am not certain. The evidence points that way, as the Linnaea would say. I think so. Except..."

"The Fade."

"Yes. The Fade. I think the Lady's Gaze destroys everything that could be someone."

Philotech made the apotrope. "Love we the Lady and fear we the Fade."

A pause lingered until it became uncomfortable. Abruptly, Philotech asked:

"What about Marrigan?"

"You mean, am I Marrigan *and* Hecate?"

"If Wailenweave was telling the truth, Marrigan was a witch. And there's never more than one witch. If every witch becomes a witch when she dies..."

Oneirotheria stared at the empty library. She tried to picture herself—or a woman like her—sitting at one of the tables, books spread out in a search for something.

What if I were? How many of me have there been? How many times did I find my way to the library? How many of me has looted it for as many books as she could carry before it ended up like this?

She envied the others, if they really had existed. Every step back the world must have fuller and clearer. And yet not a one of them had preserved any of it. Selfishly, every incarnation had hoarded stores of knowing for her own little purposes, not thinking of those who would come after. Not thinking of *her*, last in an infinite line.

Infinite? Maybe not. Maybe it's not fair to hate them for squandering what they had. Maybe they did not know there would be others, later. Maybe no one figured it out until... did Hecate know? Is that why she gave me some of her memories?

Philotech interrupted her speculation.

"Who's Upstart?"

"You've never heard of him?"

"Not till Wailenweave."

"I don't know who he is. Not really. I've never met him." She paused. "I think Hecate loved him."

"Do you love him?"

"Love? Of all the words in my brain, that's one I have the hardest time sticking a definition to."

"Don't be a witch, dodging the question."

"Do you love Matron?"

It was his turn to fumble. She let him wriggle a little before answering her own question.

"Of course you do. Don't waste time denying it. But what does that *mean?* You *love* her."

"I would die for her. I would kill for her. No one matters more. Nothing. I would step in front of any pain in Osylum to keep her safe. Take anything the Lady or Wardens had to throw."

"If that's what you mean by love, then no. I do not love Upstart."

"What then?"

"Like I said, I don't know. I feel something for him. Or Hecate did and stuck it in my brain, which I resent but can't change. The most I can do is ignore it, which doesn't seem to work because I keep stumbling over his puppets."

"What's his game?"

She hesitated a long time, debating how honest to be. The eavesdropped conversation between Philotech and Eschatos made her leery. On the other hand, he had had every opportunity to do whatever he wanted as she lay sleeping. And he chose to guard her, to stay true to Platon's Oath. Could she trust that discipline if he knew her purpose? If that purpose might put Matron in danger?

'I would kill for her.' The fire in your eyes when you said that, Peripat... you would burn the world to ash if you thought it would keep her safe.

"What's his game?" Philotech repeated.

"I heard you." In a split second she decided to tell him everything. "Escape. His game is escape. Mine too."

By rote, he responded: "The Rule of No Escape. Osylum is the world and the world Osylum. One cannot escape the world."

She waved a dismissive hand. "That's just a Peripat rule."

"The Three apply to everyone," he insisted with zealous conviction.

"After yesterday, you still believe Osylum is the world and the world Osylum?"

His eyes filled with the memory of the Unreflected.

"Osylum is the world and the world Osylum," he repeated.

"Are you trying to convince yourself or me?"

"It doesn't matter whether you're convinced or not. What's true is true. There is no escape because there's nowhere to escape to."

Trying to convince yourself, then, she thought.

"Never mind then." He went to the door, where he had piled several shelves and tables, and began moving them aside. "It's time we go. You saw what you wanted to see. I need to get back to the others."

He tossed the last barricade—a table as tall as himself—aside effortlessly. He threw open the double doors.

"Here-now!" Oneirotheria exclaimed. "The trees are in a kinder mood."

A clear path led, straight as a market road, from the library veranda across the Eighth.

"Maybe they recognize you, Marrigan."

"Two jokes in two days. You're becoming quite the flibbertigibbet, Philotech."

The new trail was even open to the wan sky, so they did not need a light. As they walked, Oneirotheria tried to picture wide, well-tended lawns ornamented by carefully curated groves and airy leisure buildings. She could not.

"It's odd to think the wood is younger than the rest of the city," she said. "It smells like forever."

Philotech ignored the idle chat. "Where are we going?"

"When I was up the oak yesterday, I saw the edge of town. This path is taking us that way. If we can get there, we can follow the outer wall to the next Ward. There won't be a gate at the corner, but if you're willing to hop, we can get to the Seventh or Ninth.

"Seventh. I don't like the Ninth. Nothing's what it seems there."

"Seven it is. And then it's an easy pad back to your Stay."

He motioned for her to lead the way.

41

The shade of the sky said it was halfway to evening Feed when Oneirotheria parted ways with Philotech. The Peripat campsite was, of course, unoccupied (the others off wandering during the day). With naught but a nod for farewell, he turned his back to her. He stood post for Matron's return.

A short stroll later, she entered the folly garden. Her hut knelt waiting, its face a blank wall.

"Izbushka, izbushka, your witch implores—open your mouth and show me the door!"

The battered plank siding rippled. Two windows and a door wrinkled into existence. It delighted her as much as the first time she'd chanted the rhyme.

Was it Hecate who made that up? Or Marrigan? Or another me?

Where did you come from, chicken-legged hut?

In an instant, her perspective on her predecessors shifted. Gratitude replaced anger at their carelessness. True, they could have left more for her. But they had left some things. And now she knew that Hecate was not her only ally across time and forgetting. A host of others had left their traces on the city. Traces she could gather up and weave into a tapestry of remembering.

And by remembering, escape.

She did not need Upstart or the oseovox or the Linnaea or a fusty monk. A crowd of imagined ghosts clustered round her. All together they might add up to enough to challenge the Lady herself.

Pike the laws of Lady and man, it's time to plot and time to plan.

She almost opened her door and ended the world there and then.

Her hand jerked back before her brain even registered the threat. The faint traces of the Lady's Eye were drawn across the jamb line. Sealed and trapped.

The windows too.

"Here-now! Who would fade a woman just for going home?"

The Wardens never thought about other entrances. This was a minor inconvenience. Oneirotheria shifted into the magpie's body. She fluttered to the sag-peaked roof. She strutted along the top-beam to the chimney pipe.

Someone else—she could not imagine the Wardens dirtying their hands—had stuffed the hole with sewer filth. The tail half of a dead rat protruded from the dried shit. She turned back into a woman. She scratched at the blockage; the solid crust was hard as concrete.

"Scabby whoreson!"

"Is everything not as it should be?" Eschatos's mocking whine replied from below.

She slid down the roof. The garden was empty. She circled her hut. He was nowhere to be found.

"Where are you, gutterlick? Come out and let's talk. I know a few words that'll turn you blue, you gong-farming mother-pimp."

"Oh, no need for that. I already know everything I need to know about you." He giggled. "And now the Wardens do too."

She paced the space, hexes at the ready. She pricked her ears to locate him. "What do they know?"

Eschatos ticked off offenses, his voice quivering with glee. "What I told them! They know you remember. They know you're looking for the oseovox. Treasons piled upon treasons. So many of our Lady's laws trampled under your nasty feet."

He cackled.

"She's not my Lady and I don't remember agreeing to her laws."

That didn't even rattle him. Smug and superior, he continued:

"They know the Upstart is back and you, naughty witch, want to see him again. Oh, that's the worst of it all, they think. I'd fade you just for rudeness to my Lady, but they need more than that. So I gave them all of it. And now my Lady's Fog will wash sweet across the city, washing all the filth like you away. She will see me and love me and I will be her Lord."

She realized his tinny mewling rang out from a spout-pipe in the dry fountain. He was somewhere in the sewers below. Hiding. Smart, she had to admit, because if she found him...

If I had that book on plumbing I'd track you back in a second—it's in my piking hut and useless now.

"Who told you all this? Was it Philotech?"

"That rough beast? No, no, no. He didn't want to dance. So Kippers can take him for all I care. I got you anyway."

A stone sank into her belly. "Wailenweave."

The simper in his snigger sickened her. "My babies seized her in the Seventh and brought her to me. Oh, how she sang. She sang and sang and sang a pretty tune, hitting every high note."

"Do you still have her?"

"I took her to the Wardens to sing her song. They did not even bother to fade her, so I gave her to my children when I was done. They do not care for eating their vegetables, but needs must when shrubby-puppets are all you have. Maybe they'll feast on fresh, fleshy Peripat when there's not a witch to defend them..."

Oneirotheria took out a tube of fire-fennel.

"She didn't confess everything, I think."

"It doesn't matter! I've got you on what she screeched. The Wardens are hunting and there is nowhere for you to go. You'll fade and my Lady will—"

She uncapped the tube and shoved it in the pipe. The metal glowed yellow instantly. She shielded her eyes from the intense burn. Seconds later she heard a shriek, far-off and muffled by earth. The spout-pipe curled over under the blast of heat. The tube fused to it and collapsed. Eschatos's screams receded.

"I am sorry for your pain," Oneirotheria whispered to Wailenweave's memory. "I hope that evens the score a little."

Thank you for not telling him about Hendiatrix and the Unreflected.

She took a last wistful look at her home. She would miss it. And everything inside. Stripped to the bare essentials—satchel, pouch, patch-work brain, and two bare feet—she prepared to flee.

"Old man, old man in the mirror," her reflection chanted in the dirty window pane, "see me now, hear me here."

Silence.

She repeated the summons.

Her dirty ghost frowned.

"Really? Now of all times you finally decide to stick to your promise never to answer again?"

She tried a third time.

The Rule of Three, apparently, did not apply to monks when they did not want to talk to you.

She reviewed her list of allies.

It took less than a second.

"I really should have put more effort into making friends. Well, no use crying over spilt ink."

The magpie stirred in her chest.

"No, dear. I don't know if the Wardens know about you. I should figure yes. And I'll need my hands and words if they spot me."

If I'd been a pigeon, this would be no problem. Blend right in. Instead I had to choose the only magpie in Osylum. A tiding of one. Well, next time.

That made her laugh. Laughter fortified her defiance. She hoisted herself up the vines along the garden wall. Keeping to wall-tops and roof beams, she crept zig-zag across the city towards the Laboratory.

42

She saw nine Wardens on the way; always singly, never in groups. They streamed through the straying streets, borne on a purposeful current. Every prisoner they confronted stopped and assured them everything was as it should be. They lingered longer than usual, requiring more than the normal amount of assurance. No one failed to convince. Or at least, no one got the Fade.

She had never seen more than three Wardens in a day.

Eschatos had not lied.

They were searching for her.

Her luck held. The Wardens stuck close to the cobbles and never looked up. She scampered from roof to roof. She jumped between buildings where she could; she scurried down and up gutter-pipes when she couldn't bridge the gap through the air. She held back the urge to fly—it was faster, true, but the bird's mind was simple and she needed every bit of wit she had. Best to save it till absolutely necessary, to cross the Laboratory's unscalable concrete and razor-glass wall.

Except, when she reached the Linnaea's garden, she found their brass gate open wide.

She did not hesitate. There wasn't a Warden or

other soul in sight. No sense in hiding till someone showed up. She sprinted from the hedges
across the boulevard, through the opening. As she
passed, her peripheral vision caught two clean
yellow lines, where the gate had stood.

Twin slivers of newly exposed metal bisected
the thick grey wall. The gate had not been opened.
It had been removed. From reality.

Pike.

She took the front stairs three at a time. The
enormous double doors were also gone. Their
hinges remained.

Within, chaos reigned.

The rowboat centerpiece that dominated the
foyer had fallen on its side. It remained intact. The
scaffolding had been scattered across the marble
floor. Scorch-marks marred the paneled walls and
shattered glass ringed all the display cases. Half the
steps up to the landing were chipped and gouged.
Gears and springs and shards of brass littered the
room. The oily odor of smoke seethed across the
scene. Amid all this, mechanical spiders toiled
tirelessly at the futile task of restoring order.

She picked a careful path through the wreckage to the Mirror Room. This door had been
broken open. Splinters haloed the other side.
Dedalus's mirror remained intact. The Linnaea's
custom-built chair lay on its side.

The room was otherwise empty.

She approached the Great Mirror. Using it to
watch her back, she called out to Hendiatrix.

No reply.

She tried all of the other monks by name, from
the Abbot to Zeugma.

Again, no reply.

Pike.

The destruction had not touched the landing either. She searched the upper floors. She had never had free range of the house before; she regretted the circumstances. Until she found the Linnaea or determined what had happened, she had to settle for cursory examinations of each room.

"Here-now!" she cried when she opened a door into an enormous library.

If she had thought her izbushka had held a treasure trove of reading, she had been preening over pennies in a beggar's bowl. Dedalus and his successors had amassed a vault of books full two-stories high and the size of a cathedral church. She could spend her life cramming her brain full of the knowledge bound in that place.

And I find you at the worst possible hour!

Bitterly, she realized it was true. The time for books was past. The Wardens on her tail, allies few, the Fade her likely fate... escape could be her only goal.

Still...

The Laboratory seemed quiet enough for the moment. Little harm in running down the shelves, noting the titles, trying to suss out the organizational scheme in case there *were* to be a free moment later on.

"You know yourself better than that," she said. *You know yourself better than that.*

It would start with a casual trail of the fingertips across spines... a quick read of the contents... maybe just a casual cross-legged sit-down in a big leather chair... and the Wardens would fade her while she sat lost in words.

"Fine and feh," she said and turned the other

way.

She couldn't help herself. She spun on her heel, sprinted across the room. She snatched the only open book on the Linnaea's own lectern. She crammed it in her satchel as she fled, slamming the door before she was snared by her bibliophilic addiction.

Back in the foyer, she heard the scrape of metal on stone coming from below. She followed the iron tracks down to the subterranean level.

Midway down the hall, Cellarius clawed the floor, dragging itself in slow circles. Half of its body had been faded. Exposed gears and tabs clicked through automatic sequences. Its faces—still intact—were stuck between agony and stoic resolve.

"Oh, you poor thing," she said.

When it saw her, it pulled itself around. It tried to deploy no-longer-existent weapons, with the whine of half-toothless gears. Its faces shivered, lacking the strength to change to rage.

She laid a hand on its shuddering brass shell. In a recess, exposed by a now-sprung flap, a small turnkey ticked round.

"Shhh," she soothed the machine. "Rest now."

She pulled the turnkey out. Cellarius shuddered to a halt. Twin half-faces stared at her. Pain and determination. Her vision blurred and her eyes burned. She turned away.

The Linnaea's butler had been guarding the door labeled 'Aeronauticia'. On tiptoes, she peeked through the porthole. Outdoor light flooded the room. The ceiling had retracted—properly folded open, not faded, for she could see its segments accordioned in the corners. Ropes and cannisters and tools of uncertain purpose were strewn about.

She tried the door. Locked.

I hope you got away. Either way, I need your place for a while.

She reckoned the Laboratory was safe. Whether the Wardens had faded the Linnaea or not, they would have no reason to be back for a while. It was more likely someone else, finding out the scientists were on the run, would try to move in on the rich kip. Not having the front gate was less than ideal. She would have to hole up in a more secure interior room to regroup and not stay long.

Needs must when the Lady drives.

She hammered the door with an angry fist.

The Lady!

She hit it again and again, to raise a bruise that would serve as a reminder. The Lady owed everyone in Osylum a great debt.

And her lick-slipper Eschatos. I'll be quit with him first.

A haggard cry rang from the foyer.

"Sanctuary! Sanctuary!"

Oneirotheria dipped into her pouch for a birnam twig. Thus armed, she marched upwards towards the panic-cracked voice. As she entered the front hall, someone dove behind the sideways skiff.

"Stop!" he wailed. "I serve the masters of this house! Harm me and you answer to them."

"I would be happy to answer to them," she replied. "Or at least to trade questions. Only they seem to be elsewhere."

Hendiatrix's head poked over the gunwale.

"You!" he croaked, his throat seized with fear.

She returned the hex twig to her pouch. "Yes.

Me."

He tried to leap over the boat. Too weak, he settled for bouncing awkwardly around it. Face contorted in a rictus of rage, he charged. She stepped out of his way—it was not difficult. He stumbled. He righted himself. He turned and charged again, liver-spotted fists swinging both wildly and weakly. Once more, she avoided him.

"Please stop," she said.

"You did this! All of this!" He grappled for her. It did not take much to bat him away. He fell backwards onto a pile of gears. He screeched, reached back, and pulled a stuck gear out of his withered right buttock.

"Please," she said again, "you're just going to hurt yourself."

He flung the gear at her. Razor teeth whirring, it whistled past, three paces to the left of her ear.

She bent down. She opened her palm in front of his face. With a gentle puff, she covered him in valerian dust.

"Take a deep breath," she intoned, "nestle in the arms of the cousin of death."

His face turned bright red. His eyes bulged. He tensed all his limbs, as though he were about to flail in a tantrum. He passed out.

"Whist!" she said. "That'll buy some peace. Maybe you'll be less frumious after a nap."

43

While the monk slept, Oneirotheria went in search of the larder. Hunger would soon be an issue, since she could no longer rely on the regular Feeding. The Linnaea had stores and there were others in the city. When the food ran out... it wouldn't matter. By the time it ran out, she hoped to be gone.

After all those forgotten lives, the die really is cast. No going back. Fade or escape and no third way for me.

No third way.

She recalled Hendiatrix's story about Dedalus's last day. The inventor had Cellarius kill him, before the Wardens could obliterate him. Then, if her theory was correct, his soul had moved into the Linnaea—without memories, but somehow still him. His work could continue and the Wardens wouldn't interfere.

That was the third way.

The Laboratory held plenty of options. Some might even be peaceful and painless. Or quick. Pain could be borne if it were quick.

No. I'm no suicide. Whatever I am, I am right now and right here. I'll not wipe the slate clean for another poor hatchling to piece things back together. No.

She pieced together two meals from the larder scraps—the cupboards were leaner than she would've liked. She brought a tray back to the sleeping Oblate. While waiting for him to wake, she ate. She remembered the lone book she'd taken from the library upstairs.

"Let's see what the Linnaea were reading before the Wardens arrived."

She retrieved the enchiridion from her satchel. The cover was simply two birch boards connected by a strip of leather; it bore neither title nor spine embossing. She had lost the Linnaea's place when she'd snatched it up. So she opened to the first page. At the top, in tiny hand, all majuscules read ON MIRRORS.

"Here-now!"

What followed was a sparse outline. It read more as a guide to memory than as an attempt to convey knowledge. She took it in, whether it made sense or no, on the chance that the gaps might be filled by experience.

I. THE REAL IS THE REAL

That seems unarguable. Not particularly insightful, but I suppose spelling everything out at the start can't hurt.

II. THE IMAGE IS THE IMAGE

1. THE IMAGE IS OF THE REAL

2. THE REAL IS NOT OF THE IMAGE

By that point, it was already an effort to corral her brain to focus. The bland truisms read like the literary equivalent of counting one's right toes and then counting one's left toes and then observing the count to be equal. Of course, from what she knew of the Linnaea, this tedious enumeration probably set their hearts aflutter.

Hearts? I wonder if they have one or two. If they had two, do they beat in unison or syncopation? Stop!

She drew her eyes back to the page.

Focus!

III. THERE IS SOMETHING NEITHER REAL NOR IMAGE

Next to that, in a miniscule pencil, the Major had scribbled:

The way out is not through the Real nor the Image. The dark space between the two?

"Oh you wicked twins..." she murmured with a grin. "This whole time you've been plotting to escape too. You played that close to your chests—which there ARE two of, regardless of your heart situation. HA!"

Her crowing laugh caused Hendiatrix to stir. She hastily flipped through the codex. More outlines and images followed, growing denser and more detailed as the book progressed. Two-thirds of the way through, the pages went blank and stayed that way. As the monk blinked open rheumy eyes, she slipped the book back in her satchel.

"Are you hungry?" she asked, bright with innocence. "You seem like you might be hungry."

He swatted at her from the ground. She rolled to her feet.

"All that carrying on must have worked up an appetite. I brought you almond cakes and dried oranges. I don't think they were meant to be dried. Nought but water to drink, I'm afraid. There are other liquids around the Laboratory but who knows what they are or what foul thing they might do if drunk?"

He sat up. With a thousand-mile stare, he gave in to his impotence. Not even looking, he fumbled for a cake. He mulled it with five good teeth. Most of it ended up on his robe.

"There you go," she said, her voice a pat on his head. "Eat up. We're both going to need all the nourishment we can get."

He slowly turned his head towards her, struggling to figure out where she was and if she were even real.

"We? I have no one to say 'we' with."

"Nonsense! You have me. You and me and—" *the Lady makes three*, she thought. Instead she said: "—that's good enough to get by for a while."

He hugged his skinny shins to his sunken chest. "Isokolon. Thaumasmus. Zeugma. Ekphrasis. Diacaelox. Graecismus. Barbarizein. Anaphora."

"Your brothers."

"They are gone. All gone. Isokolon... Thaumas mus... Zeugma..."

She lifted his plate. On reflex, he took a slice of leathery dried orange and ate it.

"What happened to them? Dead or—?"

"Not dead. And I'm here. Hendiatrix." He spat. "Hendiatrix the Heretic, his soul is sick, his soul is sick. Broke the Rule to save his hide, while his brothers died. His brothers died."

"Heretic..." she echoed. Atoms of words stirred in her brain for the first time in a long time. "From haeritikos, the verbal adjective of hairein. It means able to choose. You chose."

"I chose wrong. From the moment you—from the moment Hecate grabbed my mirror I did nothing but choose wrong. Every choice my fault. And hers. And yours."

To head off more feeble tantruming, she handed him a chipped teacup of water. He sipped, still by mechanical instinct.

She asked again: "What happened? Tell me. I can't fix it but I can remember the story and maybe there's revenge."

The teacup rattled as he set it on the floor. "Revenge? Against who?"

"Just tell me what happened."

He turned away. As chance would have it, he came face to face with his own ghostly reflection in the glass tiller-box of the overturned skiff. His trembling fingers traced reflected tears on his cheek.

"Sext. It was the Sext count. I was hungry." He glanced at her, sidelong. "Thank you for the food. We did not end up getting the mid-day feed."

"You're welcome."

Once more, basic courtesy from a witch appeared to surprise the monk. He paused a moment, then resumed his tale. "The Linnaea listened to the count. When Abbot Anaphora finished, they drew their chair close to the Great Mirror.

"'And what about finding a skull?' they asked. They ask that—asked that—every count since you told them whatever you told them to get them to look for it. Anaphora just bent his head and shook it. I don't know if he even looked. I don't know if any of the others looked. We never talked about it. I think every one of us knew it was a bad idea and were hoping the interest would pass."

"It's not a bad idea," Oneirotheria said. "I don't know what it is, but it's not that. It might be our only hope."

"Hope." Hendiatrix covered his reflection with both hands.

"What happened then?"

"The Linnaea turned around. Quick. Like they had heard something. The door behind them opened. A Warden. We all prostrated ourselves before its reflection.

"Our patrons did not even rise from their chair. They spoke, noble and proud. 'This intrusion is highly anomalous. Cellarius handles all interactions between the Laboratory and the city.'

"The Warden just stood there. The Linnaea began to repeat themselves. The third eye cracked. I told myself to jump up and run to the Chantry Mirror and pull them through. I couldn't. My muscles turned to water and my bones to sodden bread. I cowered.

"Before the Warden could open its Third Eye all the way, Cellarius burst through the door. It rolled straight into the Warden, knocking it across the room like a rag doll. The Linnaea ran to the door, the smaller one wailing in pain. It must have hurt to dangle and bounce that way.

"They disappeared and Cellarius followed hard after. The Warden, who had never touched the ground, righted itself. It floated to the Great Mirror. It stared at us, third eye wide open. I looked into Nothing. I looked into Nothing..."

A shadow passed over him and he covered his face.

"The Fade doesn't work through mirrors?" Oneirotheria heard her own breathless voice ask. The thought staggered her. She pictured the front gate and all the other objects in the building that had been sliced away by the Warden's Eye. "Or *on* mirrors either!"

"The Warden turned its back on us. Abbot Anaphora cut the connection. We stared up at ourselves, pissing with fear and babbling prayers.

"Abbot ordered us back to our cells. 'Pray for the Lady's Grace,' he said, 'and the souls of the Linnaea.'

"I couldn't hide any more. I stood there in the Chantry before my brothers and the Mirror and I made a full confession. Everything I'd done. Spying for Hecate. Entering the Reflected. All of it. My brothers hissed and covered their ears at the blasphemies I spilled. I yelled louder so they had to hear."

"Why?"

"Because they deserved to know. Because if we all got faded, they should know it was me and have the chance to hand me over. And, with another part of me, I hoped they would realize we had a way out of the Phrontistery. That if the Wardens came for us—*when* they came, we could hide in our cell mirrors and flee."

"They didn't listen."

"They did not. I pleaded with them to either force me out the door or run together as one across the Unreflected. The Abbot ordered me locked in my cell. My brothers seized me and complied."

"But they didn't take away your mirror," Oneirotheria reasoned.

"No. They left me that. I think they couldn't bear to be near me long enough to empty out my cell. They threw me in and slammed the door and bolted and barred it. I waited face-down on the cold stone till I heard the first scream. I dove into my mirror. I swam from cell to Reflected cell. I called to them. Not one would come with me. Not one of them. Not one."

His frail shoulders shook uncontrollably.

In a soft voice, Oneirotheria said: "They chose too."

Hendiatrix mourned, incoherent.

Chitters and cruel snickers drifted through the door. They sounded as though they were still in the garden across the street. Oneirotheria gathered her things. She helped the grieving monk to his feet. A wicked snarl sounded, halfway to the front stairs.

"Walk with me," she said sotto voce.

Lost in sorrow, the oblate let her guide him into the Mirror Room. She let go of him long enough to close the doors and wedge a chair under each knob. By that point, the Ratkippers' feral cries had reached the Laboratory's threshold.

She ushered Hendiatrix to the Great Mirror. She took his chin in her hand. She guided his eyes to their reflection. She drew on every bit of persuasive presence she had.

"Listen. They chose. Your brothers made their choice not to flee. You have made yours. Any moment, cannibals are going to come through that door. I can fight them, maybe all of them, but that will use up power I can never get back and will be like burning a beacon for every Warden in Osylum."

The door shook. Animalistic screeches and claw-scratches filled the air.

"Or we can go in there. And you can live. And carry the memory of the Phrontistery and the Oblates. Their..." she grasped for images that might touch his heart, "...their smiles, the way they held their spoons, the hitch in their voice every time on one note in a prayer."

By his eyes, she could tell she'd struck a chord. He softly said: "I could tell every one of them by their footsteps, even with my face down and eyes closed."

"Good! That! Keep all that! And get us out of here."

The hinges splintered. The chair legs left long scratch marks in the parquet floor.

"No more Rule. Just you and your choice and the brothers you carry in your head."

He reached out to the enormous mirror.

The door burst open.

From the Reflected island, Oneirotheria saw dozens of Ratkippers pour into the room. Gibbering, they threw filth and blood and gobbets of torn flesh, despoiling the rich and splendid space. Behind them, Eschatos swept in.

She clenched a fist.

Not yet. Save your strength. Escape.

He strode smugly up to the Great Mirror. He leaned his face inches away from the surface. She was grimly pleased to see blisters covered the lower half of his face, along angry red streaks.

Eschatos smirked. He winced—pulling his face under the still-fresh burns must have been excruciating. He spun on his heel. He raised one long-nailed hand and gestured at the Great Mirror. He paced away without looking back.

The Ratkippers grabbed shattered chairs and table boards and smashed the glass. The scene shattered and the island beneath Oneirotheria's feet broke with it. The Kippers continued their frenzied destruction, grinding the silvered glass smaller and smaller, till at last there was no reflection left.

Oneirotheria and Hendiatrix bobbed in the Unreflected. She sighted on the nearest line of light.

"There."

Together they dog-paddled through the vast dark that was neither Real nor an Image.

44

Translucent shades of potted ferns and raised seedling beds hung in the reflection plane. She was beginning to learn the difference between images captured by manufactured mirrors and those ghosts barely seen in other reflective surfaces. She realized this must be a greenhouse and they looked out through a dirty glass pane. A brass spider dribbled water along the seedling beds. Another tilled empty soil.

Still close to the Laboratory. Too close.

"We should move on," she said. "The Ratkippers could smell us if we step out here."

"Please," Hendiatrix replied. "Let me rest."

Half his body was still in the un-water. She pulled him onto the island.

"You're probably still shaking off the valerian." She took out a paper packet of dried ephedra. "It should be a tea but if you just hold the leaves in your mouth..."

He shook his head. He pushed her offering away. "No more witchcraft. All the pawing and crawling's just hard work for old arms."

"We can wait here a while. If the Wardens couldn't figure out how to come through to the Phron—" she changed her words so as not to set him off, "— they can't use the mirrors. And Eschatos might know about them and he might not. Either way he can't reach us. Alright. You can rest. I need to think."

He knelt, facing the plane of reflection. He emitted a low drone. At regular intervals, he traced simple, repetitive gestures in front of his chest. The drone took shape as syllables. Prayers, she guessed, though they made little sense to her. She pushed the intrusive sound away and focused on planning her next move.

Assets? A smaller pouch of hexes than I had this morning. A book of notes it'll take me a fortnight to crack. Pens, paper, and the rest of my satchel's oddiments. More words than things, if that counts as an asset.

Liabilities? Hut sealed. Food dwindling. Not even water for tea—or ink. Still short on memories. Still don't know how anything fits together. Missing pages in every book.

Enemies? The Lady watches. Wardens look to fade me. Ratkippers want to eat me. Eschatos wants... whatever he wants, it won't be pleasant.

Allies? A grief-hagged monk who might take the Fade at any moment just to get peace from his conscience. The Linnaea, somewhere in the city. The Peripats, though I can't ask more of them. Whatever Philotech said about Platon's Oath, they owe me a life and this is so much more than that.

Upstart? Which is he? Ally or enemy or some third thing?

Why does my mind step towards him and away at the same time?

What happens if I die here behind every mirror in Osylum? The Wardens can't claim the body, as is their right. As is the Lady's will.

The Lady. Before this hurly-burly's done, I'll take the war to her front door and spit in her eye once at least.

Ragpatch said she had a mirror before her throne.

We could get there.

I'll need everything and everyone I can bring to bear. Upstart... shake the scenery... What are my assets again?

Her mind circled like a magpie on a slow current of air, going nowhere. She stared at the Oblate, not really seeing him.

Hendiatrix cupped his hands. He reached them towards the dim shadows of the greenhouse. He drew them back, pulling light from the air and washing his face with it. He repeated the gesture thrice. He shook out his hands.

He caught her watching him.

"It's not the same," he said. "As on the right side of the mirror. This is... empty. There's a fullness in feeding your eyes on reflections. This is like eating a meal that vanishes before it passes your teeth."

"We need to find you a real mirror."

"It's not real eating," he said. "I won't go hungry without it."

"That's not what I meant. I need you to find someone. Can you search the city through any reflective surface, or do you need the one in your cell?"

"I don't know. I've never tried anywhere else."

She looked into the greenhouse. A shadowy figure moved past outside; it drifted with a Warden's graceful pace.

"We'll need somewhere safer."

Abruptly, Hendiatrix asked: "Why did you say 'they chose'?"

The question caught her off-guard. Her thoughts scattered like feathers tossed from a rooftop.

He repeated the question. She corralled her whirling attention.

"I don't understand. Why does it matter?"

"It matters. You were trying to console me—or manipulate me into hiding here—and you said: 'They chose. Your brothers made their choice not to flee.' Why is that important?"

She tried to recall what she had been thinking. "You said you were a heretic. You've said that over and over since I met you. Heretic, heretic, heretic. You carry that title around like a stone chained round your neck.

"But that word doesn't mean anything special. It just means you have a choice. We all have a choice. Every one of us. So we're all heretics. You're not any more guilty than the rest of us and you don't deserve any worse than anyone else. Your brothers chose their Rule and obedience over existence—you chose to keep living, to keep going on, without any idea where 'on' is and knowing only that the other choice was the end of choosing.

"So yes, I said they chose. Not that they deserved the Fade, but it was their choice, not yours that brought them to it. Undo that stone and chain of other people's decisions and you'll at least move more freely, whatever your end winds up being."

His eyes sunk into sepulchral pits. His lips moved with fragments of thought. One last time, he washed his face with dirty light. As his hand passed from brow to chin, determination replaced fear and grief.

"Do you think the Wardens know about that basement where I first pulled you through?"

The endless oppressive shell of the Unreflected retreated briefly from Oneirotheria's delighted laugh.

"Let's find out!"

45

They tumbled onto the musty floor. She snorted a noseful of mold and sneezed again and again. When the fit passed, she lit a moonflower and examined the cramped confines beneath the pub.

"It hasn't changed," she said.

"It's been two days."

"Really? It seems longer."

"The count went from nineteen thousand six hundred and eighty-three to nineteen thousand six hundred and eighty-two. Still over by three."

Wailenweave. I am sorry. I should not have let you go.

"She made her choice," she reminded herself.

"Who?"

"Never mind. Let's see if Tosspot blocked the hatch again."

"You know a great many people," Hendiatrix said, suspicion creeping back into his cracked voice.

"You know more than me," she replied as she climbed the ladder.

"No. I've *seen* more people than you. I know no one. Not any more." He softly recited the Faded Oblates' names, Isokolon to Anaphora. By the time he'd finished, she was pushing the hatch door open.

"Here-now!"

He stepped close to the mirror whence they'd emerged, ready to bolt if the pub held any nasty guests.

Heedless, Oneirotheria hoisted herself up. The long mirror behind the bar had been covered by a winding sheet. She tugged a corner. The linen slithered to the floor. Etched in its silvered surface were the words:

She hath travell'd and is mirror'd there

"Damn you, muddy rascal," she murmured. "You. It's been you all along, scrawling on every wall in Osylum."

In an instant, a plan fell into place. She knew how to hunt her quarry.

She poked her head through the hole. "Come on up. It's safe for now. I'll block the door."

When Hendiatrix joined her, she was just finishing dragging a table in front of the entrance. She pointed at the scratch-marred glass.

"Is that going to scuttle your magic?" she asked.

"It's not magic. It's—"

"—you don't know what it is. Doesn't matter what you call it. Is having those letters dicing up the reflection going to make it impossible for you to use that mirror to scan the city?"

"I don't know. I'm not even sure any mirror but the ones in our cells, the Chantry, and the Laboratory can even do that."

"It's in the singers," she quoted Matron. "And the way they stand."

"I don't know what that means."

"It means try."

He knelt before the glass. He bowed his head. He made the apotrope before each eye and then across his chest.

"May I see," he intoned, "and in seeing, know and in knowing, serve and in service, be free. Lady's will be done."

He lifted his head. He stared into the mirror. A silver sheen descended over his eyes. The reflection disappeared. It was replaced by a faded sign of a scarlet eagle, carrying an infant by his swaddling; the view of the pub from the window across the street. Oneirotheria stifled a victorious hoot—she did not want to disrupt his concentration.

"I suppose you want me to find a skull?" His voice was oddly detached and calm, a far cry from his usual querulous crackle.

"No. No point. It was a good plan to start with, but if the oseovox could be found that way, one of you would have found it by now. If it exists anywhere, it's hidden from mirrors. That's what I would do, if I had one."

"What am I looking for then?"

"Words. Words on walls."

The image flickered. From a higher angle, they could read the words scrawled across the tavern's façade:

A great reckoning in a little room

"Yes! Writing like that. Keep searching."

Taking a pen, inkwell, and fistful of crumpled foolscap out of her satchel, she sat at the bar. Osylum flashed by in the mirror, street after street, ruin after ruin, ward after ward. Furiously, she scribbled every snatch of graffiti'd phrase as it flew by. Pages tumbled from the counter to the floor, ticking off hours.

"Why are we doing this?" Hendiatrix asked at last.

"I'm trying to find a pattern. And in the pattern understand a man."

"And who the man?"

"I don't know. Someone who's not the Lady and not a Warden or a want-to-be and not a piking cannibal. A fellow traveler, I hope. Maybe even a friend. I need to know more about him before I risk reaching out."

Hendiatrix had paused the reflection on a limestone mausoleum in the Sixth Ward. Black lichen obscured the family name. Corroded copper doors hung open on broken hinges. Written vertically on each post was the line of a couplet:

> *Yawn and yield your dead*
> *till death be utteréd*

"See?" Oneirotheria said. "There's an edge of sense to it. Every phrase fits its scene. The words are messages. Or they're trying to be, anyway."

"To whom? From who?"

"Upstart. And before you ask, I don't know who that is. Hecate did though. And maybe Marrigan and maybe a hundred other witches. Or maybe only those two. He's who we're—"

A strange oblong shadow rippled over the tomb. It moved swiftly past. Oneirotheria surged across the bar, pointing.

"What was that? Can you find a view of the sky?"

Gravestones and statues jumped around the image. A few times the same shadow flowed over the scene. By the time Hendiatrix found a puddle showing the sky, though, there was only the same unbroken expanse of slate grey as always. He returned his gaze to the ground but the shadow was gone.

"Somebody is flying," Oneirotheria said. "And here I thought the sky was mine."

"Should I keep trying to find them?"

"No. Go back to the words. I can find the trespassers myself if I need to."

The distraction stuck with her, though. As Hendiatrix sifted images of the Sixth, Seventh, and Eighth for graffiti, she only paid half-attention. Every errant shadow drew her eye.

Who could have been flying? How high were they? You can't tell unless you know how big they are, of course. It wasn't a bird, the shape had no wings. Oblong. The form itself didn't change except as the ground went up and down.

Birds know what men never learn.

The sky is the Tenth Ward.

Thirteen walls.

Who was up high without wings?

"You may want to see this."

She snapped back to herself. Ink puddled on the page, where she'd been resting the wet nib for who knows how long. The last note she'd taken read:

Who gives anything to poor Tom?

She realized the words had defaced a tombstone, over an open hole where an Abram-Man slept in the Sixth. She had not been on task for a long time.

"He's gone now."

In the bar mirror, a scaffold dangled on the side of a brick wall. It swayed as though brushed by a gentle breeze.

"He hopped off right as you looked up."

"Who?"

"Whoever did that," he pointed.

Still-drying paint dripped down the brick.

This town is full of cozenage

She jumped onto the bar, as if she could dive into the image and chase Upstart down.

"Get after him!"

In the pane of a street-lamp, they caught a glimpse of a man's back. Running with a furtive and waddling gait, he bolted down an alley. By the time Hendiatrix found a privy window with a view, the graffitist had already reached the other end. She could see his hands were black-spattered with ink and paint.

"Quick, quick," she hounded the Oblate.

"I'm doing what I can," he replied, an edge of pique creeping into his placid meditative tone. "There are not many reflections in the Ninth."

The scene shifted from warehouse to covered market to red-hued brothel front. They glimpsed the sole of a shoe here, the flutter of a doublet there. They never saw the full man. At last, they lost even the glimpses. With mounting frustration, Oneirotheria barked instructions, which Hendiatrix did his best to follow.

In the end, the image settled on an upwards slant of sewer pipes and browning sky, seen from a swiftly drying puddle.

"Pig-swiver!" Oneirotheria shouted. She threw fistfuls of paper at the glass.

"Shall I let the reflection go?"

"Might as—"

A plain and balding man with a wispy beard and mustache peeked into frame, upside down. He must have been leaning over the empty river's edge. He winked.

"Oh, you vile..." She trailed off, her vocabulary failing her for once.

With the seriousness of a bureaucrat producing sacred forms, he held a piece of ragged paper over the puddle.

We will meet

"Where and when?" she demanded, lips exaggerated around each sound.

"He can't see you," Hendiatrix said. "I don't know how he knows you're watching."

Upstart dropped the sheaf. He tapped his nose with an inky digit. He produced another and another and another.

and there we may rehearse
most obscenely and courageously.
Take pains.
Be perfect.
Adieu.

With that, he was gone. The mirror showed only gummy clay and a vacant sky.

46

O neirotheria lay on her back. She brooded at the pub ceiling. The water-stained plaster refused to yield any secrets. She'd been staring at it for hours and the amorphous blobs would not cohere into any sensible shape.

"Why aren't we going to the Ninth?" Hendiatrix asked; not for the first time. "You found the man you wanted to find."

"Did I? Or did he find me?"

It was not the first time she'd given that answer either.

"What difference does that make?"

"It's the difference between me finding him for my plan and him using me for his."

"As long as you get what you want, why fight? Why lay around doing nothing while Wardens and who knows what else hunts us down?"

"I'm not doing nothing. I'm thinking."

Hendiatrix grumbled something unintelligible. He lapsed into silence. She continued the conversation in her mind.

Why not run to him?

I—Hecate—whoever—trusted him once. Pieces of my memories tell me I should seek him out. He's never done me any harm. Turnspade died to save

me. If a puppet can die. And Ragpatch too. Wailen-
weave. All of them helped me at the ultimate cost.

Except for Tosspot.

Who can hold the master to account for a drunk-
en lackey?

So why hesitate?

Because in a barking mad city that refuses to
make sense, he *makes sense. And that can't be*
right.

It can't be wrong.

Because he lives in the Ninth Ward and every-
one I ask says nothing there is what it seems.

Is anything anywhere what it seems?

Because his words are always waiting for me,
like he knows where I am going to be before I
decide to go.

Like a puppet.

I'm not a puppet.

Am I?

She brushed her wrists and ankles, feeling for invisible strings.

This is getting silly.

"Alright, Hen. Let's go."

He did not reply.

She sat up.

She was alone. Even as she checked the other side of the bar, she knew he'd gone into the Reflected. She could not blame him. She did not bother trying to call him back. She touched the glass farewell.

"I hope you find sanctuary, old man. You deserve it. No matter what you think."

She gathered up her things. Leaving the door blocked by tables and chairs, she went upstairs. She scratched a chip of black paint off the corner of a window pane; just enough for one eye to peek through.

Night had fallen while she brooded. Too dark to safely fly; the magpie was a day bird.

Wisps of mist trailed through the straying streets. Thin yellow-gray brume wound round the posts of street lamps. One at a time, the lights went out, extinguished by fingers of fog. She had never anything like it.

Except for the Lady's Ward.

The same vapors filled the gate between the Second and the First. She pictured the magpie's view. The same yellow-gray haze roiled over the whole central Ward; the glazed blind iris of Osylum's single eye.

The Lady's Fog. Eschatos really did it. Maybe it's the end of the world and maybe not. Don't need to toss bones to know this bodes ill. Still. Needs must when the Lady goes mad.

The upper room's chimney was narrow enough to brace and wide enough to climb. By the time the soot-stained witch reached the roof, the mist had thickened. It filled the streets around her, flowing across the city from the upper Wards to the lower. Here and there, stubborn lamps sputtered, casting yellow haloes. She crouched atop the building—its rooftop now an island in a sea of fog.

Is this because of me? It will make it hard to travel by reflection. Do the Wardens know that's how we were jumping around? Did they get impatient while I was dithering? Oh, Hen, hope it stays outdoors. Hope you are safe.

A scream tore through the streets. Someone had taken advantage of the haze to do something terrible to someone else. A clear space opened just beneath her. She flattened herself. At the center of the cylindrical gap, a Warden floated impassively. It moved directly towards the shrieks. She lost sight of it quickly in the whorls of fog. The smell of nothingness wafted across the dank miasma. The Lady's justice had been done.

In the Fifth Ward, buildings clustered close. She crawled along, stepping easily between them. Even without landmarks, she had a general sense of topography. The Ninth was downhill, so she moved that direction as best she could make out.

Sick sounds rose from the shrouded streets. Crunches, grunts, squeals, gibbers, prayers, wails, cackles...

Eschatos had squealed 'rule-breaker, rule-breaker' to every Warden in town. The Lady spewed her fog from the First Ward over the whole prison. Now Osylum's worst inmates ran amok because of it. Oneirotheria pushed the noises aside. Whatever was happening, she could not do anything about it except press on her own mission.

She reached the wall between Wards. Unfortunately, while a house on her side leaned hard against it, no structure was within sight on the other. She couldn't even tell whether it was the right Ward or not. She drew Turnspade's map in her mind.

It's Two, Three, Four, Six, Eight, or Nine. Any Ward except One and Seven. I do not like those odds. Fly away, fly away, wait for day. No. Too late for that. Pit pat, that's that. My, my cobblestone pie. Down you go, into the dark. All's well that end's hell.

She swung her legs over the edge. Her bare feet felt for gaps and outcrops. The walls between

Wards were not maintained—at least not like the smooth, implacable barrier holding back the nothing at the edge of town. It was tense going until her feet touched dirt.

A woman appeared, fleeing out of the mist. Her hair frizzed wild and her eyes burst with terror. She blundered straight into Oneirotheria, knocking her on her haunches. Before the witch could react, wide, fluttering trumpet sleeves reached out from behind the panicked woman. They grappled her shoulders. Animated by eldritch strength, an empty billowing dress halted the stranger's frenzied flight.

"Lady help me!" she cried.

Oneirotheria kindled a witchwick. Not quick enough. The resplendent gown yanked the woman out of sight. Crunches, screams, rips, snaps preceded a terrible silence.

The murderous costume re-appeared, continuing its insatiable search for living flesh. This time, it met a blue blast of fire from Oneirotheria's palm. The fabric dissolved in smoke. The skeletal farthingale continued unclad towards the witch for another heartbeat. The witchflame licked away the brittle twine that held the dry old hoops together. The sinister sartorial contraption sprung apart. It rattled harmless to the dirt.

Farthingale, Oneirotheria's oddly calm mind chanted. *From vertugado, which means green or supple wood. Although verdugo means executioner. And not at all related to vertigo. Lady, how this night spins.*

She sat very still. She pressed feet and hands to the earth, to add feel to sound as she tried to suss out her surroundings. Bootfalls receded, perhaps a block away—iron-nailed heels by the sound of them, on boards. A rhythmic whuff-whuff passed by, above the wall to her back, moving high and fast. She heard no further hue and cry. She risked the light of a moonflower. Nothing cruel was drawn to it.

Sound and fury, strut and fret, Wailenweave sang in her memory.

Keeping low, she scurried away from the wall.

She came to a series of lean-to shacks, barely holding themselves erect. She knew she wasn't in the Second, Third, or Fourth—the driftwood construction and the packed-clay streets told her as much. Ten paces later, she hadn't seen a grave-stone or tree, which ruled out the Sixth and Eighth.

Nine, then. So far so good.
Except for whoever that was at the wall.
Not so good for her.

47

Time became impossible to track. Even the beat of her heart danced too irregularly to tick by any sense of seconds. She saw no Wardens, though a time or two she smelt the new-made nothingness of their Fade. She snuck along on light feet. She cupped the moonflower, shielding its light except when absolutely necessary. The mist had a very slight pale glow to it—enough to contrast with buildings. And reveal outlines of unidentifiable things, skulking in the night.

After a while, she embraced the suppression and distortion of her usual senses. It became exhilarating. Familiarity scrambled, she unlocked new ways to take in the world. Instincts she had not known she possessed fed her information. Every part of her mind worked at full capacity, at its fastest speed, processing the madness.

She had not felt so awake since she first stepped from the dingy city into the Linnaea's resplendent home. She was suffused once more by that same sense: everything prior to that moment had been a poor stage copy. The lunatic upending of all order ripped a veil from her face.

Behind it she found a newer, truer world.

At the end of an alley, she came to a door. An

archway made of crossed ivory tusks framed it. She turned the iron knob, shaped like a weeping face. The hinges whined. The alley walls ended at the gate. A subtle shift in sound suggested a wide open expanse beyond. At the threshold, mucky ground gave way to warped boards. She stepped through, shut the door behind her, and wandered through the featureless fog.

Here-now. If I had a blank page, it would be an excellent map.

A new claggy odor clung to her lungs. She coughed. The stubborn miasma—tasting of mud and rotting fish—would not be dislodged. She hacked harder. The mist dissipated before the force of her breath. Torches flared in a ring. She stood at one edge of a wide circular expanse. Over-turned booths and tables littered the board-walk—a market fair abruptly overrun by vandals.

Across from her, the haze split in two. Like a curtain tugged open by weak or careless stage-hands, grey fabric jerked left and right. Beyond, hulked a creature four times her height. Its head—fully a third of its total size—was an enormous tragedian's mask. Its body was a crude wooden carving, sketching the barest minimum of a bipedal form. Its hands, large as the head, were made of plastered lathe. Even at the distance, she could see blood and skin and ragged bits of flesh on the palms.

"I wouldn't if I were you," she called across to the thing. "Find another bird to smash, Handsy-man."

Gasps rose around her. The misty perimeter congealed into dozens of blurred faces. An audience leaned forward. Tense expectation rippled across the phantasmal crowd.

The Handsy-man advanced with a limping shuffle. He pounded his mask with his palms. A dreadful booming thrum filled the air. It vibrated the boards beneath Oneirotheria's feet.

"Stop that. It tickles," she quipped.

"HAVE YOU PRAYED TONIGHT?" he bellowed.

She laughed.

In fury, he smashed a fishwife's booth. "DO IT AND BE BRIEF!"

The ectoplasmic audience wailed. They begged mercy on her behalf. All she could do was continue to laugh.

"THINK ON THY SINS!" He picked up a table and flung it just over her head.

"Sins? Now *there's* a word I do not know. Did you make that up just now?"

The giant tragic figure beat the boardwalk in a tantrum of grief and jealous rage.

Oneirotheria reached into her pouch. She wasn't sure the fire-fennel would do the trick. She'd hope to use the last dose on Eschatos anyway. Her fingers closed on a small poppet-like form.

Bryony root.

While the Handsy-man soliloquized about her transgressions, she riffled through her brain for the correct incantation. He reached the crescendo of his litany. The audience grabbed one another and wept and cried out to the puppet to spare her.

"Mindless as a plant, shape of a maid, take my place and I'll be away."

The root swelled. In a blink, the witch's vacuous duplicate dropped to her knees in front of the raging tragedian. She clasped her hands. In mime, she begged for a minute more of life.

Having worked himself up to sanctimonious murder, the Handsy-man charged. He seized the homunculus between his hands. He choked and crushed her. Paste, like mashed potato, squirted through his fingers. The bryony root perished in appropriate dramatic fashion. The audience erupted in applause.

The real Oneirotheria, safe across the opening, flicked them an apotrope.

"Idiots," she muttered and stepped back into the shadows.

She soon reached a bridge. It stretched over an empty river. Below, fetid vapors seethed. The wooden sign that had arched over the entrance had been shattered. It lay in individual letters, scattered around. She assembled them on the ground.

HERE NOW

A sour wind gusted by. The boards rippled and shifted until they read:

NOWHERE

"Semi-clever," she said to whoever was responsible.

She was losing patience with the illusions. Someone was having a laugh, likely at her expense. She grabbed the boards one at a time and sailed the letters over the railing. As the last one hit far below, a thunderous clamor arose. Alarums and cries sounded up and down the river's edge. Blind armies clashed, just out of sight.

The fray hemmed her in, forcing her onto the bridge. Its planks creaked dubiously. The magpie stirred at the thought of the unknown drop beneath those frail supports.

Shush now. Not yet. Flying into the night and fog is a sure way to end up tangled in a net.

One careful step at a time, she made her way along the span. The hideous cacophony of war pursued her. She ignored it. The fight had nothing to do with her. The bridge swayed and dipped under dozens of feet. She pushed on, trying to cross the bridge before the stampede of soldiers brought it down around her.

A suit of armor staggered out of the night. A crown was inset in the helmet and the tabard bore the royal arms of some forgotten line. The gauntlet was welded to a bloody sword. The visor flipped open. Only shadows filled the metal skin.

The misty audience formed again in galleries around the bridge.

"Enough!" Oneirotheria shouted.

A host loomed behind the king. He raised his blade, about to begin an exhortation to his troops. The witch was having none of it. Acknowledging neither the soldiers nor the leering spectators, she flung her birnam twig over her left shoulder.

"Bind them all in thorn and vine."

A hundred-year bramble exploded into being. It seized the king, his army, the usurper, and his men. The pointless conflict ceased, tangled in a wild hedge. Like air-bladders pricked with pins, the history behind her deflated. The audience's mishappen faces fell and melted into clouds.

"You're wasting good effort," Oneirotheria called to the night. "Find another leading lady to drag your drama out."

There was no reply.

"Yours to waste," she said and pressed on into the madness.

At the far end of the bridge, she emerged into clear air. It was the liminal hour, between light and dark. Night-lanterns still danced up and down the boardwalk on this bank. Docks jutted over the muck. Warehouses and boatsheds clustered along the shoreline. The Lady's Fog had not reached the far end of the Ninth Ward yet.

A hacking cough rattled across the pre-dawn. A grey smudge hobbled along the river-side road; a beggar, wrapped in festering bandages. He paused every so often to spasm with more coughing. No other sign of life disturbed the scene, so it was to him Oneirotheria went.

48

The lazar hunched over the boardwalk railing. A crooked crutch leaned against the railing next to him. He squinted across the river at the fog with jaundiced eyes. A doctor's panoply of pustules covered his skin—dry grey sores, oozing yellow sores, crusted green sores, scabbed-over scarlet sores, the pinkish patches of near-healed sores, wounds in every shade and texture of necrotizing flesh. Strips of mottled linen wound round most of his body. They were his only clothes.

A brutal rattle seized his lungs. He expelled an implausible volume of phlegm into the dry channel below. Wiping his chin, he pointed at the seething brume.

"It'll be here soon. And then—" he coughed again.

"Pigeonfoot, I presume," Oneirotheria said, guessing by process of elimination.

"Aye. You've heard Tosspot's song, I take it."

"Do you know who I am?"

"Do *you* know who you are?" the beggar riposted.

"Mostly."

"Mostly's never good enough. Oh well. It doesn't matter."

"It matters to me."

"How can you know what matters to you, if you don't know who you are?"

"Maybe we are what matters to us."

"May—" Pigeonfoot convulsed with another fit. Between paroxysms he tried to finish the sentence. She could not piece together his hacked-up syllables. After a long minute, he tamed his breath by beating his chest.

"Heh-heh-hanyway, this ma-hatter wi-hill be de-heh-head soo-hoon."

"Can I help? I might have a cure."

"Hoh-oh, it's not the sickness that'll kill me," he replied. "Plague is who I am. My part in the pla-hay."

"What will kill you then?"

He plucked out a blackened fingernail and flicked it at the fog. "The Lady's Breath."

"It looks like it's stopped."

"Not stopped. Slowed. I've been watching it since the witching hour." He pointed with his crutch. "Look. There. Creeping on little magpie feet."

She watched. She could not tell whether the mist was moving closer or merely seething in place. It might even be retreating. She decided it didn't matter. Slow as it must be moving (if it were moving) she would find Upstart long before it made it across the river.

"Never mind it. Let's go. Take me to your boss."

Pigeonfoot did not move.

"Don't worry," she said. "Even if it does get here, it's not lethal. Stick with me and I'll keep you safe."

"Turnspade," he replied. He shoved himself back from the railing. He caught the crutch under his arm. "Wailenweave. And the less said about Ragpatch, the better."

He limped down the plank road with startling alacrity.

"I loved her," he said. "I think. If a poxy beggar can love. Can I love? They say sickness cannot kill love. They also say love is a sickness that kills. I don't know how that logics out."

Oneirotheria jogged to catch him. "Are you taking me to Upstart?"

"You always asked too many questions."

"Is there a better way to learn?"

"Learning's a hard boil waiting to be lanced. We're just here till we shuffle off. And it's not much fun before then."

"You're a delight."

He coughed and spat and continued hobbling down the riverside. She persisted.

"Upstart? He's on this bank, right? Not back there in the mist?"

"Yes, yes. Here, there, anywhere he pleases. Won't help. Too late now. Die quietly, I say. There's dignity in that. Ha!"

The diseased beggar's relentless nihilism failed to put her off. She approached from a different direction, jumping topics to knock him off guard.

"What do you mean you loved Ragpatch?"

He was not phased. "You and Upstart know what words mean. I just use them."

"Tell me about the two of you."

He stopped. "You're asking about me?"

"Yes."

"None of you ever did that before."

"Maybe I'm not one of me."

He laughed again, this time without a bitter

hack. He resumed walking at a less breathless pace.

"I was less sick then. A small itch in my throat and a pimple or two. She and I played clowns and common folk. The fleshy stories under the grand soulmate romances of Wailenweave and her leading men. Sex and dirty double entendres. The kind of thing the groundlings could see themselves in. The balcony crowd too, though they'd deny it."

"So after acting together long enough, you fell in love?"

"We all become the parts we play. If the Lady lived in a chicken-legged hut, she'd be a witch."

She thought about the way Philotech looked when he looked at Matron. It did not feel like he was playing a part. Even dressed-up Eschatos, with his sick, possessive love of the Lady, was at least sincere about it. She twisted her lips skeptically.

"You think love is just an actor's trick?"

"You tell me. You loved someone once. And now here you are. Different face and you don't even know the way to his door."

She had not expected that. Knocked off kilter, she stammered to silence. He went on in a broken tone.

"You're here. Asking me questions, alive as can be. While *my* love is faded. There won't be another for me. All to teach you a lesson you had learned over and over. Why couldn't you remember?"

Tears streaked his mottled cheeks.

"What do you mean?"

"Upstart sent her. 'I fear Hecate failed to skip the stones of her mind past the gap of death,' he said. 'Whoever she is now must learn of the Fade and must learn it in a way that brands it on her soul. Else she'll stumble into it and all will crumble to nought.'"

"You're saying I only met Ragpatch so she would goad the Wardens into destroying her so I could learn about the Fade?"

"Aye. Ragpatch. Lovely, capering, soft, solid, yielding, delightful Ragpatch leapt up and volunteered. He wrote the script, she learned the lines. You meet her, she shakes the scene, you discover oblivion's the enemy. She vanishes forever from Osylum and I get sicker and sicker waiting for death that refuses to come."

"I am sorry. I did not know."

He plucked at his bandages. "It was she who gave me these. 'You'll need them, dear,' she said, kissing me on the head, 'with no one to soothe the sickness in your heart and keep it at bay.'"

"Why would she do that? Volunteer, I mean. To be faded."

"Because we're all pigeons, plucked and stuck to the bottom of the city's foot to draw out the plague."

"You mean the Lady?"

He stopped again. He pointed at a building with his crutch. "We're here."

Oneirotheria had been so absorbed in the beggar's sad tale, she had not noticed they had left the boardwalk. She could still smell the fishy mud—they had not gone far. They stood midway down a narrow street labeled 'Maiden Lane'.

A round three-story theatre, forty paces across, rose in front of them. Fourteen flagpoles crowned the roof, their threadbare pennants hanging slack. Each of them only showed a slice of the same emblem, which she could re-assemble in her mind; a muscled man bent under the burden of a globe on his shoulders. The same sigil appeared in carvings and barely-visible frescos around the façade. Three squat double-doors were sunk in alcoves along the front.

"Here we are, off we go. So little time, so much to know."

Pigeonfoot's crutch thwapped across her midriff.

"Not that way. The theatres have all been shut a long time. Pestilence, the official explanation."

He made the apotrope. She investigated the doors. Sure enough, the Lady's Eye marked all of them—multiple times on every threshold. She had never seen so many Fade-marks on a single place.

She really wanted you closed for good.

"How are we supposed to get in?"

He led her down a side alley. Near the back of the theatre, a door, above which read 'ACTORS ONLIE', stood propped open with a brick. She could see the two halves of the Eye, split between door and post.

"We lost a perfectly good ticket-taker getting that open," Pigeonfoot said. "Don't kick the doorstop loose or the seal will reform. And we haven't got another Grubgelt to spare."

She walked as far around the wedged-in brick as possible. The air did not smell of a recent Fade, at least.

"Here now," the beggar said and hobbled inside.

49

He led her down a ill-lit hall, barely wide enough for one person. It curved around the outer edge of the theatre. Doorways opened at regular intervals to her right. Every room stood empty, save for rows of hanging racks. Here and there, broken marionette crossbars dangled frayed strings from the racks.

They were all filled once. Let's think like the Linnaea. Every rack can hold six puppets, five racks per room... How many rooms have I passed?

"There were hundreds of us once," Pigeonfoot said, as if hearing her thoughts. "Now there are three."

"Did they all—was it other versions of me who caused—did Upstart—" She struggled to phrase a question whose answer she was not sure she wanted.

"I could tell you every story of every loss in this place. But that would take too much time and be a waste. Quick now. Up."

He stepped into the last storage room in the hall. He motioned for her to pass on to a steep, irregular staircase. Warped steps creaked underfoot. She glanced back. The beggar did not follow.

"As high as you can go. Through the curtained

arch."

He spun awkwardly. He crutch-clomped away down the hall. Alone, she coiled around the building's circumference, still mulling the notion of hundreds of lost marionettes.

My short life cost three. Turnspade, Wailen-weave, and poor Ragpatch. If there were hundreds, how many of me does that mean?

Hundreds plural sets the bounds between two and nine hundred. At three per me, that's... many. I wonder if the twins have a machine to count this high? Had a machine. If they did it's probably halfway through a Ratkipper's gut-road by now. The Oblates knew how to reckon big numbers. Picture stones in your head. One... two.. three.. many.

That's not helpful.

Hecate was old they tell me. Perhaps she needed more than three of Upstart's puppets. And I don't know much about Marrigan. So I can't assume three is a normal number.

How many of me were there?

It doesn't matter. They weren't me, those others. Not all the way. I have some of Hecate's words and memories. So what? Doesn't everyone have other people's words in their heads, coming out their mouths? If we were the same as those whose words we used, no one would be anyone. Or everyone would be everyone else.

And the puppets? Do they have Upstart's words or do they use their own?

Are any of them anyone at all? Or—here-now!

Her speculations ceased as she reached the top of the stairs. A servants' door—hidden on the other side—opened onto another hall. Candles burned steady in gilt sconces. Polished paneling doubled their light. Gauze sachets dangled from the sconces. They exuded the smell of cloves, dried roses, and mint. It was the richest space she'd seen since the Laboratory and utterly out of place.

She passed seven locked mahogany doors down the arc of the corridor before she came to the curtain; blue as a Warden's robes and velvet so plush it could make a mattress by itself. The feel as it brushed her skin was the most sensual experience of her life.

On the other side, she found a private balcony, three stories above ground level. Thick silk carpet caressed her bare feet. A single high-backed chair faced center stage; ebony frame and ivory silk upholstery. She sat. It fit her as if the chair wright had measured every line and angle of her body.

There was a curious silence—as profound, she imagined, as the silence before the world came into being.

Did the world come into being? How? Nothing will come of nothing.

Peace, witch. Be where you are.

While she waited for whatever would come next, she took in Upstart's theatre.

Light came in through a large circular hole in the center of the roof—perhaps half the total footprint of the building lay open to the sky. A shimmer betrayed that it was not *entirely* open. A fine mesh had been strung across it. Tiny coins of polished steel were sewn into the net. She could imagine at night, with lanterns lit below, they would sparkle like stars.

Stars. Is this where that word comes from? Are

all the words I know that aren't found in Osylum nothing more than a playwright's creation?

Shush. Wits sharp. That mesh may pretend to be the sky, but it'll trap a magpie well enough I reckon.

She turned her attention downward. Three quarters of the building was given over for a now-absent audience. Balconies like hers ringed the uppermost floor, each as richly appointed. Beneath that, stadium seating stair-stepped from the second to first floors. A semi-circle of packed nutshells and dirt provided standing room.

A raked stage thrust out into the groundling zone. It was built of well-fitted boards, buffed to a crisp shine. A black curtain, embroidered with the silver sigil of the man carrying the globe, cut the stage in half. It hid the remainder of the house.

Hushed voices and muffled footfalls from backstage broke the silence. The curtain luffed. A plain and balding man stepped out. He gazed across the empty seats. As though the house were full, he waited for imaginary applause to die down. He raised one hand. He puffed out his chest. In a voice that shook the rafters, he declaimed:

"O for a muse of fire that would ascend the brightest heaven of invention!"

Oneirotheria could contain herself no longer. Peals of laughter rained down on the actor. The officious little man put his hands on his hips.

"Do you mind? It's a history with tragical elements! Battles and bloodshed, witch! I'm setting a mood here."

She giggled. He glared which only made her giggle more.

"I'm sorry," she eventually managed to say. "It's

271

just... it's all so overdone. Monsters in the fog?
Armies of shadows and a king without a head? The
poor gloomy beggar going on and on and on about
his misery and suffering to stoke my guilt?"

"Oi!" Pigeonfoot cried from backstage.

"You did go on!" she said. "On and on."

A slurred voice came from between the first and
second row of seats. "Told you she's too canny,
captain."

Tosspot poked his head up. He winked a
bloodshot eye at Oneirotheria. She wished she
had something of middling hardness to throw at
him—she'd not forgiven him for locking her in the
pub basement.

"I will drown you in a butt of malmsey," Upstart
threatened the drunk. Tosspot merely shrugged.

Pigeonfoot leaned out through the curtain
crack. "Will you need me for the second act, if
she's seen through the thing? I could use sleep. It
was a long night waiting by the river and sucking
up that cold air."

He coughed consumptively to illustrate the
point.

Upstart waved him off. The playwright pulled a
put-upon face. "So, dearest witch, what gave us
away? For professional improvement, if nothing
else."

"What's the one thing everyone says about the
Ninth Ward?"

"The river was beer till the players fell in and
drank it dry!" Tosspot shouted.

Upstart flung an inkwell at him.

"Go join your idiot friend, swine-swiver."

"Aye-aye, skipper!" The drunk lurched across
the perfectly level floor as though it were a ship's

deck, tossing in a nightmare squall.

"I'm sorry," Upstart said to Oneirotheria. "A playwright can't pick his cast any more than the Lady can pick her people. It doesn't matter. What *is* the one thing everyone says about the Ninth Ward?"

"The one thing everyone says is that nothing," Oneirotheria said, hopping onto the balcony rail, "is what it seems."

As she dove into magpie form, a ripple of reality rolled across the theatre. The splendid furnishings disintegrated. Soot-smudged ruin replaced the illusion. The bird landed on the scuffed and filthy stage, backed by a patch-and-tatter curtain. She shook off the feathers and stood in woman's skin.

Upstart dropped to the edge of the boards. His feet dangled over the groundling pit. His illusions dispelled, he stared at the wreckage of his home. His shoulders slumped, as though he had carried the globe of the world for ages untold and was beyond weary of the burden.

"It wasn't always this way, you know."

"I don't know," she replied. "Tell me how it used to be."

50

I'll start in the middle, *the Player-King told the witch*, because the middle is where I started. And I'll be brief because the end is almost here. By the time I woke in a puddle of ink, the Nothing around walls was there. The Wardens patrolled the town and the Lady, it was said, ruled from the top of her hill.

The Ninth Ward was still full. The whole prison was full. So many prisoners, who would notice one or two disappearing for good? No one feared the Fade. And the Lady was just a far-off word. We jostled each other and made a life as though everything would always be the way it was. As though everything was as it should be.

The people demanded entertainment. I set nib to sheet and scribbled plays. I cast actors. We did very well for ourselves; packed houses and private masques. I discovered a power in my words. The world remade itself in my images, at least for the span of a few scenes. It was headier than sack and sugar and a midnight tumble.

How did you do it?

I do not know, any more than I know how I turn air into fire and fire into life in my frame. Same with any good magic—you can do it or you can know how it's done. I've never met a wizard yet who could manage both.

When I wasn't working, I wandered the Wards. You have to watch the world close and often to capture it in a theatre ring. I saw the emptiness pressing against the walls. I saw the same void in the Wardens' third eye when one of the quire-birds transgressed the rules of our collective cage. And then, as you've seen, there was a hole where once a man had been.

More than nothingness troubled me. As unsettling was a fullness, unaccounted for. Books, paintings, statues... they spoke of things that did not exist around us. Words for things not found in Osylum town—

—the sun, the moon, the stars!

Aye. And a dozen hundred other things that only poets and Abram-men canted about. Where had the river gone? Where were history and ships from distant lands and the faces in cathedral glass? Where did that man go, who flouted the Wardens and vanished under the Fade?

Nothing was as it should be.

I hid dark speculations in my heart. Made a mask—made scores of masks—to wear in front of my thoughts. I saw what happened to those who spoke too freely about such things. The crowd got thinner under my stage. The plays went on all the same.

One of my friends died. It was a tavern brawl in an upper room. Some stupid thing over the bill. He took a knife to the eye. Three days later, I found a man wearing his coat and making the same gestures he used to make. He had a different face. I fell on his shoulder all the same and kissed his cheek.

He did not remember me.

That is how I learned that death—just death, not the Fade—was no escape from Osylum.

I watched even more closely, as I danced around the town like a fool. People died. People were found. No one remembered things from before. And the crowds got even thinner as the years and the Fade ground us down. Who could live over and over and not break one of the Warden's rules in any life?

I despaired.

My work descended into darkness. Nothingness seeped into every line I wrote. Nothing became my only theme, my obsession. Nothing hounded my heroes and nothing consumed their love. Nothing and nothing and more nothing.

The crowds went elsewhere. Who would pay for that kind of entertainment?

I went to the outer wall. I looked into the vacuum.

"You will come for us all," I said to it. "So I will come for you first."

I drew a rapier. Melodramatic, I know, but we are what we are. I flourished. I challenged the void that would come for us all.

"Have at thee!" I cried and prepared to hurl myself into the end.

My bones turned to water. The water froze. The ice within me cracked and splintered as my body turned, against my will, away from the dark. An eagle landed on the wall. In three steps, she was a woman; gap-toothed, hook-nosed, clad in the savage beauty of strong old age.

Marrigan!

Not yet. She—you—bore the name Louhi then. *Louhi.*

Aye. And she would not let me step into the dark. Instead, she spoke a word I had only thought, and then only dared to think late at night when the city was pitch black and smothered in sleep.

Escape.

So you remember that much.

It's why I'm here.

And escape is why she came to me then.

What was she like?

Powerful. Brilliant. Cruel sometimes, if I'm honest. She was the first Osylum witch I ever met. I'd made three of them for a tragedy once but they were paltry toys compared to her.

She, like me, had watched the city for a long time. She had worked out the sums, tallied the words and phrases, weighed everyone in her balance and found the whole prison wanting. Unlike me, nothingness had not wormed into her heart and laid its foul eggs. She was so much stronger than me.

She shared some of that strength. We plotted and planned. If we were in a prison, she argued, that meant there had to be a world that was free. And if books spoke of history, there had to be a time before the Lady and her Wardens. What was, might be again.

So why didn't you escape back then?

We ran out of time. One day Louhi found a golden egg in the mouth of a cathedral gargoyle. Three days later, she was gone and a bright new witch named Gullveig blazed in her place. I went to her as soon as I heard. Foolishly, as it turned out.

That's when I learned that, wise and powerful as she had been, Louhi could not fight the forgetting that comes between death and the next life. I prattled our plans like an idiot to Gullveig, but, newling as she was, she didn't know enough to keep them secret. The Wardens found out.

Wait—they faded her? How could she be me then?

They didn't fade her. When they came, she burned half of the Third Ward to cinders and disappeared into the ash. I never saw her again. I was too busy running myself.

The puppets.

Aye. I split myself into a hundred selves and made those selves nothing more than objects. The Wardens wouldn't pay any attention to a marionette hanging in an empty theatre. I—we—cleared our minds of thought. We waited without awareness in the storage rooms of this place.

Until?

Until another incarnation of the witch would figure out what I—what we—really were. It was a gamble thrown with desperate hope. By the time it paid off, we found the city much as you see it now. So many lost to the Fade. And all those caught in the cycle of life and death remembered nothing of what came before. The world had changed and only we knew it.

Marrigan found you?

Aye. And woke us up. Though she did not know what she had found. She was... adversarial. We circled one another through the straying streets for a long time before she accepted that the Canting Crew might be of some use as a tool in her plan.

By then, her crow's egg had appeared and Hecate was on the way.

Hecate lived a very long time. Long enough to realize she would never have enough time to pull off a successful escape—unless she could hold onto her memories across the gap of death. And, with our help, she found a way.

Or so we thought.

She got partway there.

So I've gathered. But do you remember enough?

I remember the oseovox. That it comes from the time before all this. That it knows... something...

Yes! The oseovox! The skull that speaks of the time before the Lady and the Wardens and the endless, inescapable void. He's the key to the whole thing, Hecate said. Did that knowledge survive?

No! I don't know why *the oseovox matters! How is it supposed to help?*

Why don't you ask him yourself?

51

Upstart loosed a rope, tied to a cleat beneath the stage. It slithered into the air. The ragged curtain behind them fell like a dropped sail. A skull nestled on a lectern, centerstage.

"What's past is prologue," it cried, with the strange vowels of an age gone by. "What to come in yours and my discharge."

A surge of triumph yanked Oneirotheria off the boards and into the air. She flew three thrilled circuits of the theatre before landing on the lectern. She nuzzled her beak on the oseovox's occipital bone.

"Madam," Upstart said, joining the magpie and the skull, "perhaps a form better able to converse is in order."

The bird cocked her head. She whistled a thoughtful two-part tune, as if debating with herself. At length, she nodded and stepped off the platform as a woman.

"Apologies. From time to time, I fail to keep her in."

"A bagatelle," Upstart said with a graciously forgiving wave. "The Globe's a free place, I always say. For whatever you will."

Oneirotheria caressed the cranial dome. Her

fingers traced a trembling line along the mandible. A thread of silver wired the lower jaw to the temporal bone. It branched and spread from there, delicate as a spider's web. An intricate metallic pattern covered the whole neurocranium. The witch's eyes blurred with tears and a vision pressed on her brain; lips in a kind smile, deep insightful eyes, crow's-feet and mimic lines.

"I can see your face. How is that possible?"

She bent over the lectern and pressed her lips to the forehead. A welter of chaotic, unnamable feelings churned in her chest.

Upstart cleared his throat with delicate tact. "If I may ask, dear lady: do you remember what the plan for him was?"

"Oi!" Tosspot's cry interrupted her reply. Beet-faced and heaving with breath, he ran onto the stage. "Kippers coming!"

Upstart grabbed him by the lapels. "What? Where? How long have we got?"

"I was out returning my beer to the river when I spotted them crawling across the muck. Every sewer pipe and rathole birthed bedlam cannibals, far as I could see. They're hard on my heels. We're for the gullet, boss, like a hanging beef in a shop window."

"Cack!" the Player-King shouted to the sky.

He released his lackey. He placed a hand on Oneirotheria's forearm. "Don't go bird yet—that net is still up there, even if the stars need a polish."

She looked to the open roof and saw it was true. "Where to then?"

"Pigeonfoot!" Tosspot bellowed. "Arms! Arms now, damn your pusty hide!"

He stomped backstage. A clatter and

back-and-forth ensued. Meanwhile, a clamor rose down all three tunnels to the sealed front doors.

"We've a step and a half ahead," Upstart said. "Barely. Grab the boss and run behind me."

Oneirotheria picked up the oseovox. She almost dropped it. Though it looked empty, it was unexpectedly heavy; as if full of loose fine sand, shifting around unpredictably when she moved it.

Here now! What's—

The theatre doors boomed. They cracked and boomed again. She shoved curiosity hard to the side. She secured the skull in her satchel and exited stage right, chasing Upstart.

"Death already," she caught his mutter. "I wasn't close to done."

"Oh come on!" she shouted back. "Show a little spleen!"

"I'm sure the Ratkippers will be happy to help with that."

He looped a stage rope around his forearm. He motioned for Oneirotheria to wrap her arms round his neck. A poniard dropped from his doublet sleeve. With two slashes, he cut the cord free from its cleat. It whined through a pulley high above. A enormous weight crashed down, pulling them up to a catwalk. Oneirotheria leapt nimbly off the Player-King's back.

"Clever," she said.

"Thank Dedalus for that. Or whatever he's calling himself these days."

"Themselves. I think."

"What?"

"I'll explain later."

Below, Tosspot stumbled onto the stage. He bristled with an improbable number of pistols and rapiers. He pushed a small cannon. He craned his neck and saluted. Upstart produced a bottle by sleight of hand. He let it fall. With uncanny reflexes, the drunkard caught it.

"Oldcastle's Port!" the Player-King shouted. "Last bottle in existence, I think."

Tosspot toothed out the cork. He spat it into the groundling pit. He raised it in toast, to Oneirotheria and then to the pounding doors. He drained it to the lees in three gulps. He let out a heroic belch.

"Go!" he bellowed with the fury of a thousand soldiers at the breach.

Upstart led Oneirotheria along the catwalk to a small archway. She heard the theatre doors give way. Ratkippers cried out as their fellows were faded by the Lady's Eye. Eschatos ordered them forward with a nasty snarl.

Oneirotheria stopped. Upstart kept on for a few paces before he noticed. She reached into her pouch and moved back onto the catwalk.

"What are you doing?"

"I owe him fire," she said. "So do you."

"There's no time."

She ignored him. The sneer in Eschatos's tone as he bragged about torturing Wailenweave filled her memory. This time, he was not hidden in a sewer. No glass stood between them. She'd finish the job.

Pigeonfoot, blood-limned cutlass in hand, limped down the catwalk from the other side. He blocked her path back to the stage.

"You can have revenge," he said in a level, rational voice barely audible over the fray below. "Or you can escape. Not both."

An explosion from Tosspot's cannon drown out

her response. Ratkippers screamed Bones and flesh rattled and splattered on the wooden walls. Flames crackled as the seats caught fire. Acrid smoke filled the air. The mad cannibals, hounded on by Eschatos's voice, regrouped and pressed forward once more. Pigeonfoot looked over the catwalk's edge.

"There's too many for him. For any of us. You need to go and take the boss with you."

Oneirotheria knew he was right. It galled her to her core.

"Come on!" Upstart called. "It's now or nothing!"

"Fine!"

She spun on her heel. Tosspot's drunken laughter chased her up a spiral stair to the uppermost floor. She ground her teeth till the grinding blocked the sound of the drunken puppet's final party.

Upstart led her through another narrow corridor. Fire licked the floors below. He threw open a door. Once they were both inside, he slammed and barred it shut. He wedged a chair under the knob for good measure.

Oneirotheria quickly surveyed the cramped confines. No other door led out.

"We're trapped."

"Not quite."

He pointed to a clerestory window, haloed by broken glass. Red flickers and black smoke played across the plain grey sky.

"We can't fit through that."

"I can't. You can't. But a bird..."

"No. You're part of the plan. I'm not leaving you to die, Upstart."

"Haven't you figured it out? I'm surprised... you

are always so quick."

"What are you talking about."

"I'm not Upstart. I am but I'm not, if you read me."

"What? Make sense!"

He tapped the bulge in her satchel, formed by the skull. "He is me."

"I don't—"

"There was one part of my story that was absolutely true," the Player-King puppet said. "I—or rather, yon bone-box in your witch-bag—did make all of us from his imagination. We are such things as dreams are made on..."

Muffled from below, Pigeonfoot railed curses at Ratkippers. Steel clashed on bone. The blaze roared higher through the building.

"Go," earnest Upstart said. "We've all played our part here. It's taken worlds more improvisation than the boss expected, but you've been a delightful counterpoint to build a drama on."

"Drama?"

"In parts, at least. But you're right. Can't call the genre till the curtain's down." He winked and pointed at the roiling sky through the narrow window frame. "Make it a comedy, witch, with an ending no one will weep to see."

In a daze, she staggered back. An oblong shadow from outside wrinkled across the floor. The boards beneath her bare feet grew hot. Dimly, she was aware of Upstart crooning a bittersweet lullaby.

"When that I was and a little tiny boy, with a hey-ho the wind and the rain... a foolish thing was but a toy..."

The instinct for survival took control. The magpie winged up from her soul. She sailed out the window, catching one last glimpse of the smiling, weeping, singing marionette.

She flew into thick black smoke. The fire had spread from the theatre to the buildings around. Cinders scattered from roof to roof, faster than the Ratkippers could run, faster than the magpie could fly. The whole Ninth Ward below the river caught blaze. Her lungs burned. She strained to find clear high air. Beat after beat of her wings struck only noisome reek.

A black wall rushed out of the smoky sky. She hit it full on. She fell. With her last conscious effort, she released the magpie's form. Her head spun. Her stomach lurched. She pressed her face to a wicker floor and passed out.

52

A single black feather drifted across soot-streaked canvas. Blank-eyed and on her back, Oneirotheria traced its journey, as if its curving path might reveal some algebraic mystery. The errant plume crawled upwards. When it reached the edge, it suddenly flew away into empty sky. She sat bolt upright.

"Here-now!"

"Take care," Hendiatrix said. He pressed a cloth to her head and put her own hand over it to hold it. "You're bleeding. Just a scratch, but take care all the same."

Ratkippers screamed below. Whirlwinds of ash danced across the Ninth. Hot air rushed past, as if blasted from a furnace. She had not been unconscious long.

She sat in the bottom of a long, narrow wicker basket. Ropes connected the edges to a canvas balloon twice the size of the hull. The cloth stretched taut over a geometric frame, while the ropes ran through a dense network of pulleys to a central panel of levers and wheels. A hole in the bottom of the balloon opened over a steady blue flame. The fire roared out of a narrow tube atop a complex brass-and-glass contraption, next to the controls. Aft, a wooden wheel hung off the basket. It spun, driving the airship forward.

The Major hoisted a bag of sand over the edge, while the Minor eyed her with infantile calculation.

"Hendiatrix, toss one more ballast sack off starboard. That should accommodate our unexpected passenger."

"Yes, patron." The Oblate left her side and followed the order.

When she stood up, the basket swayed slightly. She carefully walked to the edge and leaned over. The Ninth Ward slipped by, a hundred feet below. The vantage felt odd in a human body.

She remembered the Laboratory door labeled 'Aeronauticia' and the room with the retracted ceiling. That explained the mystery of the Linnaea's escape.

"I like it," she said, patting the wicker frame. "Did you build it, or is it one of Dedalus's?"

The Linnaea returned to the control panel. The Major pulled a sequence of levers, while the Minor turned a dial on the fire-maker.

"It was one of Dedalus's conceptual projects, from an early escape plan. Before he realized the sky ended in the same void as the walls. I found the sketch and assembled it. I had to solve a few key problems of airflow. In engineering terms, the final product is a marked improvement over the original blueprints."

Despite their precise and formal demeanor, she could tell they were very proud of their invention.

"Well, I know flying and I think it's remarkable. Elegant and well-built."

They hid their smiles in busy-work over the controls.

Hendiatrix stood awkwardly in the stern. Leaving the Linnaea to piloting duty, she joined the monk. He avoided looking at her.

"You found your sanctuary," she said.

He nodded, still averting his eyes.

"Probably using that brass plate there, right? It looks shiny enough to step through."

His shoulders twitched midway between a shrug and a flinch.

"I found the graffiti artist," she said.

"Oh?" It was a remarkably noncommittal sound.

She threw her arms around him. He wailed in terror. She kissed his spotted tonsure and let him go. Red streaks spread from the spot of her kiss down to his cheeks.

"Silly old monk. I'm not going to do something horrible to you for leaving me in the pub."

"Hecate would've—"

"—Hecate was, by all accounts, a grumbling old bully. I get to be myself from time to time, no matter what she's stuck in my head."

"Thank you."

"You're welcome. Now," she said, raising her voice to include the Linnaea in the conversation, "where are we going and when we get there, will we have time to talk?"

"At the moment, we do not have a final destination. Hendiatrix insisted we pick you up when he saw you in the theatre."

"When he—how? The stars in the net! You dusty spy!"

He blushed scarlet.

"We needed everyone we could get," he mumbled. "What with the world ending and the Wardens gone mad."

"Yes. That."

"It seems my investigations into the nature of mirrors have prompted the Wardens to declare Fade against me."

Oneirotheria decided not to correct them; even though clearly the Lady's Fog and all the mad, murderous events of the past night had been in response to her own actions. Instead, she asked in her best innocent tone:

"Mirrors? Whatever for?"

They ignored the question. The wicker craft had reached an altitude above the fog. The Major threw a final switch. Vans on either side of the basket tilted up and down. It was difficult to tell with the featureless mist below, but she sensed the airship circled in place.

"Fuel," the Linnaea said, joining her and the monk, "is going to be a limiting factor. We will crash long before hydration or nutrition become an issue. Therefore, to expedite matters and forestall an unwanted plunge to the ground and resultant death or Fade, can we all agree that the time for cagey dishonesty and concealed motives has past?"

"I'm not worried about crashing," she said. She laughed and raised a mollifying hand. "Fine, fine. You're right. We've wasted enough time dancing around the truth and trying *not* to say things while still saying things. Everything in the open."

They waited.

"I'm to go first?"

They continued waiting.

"I suppose you are my host. Very well. You were studying mirrors. You were doing it because your goal—which is the same as my goal—is to escape."

"Correct. The absence of documented physical phenomena and the unnecessarily large scope of the city, along with a great many other data too involved to enumerate at present, strongly suggest the existence of alter‐ nate locations. Further, given the division of Osylum into Wards guarded by Wardens, I concluded that it was a prison. Having no recollection of any crime de‐ manding a life sentence, nor indeed any crime at all, I decided that escape was not only a good idea, but a moral imperative."

"I probably thought something along those lines. Apparently there have been a lot of me."

"Transmigration and amnesis?"

She split the words apart and assembled their meanings from their atoms. "Something like that. Everyone dies and then forgets and then comes back—not just me. Unless you're faded—OH!"

"Yes?"

"That's why the count! You were tracking the number of people and comparing deaths to new foundlings and subtracting Fades."

"Correct. That was one of the aforementioned collections of data that—"

"—by the way, I figured out why the Oblates went over by six." She frowned. "No. It's not im‐ portant right now. The point is, we're all trying to escape. And you figured out somehow mirrors are the key."

"I have only the beginnings of a theory. The barest nubbins of a framework of cogitation. My predecessor had a book, you see, of notes on the subject. I found it only recently, while researching something you had said during one of our nocturnal discussions. Unfortunately, the pertinent volume is now likely working its way through a Ratkipper's alimentary canal."

Despite having agreed to be open, old habits died hard. She turned away, shielding her satchel with her body. She opened it, winking at the oseovox. She pulled out Dedalus's ON MIRRORS and closed the satchel again. She held it up as she turned back around.

"You mean this?"

"HERE-NOW!" the Major and Minor shouted in unison. They snatched it from her hand.

"I couldn't figure it out," she said as they flipped through the contents. "I didn't have much time though, with all the running away."

"This, here, look," they said, pointing to a page filled with mathematical symbols. "I did not understand what this referred to, until Hendiatrix told me about the islands behind the mirrors and the Unreflected between them. Now it's all so clear!"

"Go on."

"Point one: The Reflected and Unreflected exist. Point two: The Unreflected is navigable. Point three, and this is the beauty in this equation here, as you see: The Reflected and Unreflected cannot contain Nothing."

She parsed the stacked negatives. "You mean that whatever is around the walls and over the sky, doesn't extend to behind mirrors?"

"Not only doesn't. Can't!"

"That means if you go far enough through the Unreflected you could find a Reflected Island not in Osylum."

"If any such exist, yes. There are some logistical diffi_culties of course."

"Swimming is hard work," Hendiatrix piped up.

"You have a boat," Oneirotheria said.

"I don't think the airship could be converted. The wicker—"

"—Not this thing!"

"Then wh—"

"—You've had one in your front room all this

time! What did you think it was there for? Decoration? A conversation piece?"

She made duck-faces with both hands, making them talk to one another in the voices of Major and Minor. "'Oh, nice skiff.' 'Thank you.' 'Do you ever take it out on the ocean?' 'Of course not, there isn't any such thing.' 'Then what do you have it for?' 'For conversations just like this one!'"

The scientists and monk just stared at her. She went on:

"Dedalus had it figured out. He knew you'd need a boat to cross the Unreflected. And he knew you'd have to train people to go through mirrors to get there. I wonder if Hecate led him to it or he got there himself? Probably a bit of both."

"Hec^ate?"

"Never mind. More important question: Why didn't Dedalus just go, if he had a boat and he had Oblates? What stopped him?"

"That is the second logistical challenge. The extent of the Unreflected is unknown. It may be incalculable, the equations are not clear. Moreover, even were it a finite space, without knowing so much as approximately where to go, the probability is overwhelming one will get lost. Hunger and thirst ensue and death."

"Then you're right back here in another body, without a clue."

"That may be the most optimistic scenario."

"Pike."

"Indeed. That, since we're all being forthright and open, is why I was so keen on having the Phrontistery find the oseovox. Dedalus hypothesized that its memories of the time before Osylum's isolation from the greater cosmos could be harnessed as a guide across the ocean between images."

Oneirotheria collapsed, wracked with laughter.

"I fail to see the joke. Without the oseovox, which the Oblates could not find, the Unreflected Vessel is simply one more death trap."

She could not compose herself. Whether it was exhaustion from the wild night catching up with her or catharsis as the final piece of an aeons-old puzzle clicked into place, the absurdity of it all overwhelmed her with unquenchable hilarity.

Hendiatrix bent over her. He checked the cut on her brow. He shook his head at the Linnaea.

"It's not a concussion."

"No, no, no!" she gasped. "Just give me a moment."

She rolled onto her side. She flipped the satchel open again. With a flourish she produced the skull.

"TADA!" she cried.

"O, too much folly is it, well I wot," the oseovox declaimed in his ancient accent, "to hazard all our lives in one small boat..."

53

Had Oneirotheria clubbed the Linnaea with a belaying pin twice each, they would have retained more of their faculties than they did at the sight of the oseovox. Their jaws hung slack. Their calculations fell apart in their brains. It was one thing to bloviate theories about the existence of an impossibility, based on a scrap of paper of dubious provenance—quite another to meet it faces to bony face.

The Minor reached out with grasping chubby digits. Oneirotheria moved back.

"Hup, hup. No dissecting."

The Major emitted a faint drone that might have been jargon in search of a handle on the moment. Oneirotheria cradled the oseovox.

"Isn't he lovely? Linnaea, Hendiatrix, may I present Upstart. And Tosspot, Pigeonfoot, Rag—you know, he has a lot of names."

To the skull, she said: "I'm sorry. I was too distracted earlier to ask. What you want to be called?"

His mandible chattered. "My lady, you may call me what you will."

"Will it is," she replied with a pat on his pate. "For short."

"He speaks?" Hendiatrix gasped.

"There are more things in heaven and earth, Hendiatrix," Will said. "Although come to think of it, you probably don't know about heaven or earth."

"No!" Oneirotheria said. "We don't. But you do, right?"

"I know so many things."

The Linnaea found their voice. "Is it true? You maintain memories of the time before Osylum was as it is and of the world elsewhere?"

"I do."

"Tell us. Everything."

"I could do that. I could fill your brains—both of them—with a hundred million facts. But if I'm not mistaken, don't we have a boat to catch?"

"Yes!" Oneirotheria crowed. "All the past versions of ourselves have set in motion everything that ended up here, now. We know the way, we have the will, we just need to go."

The Linnaea snapped to. They took the controls. The vans leveled out and the airship moved forward. They set a course toward the distant blue star atop their observatory tower, peeking just above the fog.

"Back to the Laboratory to collect the skiff. We drag it to the nearest big mirror, hop inside, Hendiatrix hoists it through the glass and off we go. Escape!"

"Escape! Escape!" Will and the Linnaea echoed.

The witch and scientists shook hands in triumph. She extended her hand to Hendiatrix. He did not take it.

"There's one more problem," the Oblate whispered.

The others looked at him. He stared at his

sandals. "The mirrors. The Great Mirror was smashed. The Chantry Mirror too."

"What about the pub mirror? That should be plenty big enough for a skiff."

"They got that one as well."

"They?"

"Ratkippers. They've been breaking mirrors all night. I nearly drown in the Unreflected because islands kept disappearing."

Oneirotheria clenched her fist. "Eschatos."

The Major and Minor frowned identical frowns. "Why would this Eschatos person order cannibals to break mirrors? Does he know the secret to escape? And why wouldn't he want to use it himself?"

"I don't think he knows," Oneirotheria said through gritted teeth. "Not about the Unreflected and all that. He just knows that mirrors matter to me and so he's going to wreck them out of spite."

"That is irrational."

"That's the kindest word for what he is."

"He is a prisoner who kisses his chains," the oseovox said, "to gain power over other poor captive souls."

"There must be other mirrors of appropriate size. Surely in one evening even hundreds of Ratkippers couldn't smash every sufficiently large reflective surface in the city. Hendiatrix, can you search?"

"Yes, patron."

The monk knelt before the brass plate on the control panel. He bowed his head. He made the apotrope before each eye and then across his chest.

"May I see," he intoned, "and in seeing, know and in knowing, serve and in service, be free. Lady's will be done."

The oseovox's teeth clacked nervously. Oneirotheria stroked his zygomatic bones and made soothing sounds.

Hendiatrix lifted his head. He stared into the polished metal. A yellow sheen descended over his eyes. Mist replaced his warped reflection. The scene shifted: more mist. And again. He shuffled through the city's images, every reflection shrouded in the Lady's Breath.

"Without the perspective of a image," the Linnaea said, "I cannot gauge the size of the reflective plane."

"And without seeing what it sees, we can't know where it is," Oneirotheria added.

Hendiatrix continued his search as the airship crawled slowly towards the Second Ward.

"This at least supports the hypothesis that the fog from the First Ward covers the entire city."

"And what good is that?"

"Any confirmation of a hypothesis is a good thing."

"At least we'll die with our hypotheses supported. Huh-piking-zah for that."

"Please," Hendiatrix interjected. "This is not easy with all the noise."

The witch and scientists continued bickering with glances while the monk scoured the city for a fitting reflection. They were almost to the observatory tower when he stopped.

"Here, now."

The brass plate showed a chamber with a tessellated mosaic floor. Pillars as tall as the Eighth Ward's mightiest trees held up a high-vaulted ceiling. Tattered banners—their sigils blurred by the warped brass—lined the hall. The space receded far into the distance.

"The corresponding mirror must be at least twice

my height. Unless the room itself is a doll's house. Which we'll have to risk."

"Where is that? I've never seen it."

"I am not sure. It does not correspond to any of the locales depicted in any of my books on the city."

Hendiatrix pulled back. He closed his eyes, releasing the reflection.

"I do not know this place either."

"I do," the oseovox said. "It is the Lady's home."

"Pike," cursed Oneirotheria.

"Of course," Hendiatrix said, rising. "The Cant is there's only one mirror in the First Ward. It stands free in the Lady's throne room. They said that through it, she watches us all. Only the Abbot could view it for the count. He never saw anyone, save Wardens who we do not count."

"True. The First Ward count always stood at zero. I assumed the Lady did not want to be seen."

"Wait," Oneirotheria said. She held Will up so they were eye to socket. "How do *you* know where that is? Haven't you been on a prop shelf for ages?"

"It doesn't matter how I know. That is where you and I must go."

"Somehow I always knew it would come down to me and her."

The Linnaea shook their heads.

"We cannot face the Lady. Not without every machine we ever built and perhaps not even then."

"You're not going to face her," Oneirotheria replied. "I am."

"We are," Will said.

She recognized the Linnaea's expression. They were marshalling a host of arguments; logical and empirical. The weight of a staggering waste of time threatened. She decided to pretend they'd had the discussion and she'd won.

"You'll need someone to help move the boat."

"With regards to the matter of the oseovox, however—"

"It's too big for just the two of you, even if Hendiatrix wasn't a withered bean who couldn't hoist a feather without losing his breath. Apologies, H."

"No need," the monk said. "It's true. Life in a cell does not prepare one for this much activity."

"We have not settled the disposition of—"

"—Cellarius could do it, if the Wardens hadn't got him."

"What? How?" Pain filled their voices.

Startled, Oneirotheria moderated her tone. "I am sorry. I thought you must have seen it as you were flying away. They faded half of him as he fought. The rest did not work right any more."

Their eyes closed. The Major laced his arm around the Minor. Their lips moved in sync. She realized they were enumerating syllogisms sotto voce, rocking slightly back and forth.

"There will be time for grief later," Will whispered. If a skull could shed tears, Oneirotheria's felt sure her hands would have been damp.

"Yes." The Linnaea opened their eyes. "This unexpected setback and resulting emotional response must wait. You are correct, as always, witch. We need help with the boat. And I assume you have a porter in mind already?"

"I do. Five, in fact. If they survived the night, they're still in the Second. And they owe me one last favor."

The Linnaea returned to the controls.

"Where to?"

"Look for a red ring, glowing under the fog."

"The singers," the oseovox said, "and the way they stand."

54

The fog still hung thick across the Second and night monsters walked abroad in day. Thus, the Peripats had not relinquished their protective circle at dawn. They brandished clubs and knives as the airship's propeller blew aside the mist and the basket descended to the courtyard. Oneirotheria leapt over the side and flew down before the craft hit the flagstones.

"Did you do this?!" Philotech shouted, drowning out Matron's greeting.

"Eschatos," Oneirotheria replied. She reckoned it would be easier to blame the fake Warden than explain something she only half understood herself. It was part true, anyway.

"Cack!" he replied. "This stinks of witch-work."

Ignoring him, Matron made the apotrope. "Lady sees you, Oneirotheria."

"I really hope not. Not yet anyway." She pointed at Philotech's steel blades. "Could you please put those away? Just in case anyone's watching."

He did not comply, until Matron repeated the order.

Hendiatrix and the Linnaea climbed out of the airship. Greetings and introductions were perfunctorily exchanged, before Oneirotheria got to the point.

"Platon's Oath. It's time."

"No!" Philotech shouted.

"We owe one more life, dear heart. It is our rule."

"Pike the rules! Look around. The world is ending all around us. Nothing matters but us now. The Lady's rules are falling apart."

"All the more reason to keep our own," Matron replied. "We are nothing if we do not obey our rules. You know this. If we renege on our bargain to save our lives, we will lose our lives all the same, after living in emptiness as nobody. I will not have that for you and I will not have that for me."

Caught in an agonizing dilemma—love demanded he protect Matron and love demanded he obey her—Philotech hung in terrible struggle. Bleak anticipation shattered his grim and armored face. He fought the inevitable with every fiber of his being until his beloved's steady grey eyes finally broke him.

He nodded, hopeless.

"When it comes to it," he whispered to her, "I will die, not you. That's my price."

"No one needs to die," the Linnaea interrupted. "I've prepared for this eventuality."

At their command, Hendiatrix dragged a chest from the airship. They opened it. They took out a staggering array of ordnance. Oneirotheria whistled, impressed at the destructive potential.

"With these, properly deployed, no one will kill any of us."

Matron nodded to the other four Peripats. Each of them sang their note, unwinding the round that wove the Stay Circle. As the Linnaea handed out arms and instructions for their use to the four,

Oneirotheria outlined the plan for Matron.

"Follow the twins. Carry their boat to Liminal Boulevard."

"To the Lady's Gate?"

"I will meet you there."

"And then?"

"We're escaping."

Matron dragged the apotrope across her chest to ward off evil. "One cannot escape the world."

"And yet, we will."

"It is impossible."

"That's why it's taken me so long."

The skull in her hands laughed. It was a disconcertingly human sound to come from empty bone.

Matron's voice trembled. "How can this be?"

"Don't worry about Will," Oneirotheria said. "He's with me."

"Is that meant to comfort me?"

"I suppose not."

Matron lifted her index finger ever so slightly towards the fog. Too soft for the other Peripats to hear, she repeated Philotech's shouted question:

"Did you do all of this?"

"No."

"Did... he?" She averted her gaze from the oseovox.

Oneirotheria rotated her wrist so the skull shook his head.

"This was the Lady's doing," she said. "I think. Eschatos ran to the Wardens and told them things. Probably true things, even. About me. And, this happened."

"Why?"

"If there's time, I'll find out."

"The whirlygig of time brings in his revenges,"

Will interjected.

"Yes, of course. Thank you for the reminder, dearest." She pecked the top of his head and turned her attention back to Matron.

"You once told me you don't *Stay* in the First, not that you don't *go* to the First. Is that true?"

"It is not forbidden to go to the First. But no one ever comes back through the Misty Gate. So that road, we do not walk."

"Today you will. If I meet you on Liminal Boulevard."

"And if you don't?"

"If I don't, you're free of Platon's Oath all the same. There won't be another me to collect."

Before she could react, Matron hugged her. Pressed against the other woman's body, warm and soft, Oneirotheria understood why Philotech loved her. Her arms were safety stronger than city walls or magic singing circles. Her slow dovish heartbeat settled the constantly battering magpie in the witch's chest. Together, they breathed; just breathed. If she hadn't known the world was mad and death nearby, Oneirotheria would have clung to the comfort of Matron's embrace forever.

She knew at last the cost of Platon's Oath. Her heart bent under the horrible heavy toll, should Matron be the one to die. Yet she would collect, if it came to that. For escape, she would sacrifice an endless tarry in that sweet space.

They stepped apart. Oneirotheria took the last tube of fire-fennel from her pouch. She pressed it into Matron's hand.

"If needs must. Point it away from yourself. Flip the seal off. Let the fire do the rest."

Matron gave her a farewell apotrope.

"Lady sees you, Oneirotheria."

"Oh, she will. She will."

The oseovox cackled again. The Linnaea finished the disposition of arms. The Peripats formed a march. Oneirotheria spun on her heel and danced light-footed into the fog.

55

They were doubly far out of earshot of the Peripats before Oneirotheria spoke again.

"Now it's just you and me and the Lady makes three. Since we've a private moment, I have to ask: *Did* you do this?"

"I shaped the mist in the Ninth," Will replied, "with my own words and some of Dedalus's left-over toys, aye. For the rest, though, no. This is not my work, even if it did drive you to me at long last."

"Then what? After sitting on her hill forever doing nothing, the Lady chose this day to blot the world with her power?"

"I don't have a nose. Does this magic smell intentional?"

"It smells wet. And bloody. And sour and sweaty and mad."

"But is there a method in the madness? Or is it a doorbell ringing of its own accord?"

"I don't understand what you mean."

"At a pub, there will be a bell hung over the door, right?" the skull asked. "And when the drunkards go banging in, it rings, letting the landlord know he's got more custom."

"You think all of this fog and Fade is a like bell

over a door? The Lady set up murder-mist ages ago, forgot about it, Eschatos triggered the alarm and now—the end of days?"

"It's a broad net to catch a single small fish otherwise, isn't it?"

"Fish! Another of those words from elsewhere. Nets we have, fish we've none. If we did, though, I don't think I'd be a small one."

"No. You'd be Leviathan's bigger sister if a whale was a tadpole."

"Were you this much of flatterer when you were alive?"

"Better. I had a body then and could flatter you with more than my words."

"Now there's a thought worth—here-now!"

She nearly ran full-tilt into a granite plinth. Atop it stood a hooded and hand-bound statue, still in his stoic vigil over the Feeding Square.

"How much time have we got, Will-o-mine?"

"Your porters will move slow, Lady-o-mine, under the weight of a boat and all those rockets and pistols. We can spare a grain of sand or two in the hourglass."

"I want to say goodbye to one last friend before we fly."

She ducked down the alley to the folly garden. As she passed the gate, she held Will up so he could see the charcoal graffiti:

In thy orisons be all my sins remembered

"Why did you do that all over town? Were they all messages for me—or some version of me?"

"Upstart did that because it was his character to do so."

"That's a nice evasion."

"Very well. I made his character that way because I knew you forgot with every new life. Before Hecate pieced together a spell to skip over amnesia's chasm, it was the only hope I had for jogging some recollection. Or re-creating the same thoughts on either end of the gap, which amounts to the same thing as remembrance."

"How did you get them to be perfectly fitted for the moments I saw them?"

"That's an old magician's trick and a way to gull free beer from the superstitious."

"Explain."

"Picture yourself in a tavern. Unlike the swanky place where Tosspot locked you up, there's no mirror over this bar. So you hunch on your stool with your back to the door. And every time the doorbell tinkles, you say 'Ah, Kit, so good you're here. Now be a mate and buy us a beer.'"

"Kit?"

"Or John or Mag or Oneirotheria. A hundred drunks will stumble in that night and if even one of them is named Kit, he'll think you know him and you have powers of the mind to see him without so much as turning around. He won't know about the ninety-nine sots with different names who came before him."

"So the pattern in the graffiti is just an illusion? It always seemed so on point."

"You only noticed the ones that sounded as if they were meant for you. I'd wager you a cask, if I still had a throat, that you saw a dozen scrawled snippets of doggerel a day and gave them no mind because they meant nothing in that moment. Ah, but the ones that did speak to you? Magic!"

"I regret asking."

"Most do, when they learn a wizard's tedious

secrets."

She set him on the edge of the fountain. She approached her hut. The Lady's Seal still covered the doors and windows. She knelt in front of it and rested a hand on its scaly chicken knee.

"I will miss you, little izbushka. I wish Hecate had left me more to learn about you."

"We all live in someone else's house," Will said, "and we keep it for whoever comes after."

"No one will come after me."

"One way or another, that is true."

"Still," she said with a sigh. "It would have been a sight to see her run."

Suddenly, the hut lurched up. Oneirotheria fell over backwards. It pranced around the tiny space. She scrabbled to avoid being trampled by the enormous scratching claws. She scooped up Will and tried to get to the gate. The frenzied hut blocked the way, tearing stones from crumbling mortar.

"Here-now!" she cried. She magpied, flew to the roof, and stood straddling the peak as a woman. With one hand, she clung to the chimney pipe and the other she cradled the skull.

The izbushka's talons found purchase in the torn garden wall. It scrambled over and bounced down the alley. With wild strides, it sprinted through the straying streets. Swaying and pitching on her rooftop perch, Oneirotheria sang nonsense songs and shrieked with glee. Wardens and inmates alike scattered at its approach. Swifter than a flock of swallows at dusk, relentless as a hurricane gale, the witch's hut charged to the Lady's Ward.

It stopped at the obsidian wall between the Second and First. The unbroken black stone proved too smooth to climb and too hard to batter through. Thwarted, it knelt in the middle of Liminal Boulevard, shuttered its door and windows, and went to sleep. Oneirotheria skidded off the roof.

"We know what we are," Oneirotheria read from the chalked cobbles, "but not what we may be. And what precisely, Will-o-Mine, did you mean by that?"

The oseovox thoughtfully tapped his teeth. He did not reply.

"It doesn't matter now," she said. "We're far past the time for cryptic messages and drunken puppets."

"Be kind. Only one of them was a drunkard."

"Were they really all you?"

"Yes. Fragments of imagination, given local habitation and a name."

"Even Tosspot?"

"Is every part of you the best? Is there no part foul in there?"

She conceded the point.

"Every character was a piece of me, sent out into the world on strings of thought and words. Hundreds of them. Until maybe there was nothing of me left outside of them. Except this skull. Except this skull..."

She touched his absent lips. "It's not such a bad skull."

"It made a pleasant place to hang a face. And I had very good hair once upon a time."

Again the image of living Will superimposed itself on bone; deep, sad eyes, crow's feet, a ring of wispy hair around care-wrinkled scalp. "Not when

I knew you."

Whose memory is that?

"Never mind," she continued aloud. "We need to get to the gate. I have to clear the way for the others. How I'm going to do that, I do not know. I lost my knife in the Eighth. My hexes run thin. I gave my last vial of fennel to Matron. Can fire even hurt a Warden?"

"Gullveig thought so."

"The me who burned the Third Ward and disappeared? Well, I don't know how she did that, so I'll have to come up with something else."

Keeping close to the buildings, in case she needed a sudden hiding place, she followed the boulevard around the long curve of the wall. Up here, the miasma that had plagued the city thinned; as if it had rolled down from the First Ward and exhausted its source. Seeing the sky—even the blank prison dome of Osylum—brightened her mood. She breathed relief for a claustrophobia she had not been aware of till it passed.

A Tribunal swerved unexpectedly out of a side street just behind her. She dove over a hip wall, too late. They could not have avoided seeing her. She clenched everything in anticipation of a fight.

Yet, they passed by. Between them huddled the body of an Abram-Man; naked and covered in grave mud. His death had been natural, from what she could see. His kind lived rough in holes and gutters and so did not live long.

She stood up. Still the Tribunal did not slow.

Here-now! Not even a third-eye blink?

"What are you waiting for?" Will asked.

"It'll be the shortest jailbreak in history if I get faded on the doorstep, now won't it?"

"They will never fade you."

"What? Of course they will. They've spent all night trying to do just that!"

"Do you really think so?"

"They came for the Linnaea, looking for me. And I smelled nothing a half-dozen times crawling across the roofs in the dark."

"No," the oseovox said. "They came for the Linnaea because Dedalus's heirs were on the verge of discovering the Unreflected and somebody let that slip."

"And the others?"

"Six fools broke the Wardens' rules in a mad night. I don't know what they did, but I will swear on the hands I used to have, it was not on your account a half dozen rogues went to void."

"How can you be so certain?"

"You can have an explanation or you can have an escape. Here, now, you cannot have both."

"Alright," she said, stepping off again, "I'm adding this to your tab for future reckoning."

"When the hurly-burly's done," the skull replied, "I'll pay you truths, one by one."

56

A steady stream of Wardens and corpses flowed into the Lady's Gate. The night had been as lethal as it had smelled and sounded. Only the lightest haze remained in the air atop the hill. Oneirotheria could see clearly through the archway. To her surprise, the obsidian wall was thin as an eggshell.

How does it even stand? There are still so many mysteries in this city. I almost regret escaping before solving them all.

Almost.

She sat on a garden bench in front of a vine-covered mansion. She kept her body between the Wardens and the oseovox. Despite his assurances, she still was not convinced the penalty for having him wasn't the Fade.

"So, Will-o-mine, what now?" she asked, barely moving her lips.

"Now you face the Lady."

"I thought we loved her."

"People say a great many things, don't they?"

"That they do, Will."

Still she did not move.

"Why are you waiting? The skiff will be here soon. Without the Lady's permission, the Wardens will not let them through the gate."

"Who are you really, Will-o-Mine?"

"The Lady knows me."

"Is that meant to comfort me?"

"Comfort's a blanket to suffocate by."

"That's good. So good, in fact..."

She found a nubbin of chalk in her witch-pouch. She scrawled the quote on the flagstone path. She held the oseovox up to admire it.

"A fitting tribute," he said. "Pity no future witch will see it."

She laughed. "That's the spirit of hope I needed, to screw my resolution to the sticking place."

She tucked him in the crook of her left arm. Together, they approached the gate. Two Wardens watched, a Tribunal was just passing through with a dead Ratkipper. The guardians bowed their heads as Oneirotheria reached them.

"EVERYTHING IS AS IT SHOULD BE."

"Everything is as it should be."

They made no move to stop her passing by. They did not seem to even see the oseovox.

"Did you hear them in your mind?" she asked under her breath.

"No."

"Not at all? And why does everyone else hear a question instead of a report? Oh Will-o-Mine, I am leaving behind so many things unknown."

"Everyone does."

Beyond the archway, a wide plaza encircled a vast palace. Black and white bricks, interlocked in the shape of birds, cunningly tessellated across the courtyard. The pattern continued up the sides of the palace walls, giving the enormous domed building the appearance of growing out of the ground. There were no windows. There were only two doors, one to the left and one to the right, both three times Oneirotheria's height. One was open and the other closed.

The procession of Wardens and bodies curved to the left of the great house—a dozen Tribunals, lined up and slowly moving towards the only open door.

"Better than trying to break the other one down," she said, and walked along the line of Wardens towards the opening.

As she passed, the Wardens' voices sounded in her mind. Nearly two score identical, flat, expressionless voices battered her brain with the same syncopated thought, over and over.

"EVERYTHING IS AS IT SHOULD BE EVERYTHING IS AS IT SHOULD BE EVERYTHING IS AS IT SHOULD BE EVERYTHING IS AS IT SHOULD BE EVERYTHING IS AS IT SHOULD BE EVERYTHING IS AS IT SHOULD BE EVERYTHING IS AS IT SHOULD BE EVERYTHING IS AS IT SHOULD BE EVERYTHING IS AS IT SHOULD BE EVERYTHING IS AS IT SHOULD BE EVERYTHING IS AS IT SHOULD BE EVERYTHING IS AS IT SHOULD BE EVERYTHING IS AS IT SHOULD BE."

"YES!" she screamed, brain beaten by the relentless report.

"YES YES YES!" she shouted, until at last the assault broke her lie. "NO! NO IT IS NOT!"

Twelve Tribunals recoiled back from her scream. The scattered bodies they carried fell to the ground; a dozen sick thuds. After that, silence. Silence as profound as the silence after the world ends.

She waited for the Fade. The Wardens simply hovered, hands folded in a servant's pose.

"Perhaps we should continue," the oseovox whispered.

Tentatively, she stepped over the threshold. The Wardens gathered behind her, twelve rows of three. Thus escorted, she entered the Lady's Palace.

A wide hallway receded into dimness. It was lined with open chambers, separated by a half wall; like hexagonal pods in a wasps nest. Each of the chambers had a single white marble bier and nothing more. Floor to ceiling, the entire space was covered in black-and-white tiles, replicating the brick pattern outside.

The recently deceased occupied several of the corpse-beds. Three Wardens apiece surrounded the bodies. Each group was at a different stage of a curious ritual. As Oneirotheria passed, they left off what they were doing and joined the procession of their kin behind her. Nonetheless, as if a sequential panel painting, she assembled a vision of the procedure.

The body would be laid out, facing upwards. One Warden would stand at its head, one at the left shoulder, and one at the feet. The Warden at the head caressed the corpse's eyes with its long three fingers. Dark mist trickled out of the body. The lead Warden breathed it in, inhaling continuously through its narrow slit-nostrils till the soul's memories had been entirely drawn out.

They feed on the lives we build in our minds and leave us hollow in the end.

The left Warden placed its hand over the

corpse's heart. It lifted and pinched three fingers, pulling out a translucent shade. This amnesiac remnant of the soul, it set to the side to wait.

Is that all we are without our memories? Just a pale shadow that doesn't look like anyone real?

The Warden at the feet opened its third eye. The physical body Faded to oblivion.

Nothing and nothing and more nothing.

The process repeated in every occupied cell along the hall, until disrupted by Oneirotheria's passing.

"Even death is no escape," Will said as they left the efficient mortuary.

"Hecate must have figured out some way to pull her memories from her soul before she died," Oneirotheria replied. "Imperfect, but she did it. Would I knew how right now."

"Aye. So little time, so much to know."

"Well, here we are. Off we go."

The hall beyond the mortuary narrowed. It did not branch. It switched back and forth, labyrinthine, now leading towards the center of the building, now towards the perimeter. The gradual trend was inward. Treading the wending, unbroken hall, Oneirotheria slipped into a meditative trance. For the first time in this incarnation (perhaps in all of them), her mind stopped chattering. The never-ending noise of questions and commentary ceased. She simply followed the path beneath her feet.

After untold hours, having gathered an uncountable crowd of Wardens in her wake, she reached the Lady's throne room.

"Lady," she called out before even reaching the entry. Her own voice echoed back. "Lady. I have come to demand escape."

She entered halfway down a vast chamber. To her left, the two-story mirror doubled the room. No longer blurred by warped brass, she could clearly see the sigils on the dozens of banners lining the hall.

"Eagle, hawk, crow, phoenix, cardinal, gull, sparrow, robin, vulture, kite..." Bird name after bird name tumbled from her lips as she read the images aloud.

Dazed, she strayed down the tiled floor towards the empty throne. Stark and alone, it rose a full head-height above the floor. She stepped stiff-legged up the stairs, as if she were one of the Linnaea's wind-up machines. She sat on the throne. It fit her as if made for her. Wardens filled the court. They bowed, her servants.

"Now you see who you truly are," the oseovox said, "though you still do not remember."

The skull slipped from her slack hand.

"I am the Lady."

57

A tiny Oneirotheria stared back at her from the vanishing point of the throne room mirror, an infinity away. Between them, a vast and placid sea of Wardens waited for her will.

"I am the Lady," she repeated.

She had never heard words sound so undeniably real and so impossible at the same time. She tried saying them again with different inflection, to see if she could separate the two feelings; reality and impossibility.

"I am the Lady."

"That you are," Will's muffled voice came from beneath the throne, where he'd rolled face down.

"Oh!"

She retrieved him. She set him on the chair's arm. She rubbed his mandible and maxilla.

"Sorry, sorry."

"No harm done."

She rested her hand on his parietal bone; a tender gesture. For a fleeting moment, she felt thin grey hair and warm skin on her fingertips. Then, bone again. Far, far away, the miniscule reflected Oneirotheria caressed a talking skull. She could no longer tell which of them was real and which the image.

"How? How did it come to this?"

"I can't show you images in a glass," the oseovox replied. "And I'm out of puppets to dance the tale. But I can paint your history with words, if you will."

"Yes..."

"It was another country. That fact you've discovered many times over."

"Who were we?"

"We were not young. We were not old, but we were not young. I was a poet, on a good day, and on most others I was an actor and writer of plays. And you... you had your own history before we met that I do not know. We met and you became my dark lady and I yours to will as you wished."

"We were in love."

"Aye. We were in love. Such a small bit of sound, that. Love. *Our* love was the kind of love for which they invented the word love. A love without which 'love' would wither and vanish from the world's tongues for lack of meaning."

"I know that love. It's a part of me. Before Hecate. Before Marrigan and Gullveig and Louhi and who knows how many others, that love is there. Outside memory. Outside death and rebirth. I've carried it in my bones since the moment I drew breath in Osylum."

"Since before. Your love created Osylum."

"How can love make something so terrible?"

"Not love alone."

"Then what?"

"Grief."

"You died," she said.

"Aye, Lady mine. Long before your appointed time, I died. You faced empty decades. You said no and you refused to let me go."

"How could I do that?"

The oseovox chuckled. "Oh, you have so much strength. You had come to my city with the magic of the moors on your lips and the wisdom of witches in your pack of herbs. I could conjure up a storm in a wooden circle and make five men into an army with words, but you... you had true power."

"What did I do?"

"You grieved. And the grief grew instead of dulling as the chasm of days opened between us. You could not abide it. You tore my skull from the earth. You called to the spirits underfoot and when they were silent, you shouted to spirits of the air and when they whirled by, you screamed further and further into the sky. Until something from the dark spaces between the stars heard your cry. And answered."

"And answered," her hoarse voice echoed.

"Aye. Bound in a circle, it bent to your commands."

"What did I tell it to do?"

"Too many things all at once, and each demand contradicting the other."

"I don't understand."

"Grief ripped you in a hundred thousand directions. You wanted me to live forever. You wanted to forget your pain. You wanted love to never fail. You wanted to live forever yourself, pursuing me and being pursued. You wanted to die and achieve surcease of pain. You wanted the city where our love grew to be preserved, under glass and forever green. You wanted the world to fall instantly to ruin because that would match your bleak, unending sorrow. Your pain slashed your soul with a claws of desire and you demanded all your clashing incompatible desires find fulfillment."

"And that's Osylum."

"That it is. Whatever eldritch spirit you called could not reconcile the endless impossible demands of your loss. It did its cruel best and that's this city."

"And everything was as it should be."

"Aye."

A thousand miles away, her dwindled image bowed its head.

"Everyone else in the city? Are they innocents, then? Did I bring all those other people here to suffer forever or fade to nothing."

"No. All the other souls imprisoned here heard the call that your grief-wracked heart hurled into the dark. They joined in the lament, singing their own despair and loss and wish to forget and wish to hold on to what no mortal can hold. You bound the power, they merely added to its list of tasks. Everyone in Osylum is here because they wished to be."

"Everyone except you."

"Everyone except me."

She felt wetness on the skull's dome. A torrent of tears had flowed from her, so many she had soaked her face, neck, breast, all the way down her arms. She had not even known she was crying.

"What am I supposed to do now?"

"What you always planned. What you've been trying to do for countless lifetimes. What you know is the right thing, the natural thing, the good thing."

"Escape."

"Aye. You have thrashed the bars of the cage you

built for yourself long enough. It is time."

"If I leave, then you will die. Truly die."

"Aye. Let me show you the way and then let me go, Lady-o-Mine. No one is for all time."

"And where will I escape to? A world where everything lives only once and dies and fades and is lost?"

"Aye."

"An empty world," she spat bitterly.

"NO!"

The skull's shout exploded from every echoing corner of the throne room. A wave disturbed the sea of floating Wardens. He continued in a softer tone:

"No. Not an empty world. A world filled with things you'll never know in this prison of images. The sun, the moon, the stars, the howl of a raging wind, the song of fresh water over rocks, the smell of linden trees and the taste of the salt sea spray and wild nights of bodies tangled. A world so overflowing that one thing *must* pass away so there will be room for the next and that next thing give way to another and on and on into an eternity of fullness."

She lifted the skull to her lips. She kissed him deeply and tasted the memory of his breath.

"I love you, Will."

"And I you."

"Let's go meet the others."

58

Her inhuman servants parted before her. The palace door opened of its own accord. The courtyard now was also full of Wardens, hundreds at a glance.

"Who's watching the city?" she quipped. "It'll be chaos."

"Cities are always chaos," Will replied. "That's why they make such good theatre."

The skiff, on a makeshift cart, waited in a semi-circle of Wardens just outside the gate. Exceedingly nervous Peripats stood next to it, a scant handspan away from the nearest guard and trying to pretend it was a mile. They had lost all of the Linnaea's weapons along the way—or used them up.

"It must have been hell's own fight to get here," Oneirotheria said, stepping into their view.

"Yes, it was. Although, a more positive characterization would be that it was a series of extremely successful tests of inventions that hitherto had only been theoretically feasible."

The Linnaea rose from inside the boat, where they had been examining the strange tiller mechanism. Hendiatrix hovered next to them, open notebook and pen in hand.

"I think I'm beginning to get the gist of this. Note the ovoid depression, a handspan across."

Matron stepped up to Oneirotheria. She took the witch's cheeks between her hands. She examined her with searching grey eyes.

"Are you well? Is the Lady angry with us?"

"Yes. And no. I'll explain on the way." She raised her voice to the others. "We have permission to leave. Everything is—"

It was a very soft sound that interrupted her. Almost inaudible. A grunt and an exhalation that bubbled into liquid bursts.

Philotech dropped to his knees. His hand fluttered, trying to reach up to Matron. His nerves and muscles failed. He fell forward onto the cobbles.

Eschatos, hidden amid the crowd of Wardens, stepped forward with a bloody knife in his hand.

"Nothing is as it should be," he snarled around the still-fresh burns on half his face. "You cannot break the Rule of No Escape."

Matron rushed to Philotech's side. She wet her hands in the blood of his wounds and pleaded with him to live. There was so much blood.

The other three Peripats tried to make their way around the boat to get to Eschatos, without shoving Wardens aside. Above them, the Linnaea and Hendiatrix stared in confusion, trying to understand what was happening.

"Fade them! Fade them all," Eschatos screamed at the Wardens. "You can see their guilt! Do my Lady's will!"

None of them moved.

"The Fade ends today," Oneirotheria said.

Spitting filth, the would-be Warden charged her.

Matron, drenched in her beloved's blood, shot

up as Eschatos passed. She caught him under the arm. She twisted slightly. His own strength and righteous anger hurled him face-first into the obsidian wall. The Wardens, as if still waiting for the Lady's will, made space for the fight.

Holding his shattered cheek in one hand, Eschatos clawed himself standing. He raised his swaying blade at Matron.

In answer, she held out the tube of fire-fennel. Her hand was steady as the city's stones. Her thumb poised on the wax seal.

Eschatos's single good eye widened. He hesitated.

"Assault!" he cried to the Wardens, his voice rising to a shriek. "Witchcraft and escape. Where is the Fade?!"

"I told you," Oneirotheria said. "There will be no more Fade."

He stammered. "But... my Lady..."

"I was never your Lady. You are a slave, licking his chains to convince himself he is the master."

He dropped the blade. "I don't understand."

"No. Your kind never will. Preachers of purity and panderers to power. The righteous. The holy. The set apart."

Her words drove him to the street. Her voice beat on.

"You lust for loss and death and suffering and pain—your own or that of others, you do not care which. You invent gods and angels and Ladies in your own image and you dress like them and demand the world accord you respect you could never earn. I spit on your worship and I deny your commandments and I defy your vision of my will."

She turned away.

"Matron, you may burn this trash if you like."

But the grieving Peripat leader had already dropped the last witch-weapon. It rolled into a sewer. She lay atop Philotech's body, wracked with sobs. Oneirotheria crouched with her. Together, they mourned.

Whimpering threats, Eschatos crawled into the crowd.

"Everyone who is here," Will said, pronouncing final judgment on the departing puritan, "wished to be here."

"Killing him would do nothing," Matron whispered, once sorrow let go of her throat. "Except send his soul back around to a new body to be the same man. I will not be that woman, with his death eating my heart."

Three Wardens formed a triangle over Philotech's body. It floated from the cobbles, coat trailing. Matron pushed herself to her feet, wiping her face.

"I am sorry," Oneirotheria said. "I did not want Platon's Oath fulfilled."

"Oaths are fulfilled," Matron replied. "Otherwise, words are nothing. As nothing as the space around the walls."

The Tribunal departed, taking Philotech to forgetting and rebirth. Oneirotheria gathered her remaining company and led them into the palace.

59

O nce the skiff had been dragged into place in front of the Lady's Mirror, Oneirotheria held up the oseovox for all of them to see.

"For those of you who have not met him, this is Will. He is, I believe, going to guide our little boat out of here. Correct, Linnaea?"

The Major nodded. "The depression on the tiller mechanism roughly fits a human skull. The dimensions are not as precise as one might achieve, having the specimen in hand to measure, but it should—"

"—I know you hate when I interrupt you because I'm thinking too fast, but I just have to say that I really do love your exhaustive and tedious precision. Never lose it."

"I am not sure what to say to that. Is 'thank you' appropriate?"

"Yes. And thank you. Thank all of you. I do not know much about where we are going. I do not know what awaits there, except that it is more than here, and some day, whether today or far in the days ahead, we will part ways and never meet again. Before that, just know I'm so grateful to all of you that I've run out of words for thank you."

She handed the oseovox to the Linnaea. They fitted him upright into the tiller box. Hendiatrix took a place at the prow, close to the reflected boat. Oneirotheria climbed in. She held her hand for Matron. The other woman shook her head.

"Don't worry. They don't need you. With the wheels, the others can push it through, one on each side and one behind. There should be enough momentum that they can jump onboard before we're all the way into the Reflected."

"I am not leaving," she said.

"Why not?"

"Because in three days, there will be a new-found Peripat somewhere in the city. And they will need someone to guide them. To teach them our way."

"Your way? Don't you understand? I'm the Lady. I can say you're free of your rules and you're free of them. We all get to leave. No more walking Ward to Ward in an endless circle according to someone else's pattern."

Matron's sorrow-filled face spoke wordlessly loud of two lives wound together in love for years and now lost. She shook her head.

Oneirotheria heard the echo of the Peripat's expression in her own lost places. Still, she tried one more time. "Are you sure?"

"We all follow," Matron said. "We all lead. We all walk and we all become the path in time. I cannot leave another without a path to become."

"How about the rest of you?"

The other three Peripats turned away. Oneirotheria nodded.

"I understand."

Four red-coated shoulders set to the hull.

"Oh, one more thing!" Oneirotheria said.

"Yes?" Matron replied.

330

"When you find whoever he winds up becoming, could you annoy them with frivolity every now and then? For me?"

Amid the grey dead grief in Matron's eyes, a tiny sparkle of laughter flickered to life.

"Yes, Oneirotheria. I can manage that."

"Good then. All business concluded, gentlemen?"

"Yes," the two in the boat replied.

"Into the unknown we go!"

60

The Unreflected lapped the hull. Of the myriad lights that had dotted the space, few remained. The Ratkippers had been busy, smashing mirrors. Every now and then, another twinkle would disappear. Oneirotheria wondered if any would be left, if anyone else wanted to escape.

Where there's a will, there's a way, I suppose.

The Major and Hendiatrix pulled oars. Dedalus had rigged a series of gears that made the effort significantly easier. It was hard to tell, with only distant points of reference, but her belly fluttered as though they were moving at tremendous speed.

Glowing with her last moonflower tucked into his cochlear canal, Will controlled the tiller. Apparently, Dedalus had created a machine that could read the oseovox's memories and translate them into directions across the Unreflected.

It is amazing he didn't escape himself earlier. I suppose all the pieces need to fit perfectly for the machine to run.

I will miss Cellarius.

She took a turn at oar, relieving Hendiatrix. While she rowed, the last lights of Osylum receded forever into the darkness. Hendiatrix relieved the Linnaea and they, in turn, took over for her. On

and on they cycled across a sunless, trackless sea.
The journey was long and though she tried not
to, eventually she fell asleep.

61

S he woke to the taste of sand.

For a moment, she wasn't sure who to blame for the affront. The memory rushed back and she leapt to her feet, spitting her mouth clear.

A mottled white circle of light glowed high overhead.

"Moon!" She howled. "We did it!"

She stood next to Dedalus's skiff. It had struck the shore and turned onto its side. Two sets of footprints tracked up the beach, disappearing into the distance. The wind carried the tang of salt.

Wind!

Her chest fluttered. The magpie did not emerge to climb the sea breeze. It soared only in her mind now. She and her soul were one.

She took a step. Sharp pain made her wince. All around were strewn shattered shells—the ocean's bones, flung up by the waves. The steady cadence of the tremulous midnight sea filled her ears and heart, speaking without words of endless strange places and new.

Near her, half-buried, she saw a skull.

"Will-o-Mine!"

She picked him up. White sand ran out of his

eyes and mouth, sparkling in the moonlight to match the stars above. In seconds, he was empty. Light as a skull should be. His spirit departed. She kissed his lipless teeth one more time. The vision of his face receded, drawn into the sea with the ebbing tide. Aeons late, she finally bade him goodbye.

She turned landward.

"What country is this?"

A cliff towered over her, glowing in the full moon. Enormous black letters hung sharp on the stark white chalk:

Love that well which thou must leave ere long

She whirled on the beach. She delighted in the cold foam racing over her bare feet. With peals of laughter, she filled the space between the stars.

ALSO BY JAKE BURNETT

The Chaos Court
The Dream and the Muse

ACKNOWLEDGEMENTS

First, last, and always, thanks to Ruth. Ten years before this book's release, she said: "Just sit down and write every evening. It'll be fine." She was right.

Thanks for Dena McMurdie for an amazing cover. And to her and Christa Hogan for reading the manuscript and for many good hours of starbucksing.

Thanks to Eric Hoeckberg and everyone at Omnia Paratus Health Training in Apex, NC. You kept me sane and strong despite many sedentary hours of writing. Ready for anything!

Shout-out to the Futurescapes Fall 2022 organizer, faculty, and cohort: Luke Peterson, Suzie Townsend, Christina Campbell Galaviz, Leo Korogodski, and Joanne White. Your help and encouragement on the penultimate draft of the novel was invaluable. Many thanks.

James & Doug: Sorry about the murderfog.

About the Author

Jake Burnett grew up in seven countries on four continents and now lives in North Carolina with his wife and two full-time career dogs. His debut novel, *The Chaos Court*, was one of Kirkus Reviews' Best Books of 2020. When he's not creating stories or tormenting his friends in tabletop RPGs, his ego keeps writing checks his body can't cash by running Spartan races or careening down wilderness trails.